Reese had come to the conclusion that he'd be better off working with Jade than around her.

He just hoped to hell she felt the same way.

He reached for her, but came up empty as she took another step back.

"Look, forget what I said," she told him. "You and I both know this isn't Hollywood. We're not talking danger and intrigue on the high seas here."

It was time.

He dragged her chair from the desk and hiked his boot up onto it. Reaching inside, he fished out the one piece of evidence that would change everything Jade thought she knew about him.

Dear Reader,

I'm always getting letters telling me how much you love miniseries, and this month we've got three great ones for you. Linda Turner starts the new family-based miniseries, THOSE MARRYING McBRIDES! with *The Lady's Man.* The McBrides have always been unlucky in love—until now. And it's wedding-wary Zeke who's the first to take the plunge. Marie Ferrarella also starts a new miniseries this month. CHILDFINDERS, INC. is a detective agency specializing in finding missing kids, and they've never failed to find one yet. So is it any wonder desperate Savannah King turns to investigator Sam Walters when her daughter disappears in *A Hero for All Seasons?* And don't miss *Rodeo Dad,* the continuation of Carla Cassidy's wonderful Western miniseries, MUSTANG, MONTANA.

Of course, that's not all we've got in store. Paula Detmer Riggs is famous for her ability to explore emotion and create characters who live in readers' minds long after the last page is turned. In *Once More a Family* she creates a reunion romance to haunt you. Sharon Mignerey is back with her second book, *His Tender Touch,* a suspenseful story of a woman on the run and her unwilling protector—who soon turns into her willing lover. Finally, welcome new author Candace Irvin, who debuts with a military romance called *For His Eyes Only.* I think you'll be as glad as we are that Candace has joined the Intimate Moments ranks.

Enjoy—and come back next month, when we once again bring you the best and most exciting romantic reading around.

Yours,

Leslie J. Wainger
Executive Senior Editor

Please address questions and book requests to:
Silhouette Reader Service
U.S.: 3010 Walden Ave., P.O. Box 1325, Buffalo, NY 14269
Canadian: P.O. Box 609, Fort Erie, Ont. L2A 5X3

FOR HIS EYES ONLY

CANDACE
IRVIN

Published by Silhouette Books

America's Publisher of Contemporary Romance

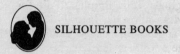 SILHOUETTE BOOKS

ISBN 0-373-07936-2

FOR HIS EYES ONLY

Look us up on-line at: http://www.romance.net

Printed in U.S.A.

CANDACE IRVIN

As the daughter of a librarian and a sailor, it's no wonder Candace's two greatest loves are reading and the sea. After spending several exciting years as a naval officer sailing around the world, she finally decided it was time to put down roots and give her other love a chance. To her delight, she soon learned that writing romance was as much fun as reading it. Candace believes her luckiest moment was the day she married her own dashing hero, a former army combat engineer with dimples to die for. The two now reside in Massachusetts, happily raising two future heroes and one adorable heroine—who won't be allowed to date until she's forty, at least.

My deepest thanks to Suzanne Brockmann, a superb writer, wonderful mentor and great friend. You'd have made one hell of a sailor, Suz! I'd also like to thank Special Agent George Festa (DEA) and Mr. Jack Coffey for their crucial assistance. Any mistakes or liberties I've taken with the information they provided are purely my own. Finally, a special thanks to Sharon Maggiore and Christyne Johnson—my critique partners, my sanity.

For my mother and father, who taught me when one door closes, another is waiting to be opened. And for my husband, who's always there to help me find the keys.

Chapter 1

"Is he here yet?"

The irony of the question slapped Jade Parker across the face as she entered the Captain's cabin. The one man on the ship who should be immune to the circus they'd sailed smack into the middle of—who should be more concerned with the *USS Baddager*'s readiness than with *his* arrival— had turned into the ringleader.

Jade stared at the crisp Navy whites the captain had donned—the ones usually reserved for sailing in and out of port. She was probably the only officer who'd declined to wear the ice-cream suit today. The faint frown as his gaze swept her khaki uniform suggested she revisit the decision.

"No, sir, he hasn't arrived." And if fortune favored her, he'd fall off the pier before he boarded the ship. She smiled at the fantasy as she handed over the sheaf of papers she'd just carted up four decks. "Here's the write-up of yesterday's General Quarters drill. As you can see, I've highlighted the changes crucial to passing the inspection in yellow. Underneath is the ship's newly revised Nuclear

Warfare Doctrine. The Chief Engineer has already signed off on the changes.''

The captain barely glanced at the top sheet before carefully arranging the ream of paper in his in-box.

Jade stifled a groan—so much for staying up until 0200. ''Is his stateroom ready?''

''Yes, sir, and the extra desk you requested has been placed in my office.''

''Good.'' The Captain dusted a piece of black fuzz from the pocket of his whites and straightened the rack of ribbons above his pocket before returning to his seat.

Jade bit the inside of her cheek as the chair found the audacity to squeak.

''Well, if that's all, Lieutenant Parker, you're dismissed. I'm sure you're eager to change your uniform and position yourself topside before our guest arrives.'' He nodded toward the door. ''Make sure you let me know when he's here.''

Jade blinked.

He had to be joking.

She had a billion things to do—hell, the entire ship had a billion things to do—and she was expected to trot up to the quarterdeck and hang out like some groupie until the star deigned to bless them with his presence? Somehow, that particular chore didn't sit well on her to-do list. Unfortunately, the captain had spoken and there was only one correct response.

''Aye, aye, sir.''

Jade shoved open the door to Medical and stalked past the two sailors in line at the counter, not even slowing down until she reached the hospital corpsman at the end of the passageway. ''Is the doctor free?''

''Yes, ma'am. She just finished sick-call. You can go right in.''

Jade nodded as she cruised by. Rounding the corner, she

headed straight into Karin's office and flopped into the chair next to the desk. "I need Valium."

Karin laughed. "Come on, it can't be that bad."

Jade plunked her forearm out over the edge of the desk. "Skip the pills, Doc, just give it to me straight. An IV bagful oughta do it."

Karin laughed harder. "Jade, he's not even here yet…or is he?"

She scowled at the hopeful note. "Oh, no you don't. Not you, too. You swore you wouldn't go all gaga on me. The whole damn ship can volunteer to baby-sit his butt for all I care, but not you!"

Karin was laughing so hard she had to pull a tissue from the box at the corner of her desk. She took a swipe at her eyes before wadding it up and pitching it into the garbage can. She tucked a cropped blond curl behind an ear as her laughter subsided. "God, you are so much fun to torment!"

Jade winced. Damn, she'd fallen right into that one. Oh well, it wasn't the first time—and knowing Karin, it wouldn't be the last. "What can I say? I live to amuse." She eyed the steaming mug of coffee on the far side of the desk and sighed. "Okay, if you won't prescribe the Valium, can I at least get a cup of caffeine?"

Karin glanced up at the wall clock as she shoved the ceramic mug over. "You sure you have time for this? I thought the captain said he'd be here by now?"

Jade snatched it up and cradled it, savoring the heavenly blend of vanilla and coffee before she took a sip. God bless Medical and their gourmet-bean grinder. "You can't trust the Captain anymore—he's turned as rabid as the rest of the crew." The coffee was smooth, so smooth she took another sip. "In fact, you should probably take a look at him. He started salivating the minute I walked into his office. We'll be drowning in drool by the time the guy makes it aboard."

"That *guy* has a name."

Jade glowered into the mug as she slumped into the vinyl chair. "Don't remind me, I'm trying to forget."

"That's probably not a good idea, considering the fact that it's your job to keep him happy for the next six weeks."

"Yeah, well, there's a lot I'm supposed to accomplish between now and then. What do you suggest I bump to make room for *Macbeth?* The fire drills? Flooding? How about the chemical-spill exercises?" She drew a long swallow from the mug. "No, wait. Why not cancel them all? Who cares if the ship isn't ready to deploy to the Gulf? It's not like defending the free world is more important than baby-sitting some two-bit actor."

"Come on, Jade, he's not that bad. In fact, he's pretty good. If you'd seen the movie, you'd know that."

"Why bother? It's a lousy B-grade slasher flick. *One* lousy slasher flick at that. I seriously doubt he'll get nominated for an Academy Award this year." She kicked out her combat boots and crossed them. "Besides, why saddle *me* with him? I didn't even want the job."

Karin laughed. "Which is exactly *why* he was assigned to you. You're the only officer who didn't spend the morning primping in front of the mirror or compiling a list of sea stories with an autograph request tacked on the end."

"Hey, I don't see you primping, either."

Karin grinned. "Trust me, girlfriend. I've seen the strapping, blue-eyed blonde up on the silver screen, remember? If I hadn't been stuck in sick-call all morning, I'd have been primping, too."

Jade glanced down at her watch and frowned. "Shoot." She hauled herself to her feet and set the empty mug on the desk. "Speaking of which, I'd better get changed. I've got a date to sell ice-cream sundaes on the quarterdeck in fifteen minutes. Thanks for the caffeine. I owe you."

"No sweat. Get me an autograph and we'll call it even."

Jade turned back as Karin ducked playfully. "Oh, I'll give you an autograph, all right. I'll sign your—"

"DCA, please lay to the quarterdeck." The disembodied voice cut off her threat.

Jade glanced up at the gray 1MC speaker hanging in the corner of the office and feigned disappointment. "What a shame...no time to change."

Karin laughed. "At least the guy's punctual. Even you can't find fault with him for that."

Jade flashed her a wicked grin before she slipped through the door. "Wanna bet?"

He did not want to be here.

Reese paused at the end of the pier, allowing himself one last moment of honesty as he stared up at the floating gray monster.

He really did *not* want to be here.

Unfortunately, for the next several weeks this ship was exactly where he needed to be, despite the fact that it was the one place he'd sworn he'd never set foot again. He tried sloughing the memories off as he reached the ladder marked Officer's Brow. But with each clank of the metal steps, the past tightened until it formed a vise about his chest.

Don't think about it!

He reviewed his mental cheat sheet as his cowboy boots counted down the paces to his own incarceration. He was Mack Reese, actor *extraordinaire*. He was thirty years old and he was here to—

"Face the rear of the ship and snap to attention!"

His right foot hovered inches from the deck of the ship as he stared up at the cluster of Navy whites and one lone khaki uniform. "I beg your pardon?"

The khaki spoke again. "I said, face the rear of the ship and snap to attention. Now."

That voice was not acquainted with disobedience. Even as he gritted his teeth and turned to comply, he wondered why the hell he was bowing to it. His spine stiffened as the position came back instinctively—almost.

"Very good."

He had to smile at the appreciation permeating the husky alto. Somehow, he knew he'd just scored a point by honoring the nation's flag correctly. "Do you want me to salute, too?"

"No."

Damn, he'd lost it.

"Turn to the Officer of the Deck—he's the one with two gold stripes on his shoulder boards—and state your name and request permission to come aboard."

Reese executed a perfect right face.

"*Very* good."

He grinned—and lost his point again. "Mack Reese, request permission to come aboard, sir."

The Officer of the Deck nodded. "Permission granted." The man held out a hand as Reese stepped onto the ship. "Lieutenant Greg Coffey. Welcome aboard, Mr. Reese."

Reese clapped his hand into Coffey's.

"Lieutenant Coffey will need to examine your luggage." The khaki stepped squarely into view, and it was all he could do to pull the bag off his shoulder and thrust it blindly at Lieutenant Coffey.

Good God, that wasn't an officer. It wasn't even a woman. It was a sea nymph. A mermaid with legs. One hundred percent slender, curvaceous proof the Ancient Greeks were wrong. All the way from her wide gray eyes and dusky cheeks to her sinfully full lips and stubborn jaw. Past the gentle slopes pushing at the pockets of her drab khaki shirt, right down to the maddening dip cinched in by a brass belt buckle.

They were dead wrong.

Aphrodite didn't spring from the foam of the sea; she was created right here, right now, on the steel decks of a modern U.S. Naval warship.

"Macbeth!"

The sharp bark split through his musings. Reese jerked

his gaze back to her face. To those gray eyes beneath a red ball cap that proclaimed *USS Baddager, AD 52*. He wondered if her hair was as black as those inky lashes.

"The name is Reese—Mack Reese." He grinned. "But you can call me Reese."

His gut tightened as her hand slid into his and returned his firm grip. She must have felt the jolt, too, because she jerked her hand back and tucked it behind her waist.

"His bags are clean, Lieutenant Parker."

So *that* was Aphrodite's name. Reese turned around at the man's pronouncement, casually scoping the quarterdeck and its security as he reclaimed his canvas bag.

Lieutenant Coffey cocked his head toward the bag. "Sorry, sir, standard procedure. Every item coming on or going off a Naval vessel must be searched."

"I understand."

"By the way, you'll need to get your Walkman checked by an electrician if you intend to plug it in."

Reese noticed the Petty Officer of the Watch the moment he exited the guard shack just off the quarterdeck. He studied him quickly—seeking, and finding, the .45 caliber pistol strapped to his waist. He made a note to find out if it was loaded as he turned back to Lieutenant Coffey and flashed him a grin. "Nope, I'm strictly an alkaline kinda guy. So, what's the game plan—when and where do I start?"

"Here and now." Aphrodite spoke again, and he turned to pay homage. "You start with an overview of the ship, Mr. Reese. A crash course in seamanship, if you will. Public Affairs felt if the Navy was to take on this particular project, it should be supported all the way."

He nodded. "And this support entails...?"

"You've been assigned a running mate—a buddy. Someone to assist you during your stay aboard the *Baddager*. A sailor to show you around, answer your questions, to aid you in your characterization."

He could feel his grin widening. "You're telling me I've got a baby-sitter, aren't you?"

Was that grudging respect flickering in those dark gray eyes? "I wouldn't put it precisely like that."

Yes, she would. For some reason, Reese also sensed she was having difficulty forming her next words. He prompted her. "So who's my baby-sitter? Where is he?"

"*He* is a she."

Reese froze. He didn't dare breathe. He was certain if he was absolutely still, that if the stars and planets were perfectly aligned in the heavens, God might smile down upon his humble form and grant him a reward for agreeing to this blasted plan in the first place.

"Me."

His breath escaped on a soft whoosh as that single husky word slithered down his body and coiled into his groin. For the first time since he'd taken this job, his world was nearly perfect and he was almost content.

But *she* was not.

Oh, she was trying pretty hard not to show it, but it was there, nonetheless. It was in the stiff, too-proper smile and in the slightly oversquared shoulders, but most of all it was in those gorgeous gray eyes that weren't quite looking *at* him.

"Captain's on deck!"

Reese turned to the toothy grin striding toward him.

"Mr. Reese—Mack. Welcome aboard. I hope my crew has told you what an honor it is to have you staying on the *Baddager*."

Reese returned the Captain's shake. "Yes, sir, they have. In fact, Lieutenant Parker was just telling me how much she's looking forward to helping me get into character."

"Good, good." He turned. "DCA, I thought I asked you to let me know when Mr. Reese arrived."

Reese didn't care if the man was her Captain, he did not like his tone. He stepped forward. "It's my fault, sir. I'm afraid I've monopolized the lieutenant's time since the second I stepped on board.''

She stabbed him with a glare.

Reese shrugged.

But her Captain turned back with a smile. ''No matter, you're here now. I suppose you'll want to take a few moments to stow your gear before the DCA shows you around. Perhaps you'd like to join me in my cabin for lunch?''

Not really. But lunch was as good a time as any to begin probing his way into the crew of the *Baddager.* Who better to start with than the Commanding Officer? ''I'd be honored to join you, sir.''

''Fine.'' The captain nodded. ''DCA, I'll expect you in my quarters at 1230 hours.'' With a flurry of salutes, he was off.

Reese followed his new running mate as she turned and lifted the lever on a heavy oval door. She stepped over the bottom lip, motioning him to follow her through the steel skin of the ship.

''Why does he call you DCA?''

She didn't even glance at him as they headed down a narrow passageway. ''That's who I am. I'm the Damage Control Assistant—DCA. A lot of officers on a ship are referred to by their position.''

She nodded a greeting as another khaki passed. ''That's Ops—the Operations Officer—he's in charge of the ship's movement: navigation, radars, communications, anything electronic that involves getting the *Baddager* from point A to point B. I work for the Chief Engineer—the Cheng. She's in charge of the mechanical side of the ship's movement— the boilers, turbines, anything and everything it takes to make the steam turn the screws.''

They rounded a corner and suddenly the entire ship went black. An eerie silence followed. Reese tensed as he felt her hand come down on his bare forearm.

"Relax." Her throaty chuckle washed over him, unexpectedly causing the most erotic fantasy to flash to life.

Her, him.

In the dark.

In a bed, against the wall, on the floor—it didn't matter. All that mattered was that he could feel her hands on him. Not just on his arms, but all over him. On his chest, on his waist. His hips, his thighs, his—

A deep mechanical keening reverberated through the ship, and a split second later, the lights came back on, searing the fantasy to embers. The background noise had come back, too. He could almost make out the sounds of individual motors and fans, as if various machinery were being restarted.

He glanced down at the slender fingers still pressed into his arm, regretting it as her gaze followed his.

She jerked her hand away and continued walking. "*That* is called dropping the load. The electrical load. Right now, the ship is on shore power—we usually only generate our own juice when we're underway."

"So what happened, someone stick a finger in a light socket?"

She was not amused.

He tried to stifle his grin—and failed.

"Listen, Macbeth—"

"Reese. I told you before, the name is Mack Reese. But you can call me Reese." He willed her to say it as he met her gaze. Never before had it been so important that he be addressed by his real name. Until now.

Her gray eyes stared right back at him for so long he was certain he'd won.

"Listen, *Macbeth,* I don't know what you think you've gotten yourself into, but this isn't some game and my ship isn't your toy."

"*Your* ship?" He took the liberty of irritating her again as he grinned down at her. "I thought this was—" he jerked his thumb behind them ''—that guy's. The one with the scrambled eggs all over his hat.''

She stopped short at the base of a steel ladder and he had to put his hands out to keep from slamming into her. The glance she blistered him with as his palms brushed her ribs could have vaporized the Pacific.

Regretfully, he pulled them back.

''That *hat* is called a cover, those *eggs* are gold leaf, and that *guy* is a Captain. Captain White, to be specific. While I may not agree with his harebrained scheme to bring you in here so you can bastardize our image in some television series, make no mistake, mister, this ship is *mine*. I train the crew to fight her fires, I stop up her leaks and I send out the welders to stitch her back together. I even clean up her air when it stinks to high heaven from the latest toxic gases. If that doesn't make her mine, I don't know what does.''

Reese stood there, stunned, as she spun on her boots and practically stomped up the ladder. His gut screamed she wasn't the one he was looking for. With an attitude like that, she couldn't possibly be.

But he ignored his instincts. He had to. He didn't have a shred of evidence to support them.

Hell, he didn't even know her first name.

''DCA, wait up!'' He took the steps three at a time and caught up with her as she stabbed a key into the lock in one of the slim gray doors lined up on parade along the corridor.

She shoved the door open and pointed inside the tiny rectangular cabin. ''This is your stateroom for the duration of your stay. Enjoy.'' That last word did not mean what it was supposed to.

Reese lifted a brow. ''I thought you were going to show me around?''

Her cheeks took on a hue that nearly matched her scarlet ball cap. Hell, she was just too darned easy to rile. It took the fun out of it—almost. Reese shoved his chuckle way down deep as she entered the room and stalked around the pea-green carpet.

"Very well. If that's the way you want it." She pointed to the bunk. "*This* is your rack. This is your desk, your chair and your sink. Feel free to stow your toiletries behind the mirror." She popped it open with her index finger to reveal the metal shelves behind, then snapped it shut before turning to the modular wall unit. "These are your drawers, and this is your closet."

She marched over to the open porthole and tapped the center of the cover hanging beneath it, a large *D* with a black *Z* spray-painted inside. "This symbol is referred to as a Dog Zebra. While underway, all doors, portholes and hatches bearing this symbol must be kept closed between sunset and sunrise—"

"Why?"

The look she gave him stopped him cold. It told him more than her words could ever say. She didn't want him here and she didn't want to change her mind.

Maybe it was time he convinced her otherwise. It couldn't hurt. And if it worked, it would certainly make his job a lot easier. Especially if she planned on taking her baby-sitting duties seriously.

He smiled.

Oddly enough, that seemed to increase the chill emanating from her.

He tried a different tactic. "I'm sorry."

That didn't work, either.

Now what?

"Look, Macbeth. We both know you had to have pulled some pretty powerful strings to land this gig. We both also know I've got a couple stitched into me by that guy upstairs." She sighed deeply. "And even though I can't find the time to sit down to re-tie my own shoes, I'm supposed to make like the happy marionette. So why don't you just cut to the chase and tell me what you really want?"

A dangerous question.

Then again, he had a dangerous job ahead. Still, he didn't know whom he could trust, and as much as his gut screamed she wasn't involved, he'd yet to convince his head. Until then, she was a means to an end. And the sooner he was able to get to her, the sooner he'd be able to use her to that end.

"Take off your cover."

Her gaze narrowed and turned steel gray. His response seemed to be down among the last she'd expected. Good.

"Why?"

He shrugged. "Maybe I get off on pulling strings."

She continued to glare up at him from underneath that damned obscuring bill. He didn't think she was going to do it. But she did.

She reached up and slowly peeled the cap back. It took every ounce of concentration he possessed not to suck in his breath as a light fringe of bangs fell forward, almost into her eyes.

Black.

Her hair was black.

The precise bluish, luminescent shade he'd first noticed way back in the sixth grade. Just catching a glimpse of the color through the years was enough to get him hot. And right now—as he clenched his fingers into his palms to keep from digging them into that gloriously fat braid—he was positively *smoking*.

Her chin came up, along with a defiant brow. "Like what you see?"

"Yes."

God, yes.

He repeated his mantra over and over as her cool gaze slid down his body, searing his skin right through his T-shirt and jeans, leaving him piercingly alert. She was a means to an end—*a means to an end*—nothing more.

She finally returned to his face. "So do I."

Somehow, he managed not to groan.

"Next question?"

He was so damned close to forgetting why he was here, it was frightening.

"What's your name?" His voice bordered on hoarse.

"Jade."

He tried it out in his mind as he restrung his vocal cords. *Jade*. It suited her. It suited him.

She moistened her lips in the silence.

As the magnet snared and drew him in, he knew without a doubt it was time to end this round. Before it went all the way. He smiled. "Well, Jade, I suggest you let me unpack or we'll never make it to lunch with the Captain. You'll have to fill me in on the Zebra Dog later."

She blinked, and in an instant the serious lieutenant returned.

He hated it.

She briskly capped her hair and glanced at a chunky sports watch before nodding. "Fine. I'll meet you back here in twenty minutes." And then she was gone.

Reese ignored the emptiness that assumed her place as he glanced at his own watch. Twenty minutes. That didn't leave much time.

He turned to the modular wall unit and released the catch, flipping down the painted steel to form a temporary desk. There it was. Just like in all the staterooms.

The safe.

He pulled the small door open and retrieved the generic slip of paper listing the step-by-step instructions on how to reset the combination. After completing the task, he backed away and lowered himself onto the side of the bed Jade had called a rack, sinking deep into the mattress as he pulled off his boots.

Yup, his bag had been clean, all right.

Too bad *he* wasn't.

Reese removed his gear from his boots and concealed it within the safe. Then he spun the dial to lock it before he picked up his bag and turned his attention to the mission ahead.

Chapter 2

Jade snapped the door to her stateroom shut and promptly collapsed back against it. She barely had time for a single breath before the tremors began. They started out small, then consumed her as she slid down against the door, not ebbing until she reached the bottom.

And there she sat. Drained and devoid of everything, except the very reason they'd begun.

Reese.

Mack Reese.

How was she ever going to make it through the next six weeks in that man's company? She'd barely made it through the last thirty minutes, and then the only thing that had saved her was her father. She could still hear him as if he were standing next to her instead of a thousand miles away.

You let him get to you, Missy.

"I tried not to, Dad."

Do you want to be taken seriously or not?

"You know I do."

Then stick to the rules. Never let 'em see the woman.

Keeps 'em on their toes. Lets 'em know you're a force to be reckoned with. An equal.

She tipped her head back against the steel door. Dad was right. She'd violated the rules, and look where it had gotten her.

In lust.

She didn't bother trying to pretty it up—at least not here, not to herself. She was in lust.

But oh, *baby,* what a man to be in lust with!

She turned her head to the left and stared intently at the bulkhead, wishing she could see through it. Wishing she could get another steamy glimpse of that golden, muscular giant.

The funny part was, she didn't even like blondes. Especially when they came attached to tanned, T-shirt-clad bodies that looked as if they'd stepped off the set of *Baywatch.* She probably wouldn't have even given Reese a second glance if he hadn't cocked that arrogant head down and stared into her eyes.

Periwinkle.

His eyes weren't blue, they were periwinkle.

She'd never thought she'd actually see the color outside a jumbo box of crayons.

But she had.

And now she had to figure out how to keep that from becoming her downfall. Because if she wasn't careful, those eyes could make her notice a whole lot more.

Like those firm, full lips. Like that cleft in his chin that deepened when he smiled. Like those long, thick lashes a model would gain ten pounds to have. And those tiny laugh lines that seemed to be permanently etched around his eyes.

Like that body.

She jerked off her ball cap and twisted it between her hands as she tried to exorcise the memory. No, she could *not* afford to look into those eyes again. How she'd manage that while he was glued to her side for the next six weeks, she wasn't sure. But she'd figure it out. She'd have to. Before she was tempted to explore a fantasy she never thought she'd have and risk breaking the Navy's cardinal rule in the process.

Absolutely no sex aboard a ship.

Rap, rap, rap.

Jade scrambled off the deck and stood panicking in the center of her room as she stared at the door.

Reese.

No, it couldn't be. She glanced down at her watch. She had over fifteen minutes left—besides, he didn't even know her stateroom was next door to his.

But just in case, she jammed her cover back on her head before she reached for the door. There was no way he was talking her out of her ball cap again. Once was bad enough.

Karin stood on the other side, tapping her foot. *"Well?"*

"Well, what?"

The boot increased its tempo. "Come on, Jade. Rumor Control posted the alert the second he stepped aboard. The entire ship knows he's here by now. *What's he like?"*

Something thumped softly in the stateroom next door, causing Jade's stomach to plunge to her toes. She snaked out a hand and tugged Karin inside as she hissed, "Keep your voice down!"

"Why?" Her blue eyes grew round. "He's next door, isn't he?"

"Yes!"

"Yippee!"

Jade glared at her.

Karin ignored her as she rubbed her hands together. "So, come on, *dish.* What's he like? Is he as sexy in person as he is on the screen?"

A filthy, traitorous heat snuck up her neck and consumed her face.

"Oh, my God. You're blushing!"

She shot off another glare. "I am not!"

Karin grinned slyly. "That good, huh?"

Jade sighed and plopped into the chair at her desk, her gaze slinking down to the carpet. "You want me to say it? Okay, I'll say it. He's gorgeous. He's sexy. He sizzles. Hell, he's so hot, I'll probably have to call in a hose team to spray him down every now and then so he doesn't ignite the ship."

"Damn."

Jade looked up. "Yeah."

"That settles it. We're changing jobs for the next couple of months. You get to slice people open and I get to stitch myself to Mack Reese."

"Reese."

"Huh?"

"It's just Reese. Don't ask me why, but he likes to be called by his last name."

Karin perched herself up on the desk. "My, my, my. We've gotten awfully close to Mr. *Macbeth* awfully quickly, haven't we?"

Jade stuck her out her tongue.

"I think you'd better save that for Reese. He may find a use for it."

"Karin!"

She laughed. "Hey, blame it on the Navy. You try explaining safe sex and demonstrating how to don a condom to a crew of dirty-minded sailors and see how pristine your mouth stays." She leaned close and coughed gently. "Speaking of condoms, need any?"

"No!"

She shook her head, smiling as she pulled back. "Don't be too sure about that. If Reese is half as turned on as you, I'll probably be a crate short by sunrise."

Jade glanced away and studied the pillow on her rack. This conversation was getting way out control. She still hadn't even recovered from her inspection of Reese.

Heck, she wasn't even sure how she'd found the nerve to

carry it off. Especially when she followed the fire in his eyes all the way down to the heat rising off his jeans. Button-fly jeans. The blush she'd managed to hold at bay in his stateroom snapped back with a vengeance.

"Okay, I'll lay off—for now."

"Thank you."

"Then again—" she tapped her chin "—maybe…"

"Don't *even* say it."

Karin ignored her, nodding as she warmed to the idea. "Why not? What's the harm in a little fling—as long as you do it on the beach and protect yourself."

"I said, *no.*"

"Well, at least think about it. You said yourself the man is gorgeous—and you can't get much better than an actor. They have affairs all the time, no strings attached. Heck, you won't even have to worry about running into him again, because he'll be long gone by the time it's over."

"Absolutely not."

The last time she'd let her guard down, it had nearly destroyed her. She was not making the same mistake again. She was *not.*

Karin sighed. "When are you going to realize Jeff was the exception, not the rule? Not every man dreams of keeping his wife barefoot and pregnant."

Jade grimaced. "Don't forget the kitchen part."

Karin reached out and squeezed her hand. "I'm serious, honey. At least you wouldn't worry about bumping into your replacement." She brightened. "As if he *could* replace you."

Oh, he could, all right.

And probably would.

History did have a tendency to repeat itself, after all. But that didn't mean she had to suffer through another humiliating lesson.

"Jade—"

A series of high-pitched musical whistles and trills filled

the stateroom as a Boatswain mate piped "chow" over the 1MC, cutting off the rest of Karin's argument.

Thank God.

Jade glanced at her watch, then tugged her cover securely to her eyes as she stood. "Well, Doc, gotta go. Macbeth and I have a command performance at the Captain's table."

Karin wrinkled her nose as she stood. "Ick. I'm not sure even sitting with Reese would be worth putting up with that."

Jade was certain it wasn't—for several reasons. But duty called and that was enough for her.

It had to be.

"Just one more chance, DCA. That's all I ask."

Jade bit down on the inside of her cheek as she stared across her desk. She'd give anything to be able to look away from Benson's tortured gaze. But as his division officer, she couldn't. She owed it to him to look him in the eye while she delivered the blow.

"I'm sorry, Benson. You're going to Captain's mast on Monday."

"*Please,* DCA. Please, don't do it. I'll lose a stripe for sure."

"Maybe you should have thought about that before you were late for General Quarters."

She bit down harder as his eyes took on a glassy appearance.

Oh, please, God, don't let him cry. You know I can't handle that.

He didn't, but his voice broke, slicing into her just the same. "P-please, DCA, I-I need the money. Shelly hasn't gone back to work yet."

Her teeth drew blood as she tried to get the picture of his sweet, adorable infant out of her mind. She reminded herself again that this was for the best—for the baby as well as the father. She drew a deep breath. "My decision is final. Save your arguments for the Captain."

Benson jerked back from her desk, bitterness permeating his voice as well as his stance. "Why bother? We both know he'll take your recommendation."

Jade nodded, not bothering to deny it. Reaching across her blotter, she scratched out a number and handed the scrap of paper across the desk. "Here's the number for Navy Relief. They'll help you out with the money if you need it."

Benson stared down at the paper as if it was a python. It was a full thirty seconds before he snatched it up and stuffed it into the side pocket of his coveralls. "Thanks a lot, *ma'am.*"

Jade ignored the deliberate slur as he turned and stalked out of her office, concentrating instead on the fact that he'd actually taken the number. It was a start.

She tipped the bill of her cover up so it wouldn't hit the desk and dropped her face down into her arms.

"Don't you think you came down a little hard on the guy?"

She bolted straight up in her chair, scowling as she yanked the bill back in place. "How long have you been standing in the passageway, Macbeth?"

"Long enough."

Jade grabbed on to her anger with both hands, using it to shield herself from the shock of seeing Reese in her office, looking thoroughly at home and too damn masculine in a pair of dark blue Navy coveralls and a *Baddager* ball cap— red.

Why did her chief have to give him a *red* one? "Well, next time you get the urge to eavesdrop, take a page from Miss Manners and announce yourself."

"Thought about it. But I didn't think the man would appreciate knowing he had a witness to his groveling."

Great. Another meddling he-man who thought he knew

it all and didn't approve. It shouldn't have gotten to her. It shouldn't have stung.

But it did.

Until now, she had to admit, she'd harbored hopes that Reese was different from Jeff. Obviously he wasn't. "You know, I don't recall the Captain telling me I had to let you run my division."

"Maybe he should have. Maybe then Benson could get a little slack."

The accusation didn't sit well in her craw—and neither did the injustice of it. "Trust me, slack is the one thing Benson *doesn't* need."

"Why? Are you afraid if you sympathize with the guy, word will get out that you're soft?"

The accuracy behind that arrow *really* stung. Reese was foolish enough to try and drive it in further as he loomed over her desk.

"You know, when I stepped on this ship yesterday, I didn't have you pegged for a cold one—uptight, maybe, but not cold. It was a drill, Jade. A lousy drill. Did you have to punish him in the wallet? The man has a wife and kids."

Uptight? Cold? She'd give him *cold*.

Jade came to her feet with the power of an aircraft carrier and steamed around the desk at ahead full. "Yes, he has a family. But he also has a drinking problem, not that it's any business of yours. The reason he missed General Quarters is because he was out so late carousing the night before, he was still stinking *drunk* the next morning. It took two sailors and a chief to pull him out of a rack that was filled with vomit. Sailors I could ill afford to lose had that been the real thing and not a *drill*."

Reese knew he'd blown it. He'd realized that as soon as the words left his mouth, but it was already too late. Hell, he wasn't even sure why he'd done it.

Okay, so he was sure. But he wasn't proud of it. Too many old memories had come slapping back at once. He probably could have handled them if he wasn't still smarting over the Captain's lunch—and the treatment that had followed.

Some running mate. Jade had been pawning him off every opportunity she could. First, she'd seated him next to the Captain and then abandoned him for a spot on the far side of the table next to Lieutenant Coffey—the same officer who'd checked his bag. Afterward, she'd dumped him on her chief.

Following a lengthy tour of the ship—*except* the areas he'd really needed to see—they'd settled in the chief's mess. He'd spent the rest of the day in the lounge, fielding questions about famous actresses. While the chiefs were a friendly, jovial group, they didn't seem prone to the kind of gossip he was interested in.

At least not with outsiders.

Investigation-wise, the day had been a bust. He hadn't learned a single thing he could use to accomplish the job he'd been sent to do. And now he'd managed to blow it with Jade—so far his only obvious, albeit reluctant, bridge to the inner sanctum.

Way to go, buddy.

Well, he couldn't take the words back now. But he could apologize. "Jade—"

"DCA? The Command Duty Officer can't find the draft report *again.*"

Damn.

Reese backed away from Jade's cluttered desk and retreated to the naked one she'd assigned him as a young sailor breezed up and passed her a slip of paper.

Jade glanced up as she scrawled her signature at the bottom of the sheet. "Let me guess, Lieutenant Dillon is Command Duty Officer today, isn't he?"

Dillon? The *same* Dillon he was here to investigate? Reese forced his body to relax.

The sailor grinned as if she and Jade shared some private joke. "How'd you guess?"

"Tell Lieutenant Dillon I said the next time he loses the draft report, he should look over the side of the ship. If it's still floating, we're okay."

The sailor laughed as she retrieved the paper. "Yes, ma'am." She turned to Reese and handed him another slip of paper and the pen. "Do you mind?"

Mind what? Oh, *right*. He grabbed the paper and scratched the name he was using onto it. "Here you go, hon."

"Thanks, Mack."

He took the invitation in her smile as a compliment, even if it was a bit zealous. No doubt it was more than he'd get from Jade. At least until he figured out how to repair the damage he'd done—and turn the conversation back to that draft report. And Lieutenant Dillon.

He turned back as the sailor left, smiling as Jade sat down and shoved a stack of papers around her desk, then rearranged a mug of pens. That had to be a good sign.

Especially the pink highlighting her cheeks.

"Jade, we need to talk."

She slapped the mug back onto the corner of the desk and stood. "Sorry, Macbeth, no time. Got a meeting to attend."

His jaw set again at the nickname she'd baptized him with. It hadn't bothered him as much yesterday—until he'd figured out she was the only one using it.

He rounded his desk before she could slip past without him. He'd just have to apologize on the go. "I'm ready, running mate."

Her brisk wave stopped him. "No can do. Some of the information's classified." She smiled. "Sorry."

That smile didn't look sorry. It looked relieved. There was something else in there, too, and whatever it was, he wasn't sure he liked it.

"Don't worry, Macbeth, you won't even miss me. I've got a nice character-building experience lined up for you today."

He was sure now; he didn't like it. The wariness in his gut crept into his voice. "What kind of experience?"

"Petty Officer Swanson will tell you all about it when he gets here." She stepped over the lip of the watertight door and turned back. "Oh, and one more thing? Don't forget your toothbrush."

Jade adjusted her oxygen mask and hunkered down into the darkened corner of the nearly empty lube oil tank before she cracked off the ends of her last hydrocarbon tube and shoved it into the handheld bellows. She forced the ambient air through the thin glass and then pulled a flashlight out from under her arm and checked the results to see if the air was breathable.

It was.

She squished her way back to the access port and gave her tether three good yanks. Two large, beefy hands slipped through the hole to claim her gas-free gear, then came back for her.

Finally free from the tank, she ripped off her mask and took a deep gulp. "God, I hate canned oxygen."

"You and me both." Her chief nodded down to the access port. "How's the air?"

"Fine. It's breathable." She handed him the slim tubes. "But tell Callahan to drain the tank better next time."

Chief Haas grinned at her white paper suit. Only it wasn't white anymore. Thick yellow streaks of oil clung to her from her shoulders down to her toes. "Yeah, I've seen turkeys with less basting."

"No kidding." She ripped off the soggy booties and slipped into her boots. "Speaking of turkeys, how's our boy?"

"Fine, last time I checked."

She peeled off her hood before snatching her ball cap off the air compressor and shoving it on. "You mean he's actually *doing* it?"

"Doing? Hell, he's almost done."

"No way. This I gotta see." She rounded the electrician's station and headed up the ladder. When she reached the top, she broke the air lock on the swinging door and struck out across the machine shop.

She really hadn't expected to get away with it, but it was just too darn tempting not to try. All afternoon she'd kept one ear cocked toward the 1MC, expecting to be ordered to the Captain's cabin so he could chew her up and spit her out on the carpet. At the very least, she'd expected Reese to throw a tantrum.

She passed the last drill press and stepped into the midships passageway and stopped short. She'd expected fallout, all right. What she hadn't expected was *this*.

Her jaw dropped as she stared out over the forty-foot passageway—a glistening, spit-polished, scrubbed-so-hard-you-could-eat-off-it passageway. On the other side, in a jungle of brooms, mops and buckets stood Reese, buffing the heck out of the brass bell at the opening to the midships brow.

Not only was he oblivious to the steady trickle of sailors boarding and disembarking the ship around him, he didn't even look up until she was almost on top of him.

Reese finally glanced up as she cleared her throat. He slapped the cotton rag over his shoulder, grinning as he tipped his ball cap to her. "What do you think, DCA? Will I make a convincing sailor?"

She didn't know what to say.

Midships was the ugliest, dirtiest, busiest passageway on the ship. With the post office and mess decks off one end, and the engineering and berthing compartments off the other, all nine hundred and fifty-five sailors had to pass through here at least a dozen times a day.

And he'd cleaned the whole thing by himself?

There was only one thing she *could* say.

She crossed the last couple of gleaming tiles and stuck out a hand. "Not bad, Macbeth. I'm impressed."

It was a mistake.

She realized it the second his hand enveloped hers. Whatever had sparked between them when he'd touched her on the quarterdeck yesterday hadn't been a fluke. She tugged her hand back and tried to ignore the tingling in her palm.

Apparently it was time to add one more rule to her growing list concerning Mack Reese. Don't look at his smile. Don't stare directly into his eyes. And, for God's sake, don't *touch* him.

She covered with a laugh and swept a hand around. "Let me guess, you worked as a janitor to put yourself through acting class."

"Nope, dishwasher." He reached out and seared a finger down her cheek, chuckling as he held up a smudge of lube oil that had transferred to him. "Looks like you could use a good washing yourself. Care to take advantage of my expertise?"

Jade evaded the suggestive gleam in his eyes as she tried to scrub the image of the two of them, naked and slick, from her mind. By the time she'd glanced back, his gaze had smelted to dark blue.

She took a deep breath, amazed she still could. "I think I'll pass, for now."

"Feel free to take a rain check—*anytime.*"

The decadent image slammed into her again. Yes, it was definitely time to change the subject.

He must have thought so, too, because he took a deep breath right along with her that time. "So what is that gunk?"

"Oil."

He chuckled. "*That,* even I can tell. Why are you soaking in it?"

"Believe me, I wasn't trying to. I had to gas-free a lube oil tank—test the oxygen—so it could be entered and cleaned."

"Didn't you guys used to use canaries for that?"

Jade grinned. "We still do. I'm the canary." Her admiration for Reese grew as she stacked that knowledge atop his precision movements on the quarterdeck. "When you research a part, you go all the way, don't you?"

Something flickered in his eyes—almost as if he was uncomfortable with her praise—but as quickly as it came, it was gone. He shrugged. "I try."

An actor who couldn't take a compliment? Odd. Shouldn't he have the opposite reaction? Shouldn't his ego be swelling right about now? Maybe she'd misjudged him more than she'd thought.

"Listen, Macbeth—"

"Hey, Mack, what's up? You finish cleaning for the Wicked Witch of the Pacific?"

Jade gritted her teeth and turned sharply.

"Hey, DCA. Didn't see you there."

Right. And she couldn't spot an aircraft carrier twenty yards off the bow. "Dillon." Her glare warned him to back off—now.

He ignored her and turned his cheesy grin on Reese. "So, how 'bout it? You up to a couple of beers after knock-off?"

"*What?*"

Crap. Reese almost uttered the curse aloud as Jade stiffened and turned to stare at him, disgust lacing more than her voice. Personally, he felt the same way about Lieutenant Dillon. And he'd only known him for two hours. Unfortunately, befriending the man was more than necessary—it was downright vital. But that didn't make stomaching the task any easier.

He just wished Dillon had better timing. Why did he have to show up now? Just when he was finally getting somewhere with Jade.

Reese shoved his loathing aside and nodded. "Sure thing." He cocked his head toward a still-seething Jade. "Just as soon as the boss lady gives the word."

He almost winced as Jade's eyes narrowed. He had a feeling he'd rather not hear the words she was burning to give.

But before she had a chance to let them rip, Dillon took a deep sniff of the surrounding air and shuddered as he eyed her oily garb. "What *is* that stench? Oh, sorry, must be *eau de DCA.*"

Jeez, the man was an ass. Reese latched on to the mop leaning against the bulkhead, strangling it in lieu of Dillon's neck. He loosened his grip in surprise as Jade laughed.

"That's right, Mike. I'm not surprised you don't recognize it. It's the scent of good old-fashioned hard work." Reese almost chuckled as she leaned into Dillon. "Take another whiff. It's as close as you're likely to come, if you can help it." With that she turned on her heel and strolled down the passageway.

Dillon turned back to Reese, still scowling. "Did I say Wicked Witch? I meant Wicked Bitch."

Reese clamped down on the mop again, perilously close to snapping the smooth wood. "What's up with you two? You guys have some kind of mutual contempt society going?"

"Contempt?" Dillon laughed. "Yeah, you could put it like that. So, who's driving?"

Reese loosened his grip on the handle but kept it at the ready—just in case. "Why don't I just follow you?"

"Sounds good to me. See you tonight."

Reese waved back as the guy headed down the passageway, wishing for a fleeting moment he was meeting Jade instead. Unfortunately, Jade couldn't take him where he needed to go. At least not as easily as Dillon could.

Yeah, he'd have a few beers with the guy. He'd pretend to be Mike's new best friend and let the blowhard brag about his Hollywood connection all over San Diego if that's what it took. Hell, he'd even smile and laugh when he did it.

Because he knew from experience he'd get a heck of a lot further with the guy as Mack Reese, the actor, than he ever would as Reese Garrick, the undercover agent.

Chapter 3

Jade groaned and slumped back into the corner of their dimly lit booth. "Oh, Lord. What is *he* doing here?"

Karin jerked her head up from her strawberry daiquiri, scanning the entrance to the bar of the Officer's Club. "Ick, Dillon." She shuddered. "I have no idea, but it can't be good."

"I know it isn't." Like the nightmare that had plagued her for two days, Jade knew what—or rather, *who*—was bound to show next.

Sure enough, he did.

"Pinch me."

Jade glared at her. "Knock it off—and wipe your chin."

"Oh, come on, we both know you're drooling, too. You're just better at hiding it."

Jade glanced away from the truth—only to run smack into it again across the bar.

Reese.

It was bad enough he was here with *Dillon;* why did he have to compound the sin and look so damn good? It looked as though someone had skipped the loom and woven that white T-shirt and jeans straight onto his muscular frame. Good Lord, she could make out the definition in his broad chest from here.

She jerked her gaze back to Karin as the two men crossed the room and claimed stools at the bar—not more than fifteen feet away—and took a hasty sip of her soda. "What's to drool over?"

Karin laughed. "I hope you mentioned you were a pathological liar when they granted your security clearance."

Jade was about to stick out her tongue—then thought better of it. She shook her head instead. "You know, I just don't get it. Of all the people Reese could have hooked up with, why *him?*"

Karin shrugged. "What's to get? He *is* studying how to be a professional sailor."

"From Dillon?" She laughed. "Right—and I've been known to drive a team of huskies across the Yukon."

But Karin wasn't laughing. "Maybe he's the only one who offered."

The gentle accusation stopped Jade cold. She stared over at the men. Though they were both turned in toward each other, Dillon seemed to be the only one talking. Nothing unusual there. He probably hadn't gotten past himself yet.

But as she continued to watch, she *did* notice something unusual—or was it her imagination? Each time Reese laughed at something Mike said, she had the distinct feeling he didn't mean it.

Oh, he looked amused.

On the surface.

But she had the strangest feeling he was just going through the motions. Maybe it was his hands. They hadn't moved an inch from their position on the beer bottle the entire time she'd been watching him. As she studied them closer, she could have sworn they were tense.

But why would Reese be socializing with Mike Dillon if

he didn't want to be? Jade shook her head. Oh, hell. Even if she knew the answer, it wasn't any of her business.

She turned back to Karin. If Reese was willing to hook up to Dillon, bully for them. Unlike Mike, *she* didn't have time to play mentor to anyone, let alone some two-bit actor. Even if she *did* have the time, she had no business tutoring that particular actor.

Nope. No business at all. Not with the way her body reacted whenever he was around.

She'd worked too long and too hard to blow it now.

"Oh, man. How did *she* get in here?"

Reese knew exactly to whom Dillon was referring. He'd known since the moment they'd walked into the bar—he'd just had to search around a bit to home in on her precise location.

Jade.

He'd like to be able to chalk his instinct up to some psychic sixth sense. But he knew better. It was tied to something a bit more physical, a bit more concrete. He just wished it wasn't quite so *concrete.* Because he was having a hell of a time concentrating on anything else.

And he needed to concentrate. If he didn't, he'd never get Dillon past his life story.

Reese shrugged. "This is the Officer's Club. She *is* an officer."

"Barely."

He raised his brow at that. "What is it with you two? You got something against gorgeous women?"

Dillon sneered without looking back at her. "Gorgeous, yes. Woman, no. Hell, I'm not even sure she's human."

Reese was inclined to agree with the assessment. Even two days of getting the brush-off hadn't changed his opinion. Jade was a goddess. But where was the crime in that? He sure as heck didn't mind working around stimulating scenery for a change.

"I'm serious, Mack. Look at her. What do you see?"

Oh, no, he was *not* going there. Not now. And certainly not with this moron. Those were confessions best left to the privacy of his own mind—and body. And *only* after the job was done. "I told you, she's gorgeous."

"No, look beyond that."

He didn't understand.

"The Navy, Mack, the Navy. That's all there is. That's not a woman sitting there, it's the Navy—all rolled up in one neat little package. And she's never gonna let you forget it."

Reese planted his boots into the rung of the barstool to keep from shifting against the declaration. Dillon had lit on the one thing that could still make his blood run cold—even after all these years. He diverted the subject out of self-defense. "You mean she doesn't date? No boyfriend?"

He resisted the urge to clap his hand over Dillon's mouth as the man's laughter barked out. "Boyfriend? Jade? Oh, excuse me—*Lieutenant* Parker. With her attitude? No way, man. No way, no how, no time. We're talking hard-core Navy. Hell, she's so gungi, she's probably got saltwater running through those veins."

No way. A woman like that, living only for her career? Dillon was exaggerating. He had to be.

Reese picked up his beer and tipped back a swallow. Heck, he oughta know; he'd spent an hour on the ship and another half hour here listening to the guy spin sea stories out of his rear. Stories he knew were fabricated—because he'd read the man's personnel jacket not more than seventy-two hours ago.

Dillon leaned closer, blasting him with beer. "Take a good look, Mack. It's 1900 hours—7:00 p.m.—and she's still in her uniform."

To tell the truth, that *had* bothered him, but not for the reason it seemed to bother Dillon. Reese just wanted to see her with her hair down. Small-enough reward for having to sit here and listen to this blowhard all night.

He jerked his gaze back to Dillon. Then again, maybe it was the same reason. Maybe Dillon had struck out with Jade—and hadn't taken it well.

Sour grapes. That had to be it. It made a lot more sense than Jade Parker cutting herself off from men—and thus his own plans for her. *That* he wouldn't consider. He couldn't afford to.

Something must have showed on his face, because Dillon leaned back and sent out a fresh blast of beer breath. "It'll never happen, Mack. I've got a hundred bucks on the table that says you won't even get to see her hair down." He barked again. "I oughta know, I haven't even seen it—and I've known her for three years."

For some reason the revelation made him feel better, not worse. But a bet? You didn't bet over a woman—and never a woman like Jade. It went beyond crass.

Then again, so did Dillon. All in all, the man was perfect suspect material. Now he just had to find the evidence to connect him to the crime. But not here and not now.

Tomorrow.

Reese slapped a bill on the counter and drained his beer. "So how 'bout it, Mike? You going to give me that tour tomorrow?"

Dillon seemed surprised, then glanced over at Jade and laughed. "You're gonna try it anyway, aren't you?" He snickered as he stood.

Reese wanted to cut the sound out of the guy's throat—with his bare hands.

"Sure thing, buddy, I'll give you the grand tour tomorrow. And then you can give me all the gory details on how you ran aground tonight."

"Oh, my God, he's coming over!" Karin's stage whisper nearly drowned out the country music belting from the jukebox across the bar.

"For God's sake, *chill out.*" Jade clenched her fingers around the base of her soda and ordered her heart to do the same.

Karin's voice lowered. "How can you even say those words while looking at him? That man is hot. H-O-T, hot."

"Evening, ladies. Jade."

What the hell did Reese mean by that? "Hey, Macbeth, what's up? Lose your date to a prettier face?" Jade winced as Karin kicked her under the table.

Reese grinned, his gaze sweeping them. "I was hoping he'd lost *me* to a pair of them."

Jade kicked Karin back before she completed her swoon. "Would you like to join us, Reese?"

Jade kicked her again, harder this time.

Karin retaliated by showing off her dimples and scooting down the short leg of the L-shaped booth. "Jade, move over so Reese can fit in."

Jade panicked as his grin widened to Cheshire proportions. If she did as Karin suggested, she'd be trapped between the two of them. Not bloody likely.

She grabbed her glass and slipped out of the booth. "Take my spot, Macbeth. I need to get another drink, anyway— this one's flat."

She could have sworn Reese winked touché as he folded his frame into the booth.

Karin handed up her glass. "I'm running low, too. Why don't you get us all another round while you're at it?"

Jade nodded, biting down on the inside of her mouth as she headed for the bar. What she wouldn't give to be sitting next to Karin just so she could whale on her leg again. She slapped the glasses on the counter. "A virgin daiquiri, a Coke and a Bud Light. Please."

As she waited for the bartender, she turned back to glare across the nearly empty bar at the booth. Reese and Karin's huddle would have done the 49ers proud. Whatever they were discussing, she'd better get back soon, because it couldn't be good.

"Look, we don't have much time, so I'm going to give it to you straight. It's up to you to listen and follow through."

What the hell was she talking about? For a brief moment, Reese considered asking, then thought better of it. He was curious to see where Karin would lead if he left her on her own. "Shoot."

Karin smiled. "Good. I was afraid I'd have to bring up that rash of smoldering glances to get you to listen."

Ouch. So much for his surveillance expertise. His partner, TJ, would get a kick out of this one. Reese grinned back. "What makes you so sure they weren't for you?"

"Because your gaze lost about a thousand degrees when Jade left. Now, shut up and listen."

"Yes, ma'am."

"First of all, you're going about it all wrong—and, by the way, that's pretty disappointing. As an actor, you of all people should be able to figure it out."

Now he *was* confused.

"You really don't get it, do you?"

He glanced over to the bar and shook his head quickly, wanting her to get to the point before Jade returned.

Too late. Jade gathered up the drinks and headed back.

"Damn, no time to explain—you're just going to have to follow my lead, okay?"

Reese nodded, more confused than ever. Follow her lead? To where? And what? He shrugged and settled back into the booth, curious to find out.

Jade ignored him as she thunked the triangle of drinks on the table. She hooked a boot into a nearby chair and dragged it up to the table to straddle it backward.

That must have been the mysterious signal Karin was

waiting for, because she glanced at her watch and gasped. "Oh, Lord, I almost forgot. I was supposed to stop by the base hospital for some test results after knock-off tonight." She slid her daiquiri in front of Jade as she stood, effectively pinning her down. "Here, you finish it for me. I'll catch you guys after sick call tomorrow, okay?"

Reese grasped Karin's plan immediately, almost feeling sorry for Jade as her eyes widened to those of a snared rabbit. Perfect. He couldn't have arranged it better if he'd tried.

He stood quickly, blocking Jade in on the other side as Karin grabbed her purse from underneath the table and slung it over her shoulder.

He was rewarded by a smile and a filthy glare.

"See ya!"

He settled back into the booth, squelching a grin as he snagged the Bud Light—the same brand he'd had with Dillon. Apparently, he hadn't been the only one staring. He took it as an encouraging sign and saluted Jade with the bottle. "Thanks."

She nodded, her gaze finally cooling to normal. "No problem. I owe you."

"How's that?"

"Midships."

"Ah, that. Actually, I think I should be thanking you."

She blinked.

He could tell he'd stumped her. "My character? The series? I learned more about the *Baddager* in two hours on my hands and knees scrubbing that deck than I did sitting in the officer's and chief's lounges the last few days."

Amazing things.

Reese almost smiled at her surprise and decided to take another stab at honesty—as much as he could give, anyway. "Jade, I know I'm just a joke to you—some *collateral duty* you've got to schedule into your day—but I've got a hell of a lot riding on these six weeks. Like my job."

She blinked again. But she didn't answer.

Damn.

Tomorrow was Friday, his third day aboard the *Baddager* and he still hadn't been able to get Jade to face the underlying issue between them.

Trust.

That and the fact that she simply did not want him around. Personally, he could take a hint. No matter how beautiful the package, if it wasn't interested, it wasn't worth the time and trouble it took to open. Unfortunately, Jade wasn't just another pretty package. Other than Dillon and Lieutenant Coffey, she was the only officer on the ship who could get him where he needed to go.

So it was up to him to *make* her interested. He'd spent the rest of the afternoon turning the problem over in his brain until he was pretty sure he'd figured out how. It was a gamble. But he didn't have much choice, because he was running out of time.

He was going to have to force the confrontation. He'd have to *make* her trust him. From there, he might be able to establish their first real connection. And since they were already together, he'd just change a few of the steps and initiate the plan sometime tonight instead.

But for now, he'd wait. Waiting was all part of the game. Fortunately, not only was he used to it, he was an expert at it. Yeah, he'd wait. He'd wait for an opportunity when her guard was down and *then* he'd pounce.

"So what's with the red ball caps?"

He could see the question had caught her off guard. His breath caught as her eyed widened. He should never have accused her of being cold. She wasn't. All her emotions were right there in those smoky eyes for anyone who took the time to notice.

"Red," he prompted. "The ball caps? Dillon seemed surprised you'd let me wear a red one."

Damn. He realized his miscalculation the second her gaze

narrowed. He should have waited before probing her about Dillon. Well, he'd already killed the mood he'd been working toward. "What is it with you two? I know the guy's a bit of a brown-noser, but—"

Her snort cut him off. "*Brown-noser?* That's an understatement. Mike's got ring around the collar."

He had to chuckle. "Okay, I'll give you that. But, seriously, what's with you two?"

She leaned over and fished her cap from under the table. For a split second he thought she was going to leave and he panicked. But she didn't. She plopped the hat on the table instead, effectively deflecting the subject from Dillon.

Interesting.

She smoothed a wisp of hair into her braid and pointed to the hat. "Red is the color of the flying squad—the rapid response fire team aboard a ship, the first line of defense. My division. Everyone else on the ship wears blue. You have to earn this one."

No wonder she looked as though she'd wanted to rip the thing from his head the first time she'd seen it. Well, she was wrong. He'd learned a long time ago not to put too much stock in symbols. It was a lousy hat—and a *Navy* one at that.

But since she seemed to think it was more, he should probably offer to return it. Or at least promise not to wear it aboard the ship. He would.

But not now.

He'd hold on to the concession awhile longer—until the time was right. Until he found a way to use it. However, he could give her something else that belonged to her. "Jade, I really *am* sorry about Benson."

Her self-deprecating chuckle caught him off guard, locking into his gut and refusing to let go. "I know. I realized that about ten minutes after I left the office. But I'd already plotted my revenge and set the plan in motion." She shrugged sheepishly. "I'm sorry I wasn't big enough to cancel it."

That was his opening. Reese glanced over to the tiny dance floor and went for it. "Make it up to me."

He almost laughed as she blinked. She was getting easier to read by the minute. *Now, push her now.* "If you're really sorry, dance with me."

Her brows furrowed as she stared at the darkened floor, then back to him. "But...no one else is dancing."

He tsked the challenge. "I had the feeling you weren't the type of person who waited for someone else to do something first."

She was wavering, he could see it in her eyes.

He pressed the advantage. "Come on, who's going to know? The only three guys left in here besides us look like they're World War II retirees."

He counted his heartbeats as he waited.

Thirty-seven-and-a-half later, she stood. "Why not?"

Somehow, he beat back a grin as he took her hand and let her lead him across the carpet. Garth Brooks started crooning out a ballad as they reached the wooden floor. He steeled himself as she looped her hands behind his neck and slid effortlessly into slow two-step.

Several beats later, he grinned down at her. "Do you lead in bed, too?"

She faltered.

Chuckling, he capitalized on her surprise and pulled her in close, bending his head to brush his lips across her temple. "Relax, I don't mind."

He held himself in check as his breath drifted back, laden with her scent. *Damn.* Maybe dancing wasn't such a great idea after all. It was a good thing her hair wasn't down; it would have been his downfall for sure.

The tension seeped from him as Jade pulled back slightly, surprising him as she relinquished the lead. "Maybe I just like to take turns."

He sucked in his breath as the smoke in her voice led to a fantasy he was forced to strangle at conception.

The means to an end, buddy, the means to an end!

His lungs finally kicked back in, and he sent up a fervent prayer that he was able to solve this case quickly.

Jade took a deep breath and clamped down on the disloyal tremors sneaking through her before they reached her stomach. She shoved them back into their box and slammed the lid.

What was she doing? And what was she *thinking* when she'd let Reese take the lead? Apology or not, she should never have stayed when Karin left, let alone agreed to dance with Reese. But she was afraid if she didn't, he'd figure out he'd gotten to her. If he hadn't already.

Still, even that would have been better than breaking her own rules. Hell, who was she kidding? She'd done more than break them. She'd shattered them. Her first mistake was noticing his smile, then she'd stared into his eyes. And now they were touching.

Everywhere.

At least it felt like everywhere. There wasn't a nerve in her body that wasn't thrumming in perfect, agonizing pitch —and it had nothing to with Garth's crooning. It did, however, have everything to do with Reese. It had to do with the iron arms he'd locked about her. The hands caressing her back through her shirt.

The row of studs on his button-fly jeans.

The same ones that were searing into her belly, locking heads every now and then with the brass buckle on her trousers. Each chink reverberated through her, tormenting her with the possibility that at any moment, one of them *might* snap free. She shuddered and shoved the image deep down into her box and drew a shaky breath.

''Cold?''

She shook her head, not realizing until then that she had

goose bumps. That was strange. As hot as it was, her skin should be having the opposite reaction.

She felt more than heard Reese's chuckle. "Me, neither. In fact, I suspect it's cooler in the Sahara right about now."

She pulled back. "Does that always work?"

"Does what work?"

"Humor. I've seen Karin use it to diffuse a situation, too." And she'd always envied her for it.

Reese trailed a finger down her cheek and smiled. "Oh, is that what's smoldering here between us—a situation?"

"Can you be serious for one minute?"

For a moment, his smile deepened, egging her closer to the edge. And then suddenly, it disappeared. "Sure, I can be serious. Can you be honest?"

"*What?*"

"Why don't you like me?"

Where had *that* come from?

"Come on, we both know it's true." He guided them back to the center of the darkened floor. "You haven't liked me since the moment I stepped aboard the *Baddager*—maybe even earlier."

For a split second, Jade suspected Karin had opened her mouth, then immediately felt guilty. Karin would never do something like that. So how—

"It doesn't take a genius to figure it out, Jade. You've been avoiding me like the plague. At first I thought it was because you were busy—God knows, you are. But sometime this afternoon, I realized it was more." His tone was light, almost teasing—but his hands were tense on her back.

She was definitely baffled. "Reese, I never—"

He stopped dancing and released her, folding his arms across his chest. "Yes, *you did.* Let's face it, I'm the great Unwashed. And you? Why, you're the Master. Only I get the distinct impression you'd rather let me rot in hell than lower yourself to save me."

"That's not true!"

"It *is* true. I've been busting my butt for days right along with your guys. Did it help? No." He jerked his head back toward the booth. "Instead, you imply I'm not good enough to wear your precious red *cover*. Well, guess what, lady? I don't want it. You can have it back in the morning. I also think it's best if I see the Captain about a new running mate." With that, he turned around and calmly walked off the dance floor.

She stood there, alone in the middle of the floor, razed by his cool words as he approached the bar. He glanced back as he reached the cash register. She sucked in her breath as his steady stare skewered into her, impaling her with the truth.

Reese was right.

And so was Karin.

She *hadn't* been fair to him. Hell, she hadn't even given him a chance. Not since the moment she'd discovered he was coming aboard. Yeah, he was right about that. She'd been so certain he was nothing more than a life-size Ken doll, she hadn't offered him an opportunity to prove otherwise.

Worse yet, she'd ignored the growing proof that there was more to Mack Reese than his perfect blond exterior.

She wrapped her arms about her stomach as the full force of her crime socked into her. She'd been treating Reese the *same way* men like Dillon had been treating her for years. It was no use telling herself she should be ashamed.

Because she already was.

Reese tamped down his regret, repeating his mantra yet again as he turned from Jade back to the bar. He passed a twenty to the bartender to cover the tab and then headed out the door. He had no intention of giving her a chance to recover while he was here. Let her sleep on it. It certainly couldn't hurt.

He sighed as he crossed the lobby and headed out to his car. He wasn't particularly proud of the way he'd just manipulated Jade. Unfortunately, it was an opportunity he couldn't afford to pass up. Especially if tomorrow's excursion into Lieutenant Dillon and Lieutenant Coffey's domain didn't pan out. Nope, despite his hopes, *that* wasn't likely. He seriously doubted either lieutenant would be eager to lead him arm in arm to the real reason he was aboard the *USS Baddager.*

Her nice, lethal stash of heroin.

Chapter 4

Jade shoved open the heavy watertight door to her office and stopped short. There it was. Right there, perched on top the wedge of papers crowding her in-box.

Reese's cover.

The scarlet ball cap taunted her as she stepped over the lip and entered the space. It flung accusation after accusation into her face as she approached it, practically screaming at her when she finally reached out to pick it up.

It was still warm.

No, that had to be her imagination—maybe even her guilt. Reese wasn't anywhere near her office. She'd seen him heading in the opposite direction shortly before she'd come down here.

Jade sunk into her swivel chair and kicked her boots up onto the edge of her desk as she stared at the plastic adjustment band. She slid her index finger beneath the tab, popping the tiny plugs out of their holes.

Reese was serious.

She'd suspected as much when he left the bar last night

before giving her a chance to explain. Finding him on the ladder leading to the Captain's cabin this morning nudged it closer to fact. But turning in his Flying Squad cover? That pretty much sealed it.

He probably already had a new running mate. And she had only herself to blame.

When you blow it, Missy, you blow it good.

Oh, God, not *him*, too! "I know, Dad. But I was just trying to do my job."

She could hear the sharp snort from here. *Doing your job, my ass. The man got under your skin and you turned chicken and ran like hell.*

"Well, what was I supposed to do, let him *know?*"

No. But I didn't expect you to treat him like dog dung, either. I thought I taught you better than that.

He had.

Jade took a deep breath and tipped her head back onto the edge of her chair. Just then, the steel lever screeched up and the door to her office swung open. She yanked her boots off the edge of her desk and speared straight up in her chair.

"*Reese.*" She bit down on her cheek as the breathy word slipped out.

He stared back at her, his face a blank mask as he stepped over the lip and pointed to his desk. "Sorry, I'll be out of your hair in a minute. Just need to get something I forgot."

For a split second, hope flared inside her and she held up his cover.

It snuffed out as he shook his head. "Nope, that belongs to you." He leaned over and pulled the side drawer open, fishing out a blue ball cap her chief must have given him this morning. "Mine's right here."

Jade clenched the scarlet cap between her fingers and met his steady gaze. "Are you sure?"

Something flickered there.

Pain?

Regret?

She should be so lucky. She took a deep breath and plunged in before she lost her nerve. "Look, everything you said last night—well, you were right. I haven't given you a chance. But I want to now. If you're willing to stick it out, I'd like to make it up to you."

She stared into those crystal blue eyes and waited. The taste of metal slid slowly over her tongue as she bit into her cheek. Still, she waited. Several moments later, he *still* hadn't answered, so she offered him the one thing she'd selfishly held back.

"I'm sorry."

Whatever had flickered in his eyes before was back. Reese shook his head. But from his expression, she wasn't sure if he was clearing it or saying no. Then it was gone and he finally answered. "I'm not sure. I've got some stuff already scheduled with your chief today. How 'bout I let you know Monday morning?"

Had she missed something? This time she shook her head. "You mean, you haven't already requested another running mate?"

His gaze was still steady, still boring through her. "Not yet. So, what do you say? Can I give you my answer Monday?"

She nodded reluctantly. "Sure, I can wait."

She really didn't have much of a choice.

"What the hell do you think you're doing?"

Reese froze, his fingers inches from the keypad of the electronic lock as he swallowed a dozen colorful expletives. When he'd managed to digest them all and replace them with a smile, he turned to face Jade.

She stood halfway down the fifteen-foot passageway with that damn ball cap pulled clear to her eyes, and she did *not* look pleased. Maybe it was the glacier in them, maybe it was the suspicion. Either way, he knew he'd better come up with something good.

And fast.

"Would you believe I'm lost?"

"No."

"Didn't think so." He shrugged. "Okay, I was invited."

Her eyes chilled to sub-zero as she advanced on him. "Do you have *any* idea what's behind that door?"

No, but he'd sure as hell love to find out—up close and real personal. "Let me guess. You could tell me, but then you'd have to kill me, right?"

That one did not go over well. She stalked closer until she was almost on top of him. *"Mr. Reese,* when you came aboard this ship, you were expressly forbidden to enter two areas—Radio and the Nuclear Support Facility. Now, I asked you a question. *What* are you doing here?"

Just then the electronic lock buzzed and the seal to the NSF was severed. Lieutenant Dillon popped through the opening into the passageway, the door snapping shut behind him. "Hey there, Mack. Right on time." His lips twisted into a sneer as he spied Jade. "I see you've brought your baby-sitter along. Forget your broomstick, DCA?"

Jade ignored him.

Reese unclenched his hands as he turned back to her and forced a grin. "See? Invited."

Her eyes did a volcanic one-eighty, churning up molten lava so quickly, he was tempted to unhook the nozzle from the fire station across the passageway out of self-defense.

"Well, Macbeth, now I know *why* you needed time to consider my offer. If you'll excuse me, I have rounds to make."

Reese could have sworn her boots left sparks on the deck as she spun about and marched down the corridor to the metal ladder. He sighed as she climbed up, cursing his luck with every step until she was out of sight.

Why did Jade of all people have to catch him casing the lock? He ignored the fact that she was the Command Duty

Officer today and that it was her job to make routine rounds of the ship.

Wait a minute. If Jade was the duty officer, she was sleeping onboard tonight. That meant he could link up with her later and try and implement a little damage control of his own. He grinned, his spirits lifting as he turned back to Dillon.

"Whoa, Mack. What's up with you two? The Witch snarls and you smile? You're an even bigger masochist than I thought."

Reese ordered that same smile to hold its place as he clapped Dillon on the shoulder. "You know how it is, Mike. Some like it hot."

Dillon grinned back. "Buddy, you must like it smoking."

Reese laughed. As a matter of fact, he did. But that was none of Mike's business. He pointed to the door. "So how 'bout it? It's after knock-off and the ship's deserted. Do I get my tour?"

Dillon nodded and turned, blocking Reese's view as he punched a set of numbers into the keypad.

Reese cursed silently. No matter how hard he tried, he couldn't get a clear look at the pad until Dillon finished. He grudgingly nudged the guy up a notch in his estimation at the obvious precaution.

Then again, his actions could have been for show. Dillon did seem to thrive on it.

The door buzzed again as the seal broke. "Come on in."

Reese could feel his heart thundering in anticipation as he stepped over the lip of the doorway. Though he seriously doubted he'd locate the heroin today, there was always the chance he'd discover something he could use to come back later.

He entered the space eagerly, only to frown when he was fully inside. He turned around slowly, scanning the interior, stopping when he came back to Dillon's smug face.

Nothing.

Not a damn thing. The room was a stinking office. An ugly one at that. Two green desks dominated one side of the space, and the other side was occupied by nothing more than row after row of perfectly boring, perfectly *ordinary* gray cabinets. The only thing of interest in the entire room was the second door located on the far side—with yet another electronic lock wired to it.

Yup, that door definitely had his interest. The heroin was in there. He could feel it in his gut. Of course the frantic statement from his informant hadn't hurt, either.

He slapped a smile on his face. "So, where do you keep the nukes?"

Dillon laughed. "I had a feeling that's what you expected. This is a repair ship, Mack. While we never confirm nor deny the presence of the truly heavy-duty stuff, we're usually stuck with more routine, run-of-the-mill repairs."

Reese leaned back against the edge of the closest desk. "Such as?"

Dillon shrugged. "Mostly testing or repairs of valves, pipes and other equipment used in the propulsion plants of nuclear-powered ships."

Reese tweaked his expression into surprise and mild shock. "That's all? Sounds pretty boring."

Dillon laughed. "It is. But it's a living."

He shifted his face into hopeful and glanced at the second door. "I don't suppose you'd care to show me where you work on those valves and that other equipment?"

"No-o-o can do, Mack. Not even for you. That's strictly classified."

This was it? All that sucking up, and this was as far as the guy was going to let him get? *Jeez!* Reese shoved his palms down onto the desk and dug his fingers beneath the edge.

It was a damn good thing he'd left Jade dangling on his hook this morning. At the time, he'd felt pretty rotten about it. But now he was blessing his caution from here to Mars.

He could only hope he'd still be able to reel her in after that little scene in the corridor.

"I understand, Mike. No hard feelings." He pushed off the desk. "Well, if that's it, I'd better head out so you can get home. Thanks for the tour."

Dillon nodded. "No problem. You want to hit the club again and toss back a few?"

Not in this lifetime. "Not tonight. Got something else on the ol' agenda."

"Yeah, I can just guess who's on *that* agenda."

Man, what he wouldn't give to wipe that oily grin off Dillon's face. Reese hooked his thumbs into the pockets of his jeans and concentrated on keeping them there. "You got it, buddy."

The lout opened his mouth, but his retort was mercifully severed by a loud buzz. This one from across the space.

The second door.

Reese forced himself to turn slowly, casually, toward the magnetic sound.

"Dillon, Mack, what's up?"

Lieutenant Coffey.

But what the hell was *that?*

Reese tensed as the strawberry blonde who'd cleared his bags the day he'd come aboard—and then laughed and smiled at the Captain's table with Jade—strolled into view with a corpse tossed over his shoulder. He flopped it down across the desk, its head landing with a solid thud.

Yuck. It wasn't real, but it *was* gross.

Dillon laughed at his expression, nodding his head toward the full-size replica of a person with a chest wound, third-degree facial and neck burns, and one eye dangling nonchalantly from its socket. "Mack, meet Lieutenant Greg Coffey and the DCA's boyfriend. Greg, Mack Reese."

Boyfriend? Reese held in his breath as he tried to contain the visible effects of the sucker punch. Jade wasn't supposed to have time for men.

He was dimly aware of Coffey glaring at Dillon. "Very funny, Mike. Knock it off." He turned to Reese and grinned as he extended his hand. "We've met. I was the Officer of the Deck when you arrived. We also had lunch at the Captain's table."

He remembered. Reese shook the freckled hand, wanting to crush it.

"Great to see you again, Mack." Coffey jerked his head toward Dillon. "And don't worry about him, he's had it in for Jade since the night she shot him down." He laughed. "You should have seen him crash and burn."

"Shut up, Greg." Dillon glanced down at the dummy. "What's up with the Witch's boyfriend?"

Relief and fury flooded Reese at exactly the same moment he realized Dillon was referring to the fake corpse and not Lieutenant Coffey. He folded his arms, tucking his fists out of sight as Coffey glared back at Dillon.

"Just planning a little birthday surprise for Jade." Coffey turned back to Reese. "Hey, didn't she give you the stateroom next to hers?"

She'd put him next to her? He swallowed the burst of pleasure and nodded cautiously. "On the right—uh, to starboard."

"Perfect!" A wide grin split the guy's face, causing a nasty premonition to seep into Reese. "Mind if I use your room to prestage a little birthday present for her?" Coffey chuckled. "Relax, Mack. It's a joke. I thought since Jade hasn't had a date in a while, I'd slip a little something into her rack for her to snuggle up to at night."

Reese stared down at the mutilated corpse, then back up at Coffey's freckled grin, every instinct in his gut tightening to full alert—and it had nothing to do with his mission. He repeated his mantra again as he nodded reluctantly.

A means to an end, buddy. She's just a means to an end. So why the hell did it feel like more?

* * *

Jade tucked the last strand of hair into her shower cap and slapped her towel over the top rail of the shower before stepping inside. She jerked the curtain closed and flipped on the lever, welcoming the blast of frigid water. She could use all the help she could get to control her temper.

Mack Reese.

If she so much as saw his arrogant mug again tonight, she was going to rip that sanctimonious smirk right off it. And she didn't care if she took a few pounds of flesh along with it. She squirted a dime of soap into her palm and lathered up her neck.

Invited into the NSF.

What the hell was Dillon thinking? She didn't care if Reese was some harmless two-bit actor. That was no excuse for granting him access to the *Baddager*'s nuclear spaces. Okay, she didn't think Dillon was stupid enough to let him past the first door. But what if he wasn't? What if his co-lossal ego kicked in? Would he be able to resist the temptation to initiate a bragfest?

Aren't you going a bit overboard here, Missy?

The gentle jibe pricked her anger, swiftly deflating it. ''Yeah, Dad, you're right.'' Mike might be a sleaze, but he wasn't a security risk.

She shoved her face into the shower spray and rinsed the suds from her face, wishing she could wash Macbeth down the drain right along with them. Maybe it was for the best that Dillon was going to take him on as a running mate. At least the two guys got along. *They* sure didn't.

So you've taken up lying now, too, eh?

She ordered her father out of her head and lathered up her body sponge. Too late. She'd already remembered Reese's offer to wash her himself. She scrubbed the sponge down her stomach, trying to scour the sight of his wide hands smoothing a slick, soapy path down her body.

It didn't work.

Argh! She had to find a way to get that man out of her head!

Jade torqued the water down to subfreezing and finished her shower in record time. She flipped the faucet off and pulled the cap from her hair before wrapping it with her towel and donning her green kimono.

The entire way back to her stateroom, her thongs snapped out a list of why she could never allow herself to even fantasize about Reese. He wasn't her type. He wasn't interested in her. He wasn't sticking around.

And even if he was, he did *not* fit into her plans. No man did. Jeff had driven that stake into her hard enough to last a lifetime.

Reese heard the door to Jade's stateroom as it closed. She was back. Great. He shoved his notebook back on top of the other items in the safe and snapped it shut, spinning the dial for good measure before settling it on his home number. Then he took a deep breath.

His entire plan now hinged on whether he'd gotten to Jade as much as he thought he had. The odds had been in his favor this morning, but after their run-in outside the NSF, he wasn't so sure. When he'd first lit on the idea of demanding a new running mate, there were two probable outcomes.

One, she'd own up to her actions and he'd use her subsequent guilt to forge a bridge between them. Or two, she'd deny everything and tell him to shove his ball cap where the sun didn't shine. Though not his first choice, the scenario still would have worked. He'd simply have wondered aloud how her Captain was going to take the news that she'd been ignoring his direct orders for the entire week.

Reese flipped up the lip to the temporary desk, concealing the safe and then rubbed his hands over the back of his neck. Now he wasn't sure of anything. But he couldn't let that stop him. Nope. He was going to head next door and start laying the ground work for plan B.

Sex.

He knew Jade felt it, too. He could see it in her eyes—especially when she was trying *not* to look at him. Hell, he could smell the attraction on her. And he oughta know, he'd been wearing the same deodorant since the minute he'd stepped aboard. Yup, sex. That was the plan. He'd just find an opening and push it one step further. A kiss should do it. One simple kiss.

He locked his stateroom and headed for hers.

Knock, knock, knock.

''Enter!''

He took one last deep breath, turned the knob and pushed the door in—and promptly came as close to fainting as he ever would in his life.

Good God almighty.

''I left the folder right there on the desk, Chief.'' Jade was standing with her back to him, next to her modular wall unit, in front of the closed porthole. She didn't even turn around. And he *couldn't* move.

Her hair.

Every glorious, *achingly* long strand. Every last one of them was down—way down. All the way down her back. In one thick, glistening line. If she wasn't wearing that robe, he swore the edge would be brushing the upper curve of her rear. His groin hardened with lightning speed at the image.

God, what an image.

She must have realized he wasn't the chief she'd expected because she turned around then, shock widening her eyes. Dismay quickly followed as a white T-shirt slipped from her fingers and fluttered to her feet. *''Reese.''*

The husky whisper ripped through him, laying waste to all his carefully constructed arguments, his meticulously outlined plan. He fumbled around his brain, frantically pulling the frayed threads of his thoughts back to some semblance of order.

The plan, buddy, remember the plan!

Screw the plan. Where the hell was his mantra when he needed it?

Improvise!

He glanced around the room—as smoothly as he could manage, as quickly as he dared—looking for something, *anything*, to fuse his gaze to long enough to right his spinning brain.

That was it! Her keys. Right there in the center of the brown comforter on her bed. Those keys were exactly what he needed. Somewhere on that fat cluster was the one he needed to access the NSF. Okay, so he also needed the electronic codes. But those keys were a start.

His gaze slipped past the keys to the white satin bra and panties spread out next to them. He yanked it back to the keys, burning their image into his brain.

Think of the keys. Only the keys.

"Did you want something, Macbeth, or are you just going to stand there all night?"

Reese snapped his gaze back to her. How the hell did she do that? How could she stand in front of him, with three feet of blue-black silk shimmering around her, and give him that Serious Lieutenant glare?

Didn't she need her uniform and ball cap to pull that off?

Evidently not. And it was a damn good thing she didn't. Because that icy stare was just what he needed. He welcomed it. He locked on to it and used it to shove the remaining steps of his plan back into place. And then he advanced.

"I came to give you an answer to your offer."

He'd surprised her. That much he could tell when she blinked. "I see. I was under the impression you wanted another running mate. Someone like Lieutenant Dillon?"

He smiled. "That's not the way I remember it. I told you I'd think about it. Well, I've thought."

"And?"

He moved in, until there was less than two feet of air left between them, until he could smell the fresh dewy scent of her bath. "I don't want another running mate." He leaned closer—and tried not to inhale. "I want *you*."

Reese bit back a groan as his words produced the effect he was after. The precise one he'd planned. Everything Jade was feeling was right there in her eyes. He watched them darken until they nearly matched the fringe of bangs brushing into them.

He had to dig his fingers into his palms. To keep from reaching out to sweep the wisps aside. To plow his fingers into the rest of that glistening hair. What would it feel like?

Silk?

Was it as heavy as it looked?

Heavier?

His palms began to ache as his mind tormented him with the ghostly sensations. No matter what, he must not touch her hair. If he did, he'd be lost for sure.

The keys. Focus on the keys, dammit!

It wasn't working.

The keys disintegrated from his mind as his gaze slid down the damp, dusky column of her neck. Down even farther into the tantalizing vee formed by her robe. He was so close he could see the curve of one breast peeking out, creamy and full where the stark line of her tan ended. And there was something else, too. Something slender and gilded.

A necklace.

Driven by a need he had no desire to examine, he reached for it, burning the tip of his finger on her flesh as he slipped it beneath the chain and slowly tugged it up from the nest between her breasts. A heart. A solid heart carved from a chunk of dark green jade.

"*Beautiful.*" His voice was hoarse. He was not referring to the pendant.

"Thank you." Neither was she.

He wrapped the slender chain around his finger—over and over—pulling her in slowly, inch by agonizing inch. So slowly, they both knew she could stop him at any moment. But she didn't.

And neither did he.

When there was nothing left to wind, he slipped his finger beneath her chin, tilting the stubborn curve up until he was staring deep into her eyes, piercing the cool gray shadows until he plundered the heady truth below.

She wanted him.

Jade stared at Reese as he held her gaze. She refused to look away. Refused to close her eyes for the kiss she knew was coming. She simply waited—determined not to move, not to breathe a word. Certain if even a whisper escaped, she'd shatter the moment. That, she could not allow. Because she wanted it.

Needed it.

She needed it so she *wouldn't* want it anymore—wouldn't want *him* anymore. There was no way Reese could possibly live up to the fantasy her mind had created. And the sooner she proved it to herself, the sooner she'd exorcise him from her thoughts and get back on course.

So she simply arched her brow and waited.

Confidence gleamed in his eyes as he accepted her gauntlet. And then he bent his head and delivered his answer in person. He captured her lips, slowly claiming them as his own as he branded her with his tongue. He traced the outer curves over and over, bathing her mouth with long, lazy strokes. Strokes that did nothing to soothe and everything to inflame. He stopped the delicious licking long enough to flay his tongue between her lips. But then he withdrew and resumed the slick, steamy torment at her lips, feeding on them until they were swollen and ripe.

Against her will, her hands took on a life of their own. They crept up his arms to knead the solid muscles of his shoulders. Still not satisfied, they snuck up even farther, threading into his golden hair. She followed, tiptoeing up and inhaling his musky scent, pressing herself against him, trying to deepen the kiss.

He groaned then, low and deep, and something seemed to snap. He shuddered and pulled back slightly as he jerked his fingers from her necklace, winding them into her hair instead. He muttered something about a mantra, and then cursed it just before his mouth came crashing back down. All trace of teasing evaporated as he finally, deeply, thoroughly, plundered her mouth. His tongue collided and tangled with hers, and his kiss turned even harder and more demanding. With each fiery stroke of his tongue, he forged her burning desire into a churning pool of molten need.

And then she tasted him.

All of him.

Her breath caught as he dug his hand deeper into her hair, wrapping the other arm around her waist, sealing her body to his. Shuddering, she memorized his rigid contours through frustrating layers of silk and denim. She shuddered again as he cupped her bottom and anchored her there— right there. His teeth scraped hers as he deepened the kiss, and she surrendered willingly to the taste, sound and feel of Reese—fully aroused.

She was mindless with want by the time his fingers left her hair to sear a path down her neck. They were hot and seeking. She gasped as they slipped into her robe. But instead of cupping her breast, he suddenly yanked his hands up, clamping them onto her shoulders as he tore himself away.

They stood there, stunned—her breath not nearly as loud as his in the stark silence, but just as shallow and just as ragged. The shock in his eyes didn't surprise her at all, for it was mirrored inside her mind. And then it was compounded by sheer panic as the painful, bald truth socked into her.

His kiss *wasn't* as good as it had been in her fantasy.

It was better.

Reese sucked his breath in slowly, trying to retrain his lungs as he stared down at Jade.

He'd blown it.

For the first time in his career, he'd really blown it. He'd lost control. He'd meant to keep the kiss slow, soft and light. Everything depended on it—on luring her in gently, establishing her trust, making her feel safe. But there was nothing safe about that kiss. Nothing at all.

Not for her and certainly not for him.

He needed a plan—a new one. Now. Before she kicked him out of her room and out of her division. He opened his mouth to speak, but his words were drowned out by a series of heavy thumps on her door.

Her inky lashes flew wide and her knuckles turned white as she clenched the edges of her robe. "Oh, my God, *that's my chief.*"

And right then, he knew he had her.

He smiled. "So?"

Her gaze turned frantic as she cased the room. Finally, she snatched up the manila file from the edge of her desk and tugged him over to the sink while hissing, "Stay behind the door."

"Why are we whispering?"

"Move!"

He covered her taut hands as she tried to shove him back against the bulkhead. "Does this mean we have a truce?"

She froze, her short nails driving into his chest as her gaze narrowed. "You *wouldn't.*"

No. But she didn't know that. He cupped her chin and stared into her eyes. "Does it?"

Lightning flashed in her eyes. "You're *despicable!*"

Her chief knocked on the door again.

"Does it?"

"Okay!"

He smiled as she tried to jerk her chin away. "And you'll take me everywhere and teach me everything you know?"

"Yes."

"And you'll be *friendly?*"

One more knock, louder this time. "You awake in there, DCA?"

She closed her eyes. "Yes, yes, *yes!*" And then opened them. "Now, will you *please* hide?"

He nodded, grinning as he released her chin and slipped behind the door. "Of course. Anything for a friend."

Chapter 5

"Relax, this won't hurt a bit."

Reese eyed the needle as Karin plunged it into the vial of anesthetic. "You know, Doc, that's probably the worst lie known to man."

Laughing, she pulled the needle out and recapped it before laying the syringe on the stainless steel tray attached to his chair. "No, I think 'I'll call you sometime' holds that spot."

He wasn't about to argue. It violated the first rule of his gut. Never argue with a woman while you were at her mercy. Especially when she needed to concentrate on compensating for the pitch and roll of a twenty-thousand-ton ship while stitching your forearm back together.

She rounded the examination table and pulled a pair of rubber gloves from a box near the head. "So how'd you manage to slice yourself open?"

She didn't know? Surely Jade had confided something to her best friend. Maybe not the kiss, but *something*. He studied the calm blue eyes staring back at him as she snapped on the gloves. Nope. Not a flicker. Karin had no clue what had happened.

Fascinating.

He shrugged. "Apparently the DCA's had a change of heart. I've been working alongside her leading Petty Officer since the ship got underway this morning." He glanced down at his three-inch jagged cut as he finished rolling up the sleeve to his coveralls. "Got this down in Engineering helping one of the guys repair a steam line."

Ah, there it was. The flicker was there now. Except it was more a full-blown blast of shock. "*What?* Jade let you work with her *welders?* Right. Next you'll be telling me she wants you to tag along when she stands bridge watch."

He grinned. "As a matter of fact, she did mention something about driving the ship later tonight."

Karin's eyes grew even wider as she ripped open an antiseptic towelette and swiped it around his cut. "That must have been some drink at the Officer's Club the other night. Guess you didn't need my advice after all."

He wasn't so sure about that.

She injected the Novocain around the cut on the top of his forearm. "But as long as we're on the subject, what happened after I left?"

Reese suppressed a smile. This was getting more interesting by the minute. Jade was as good as he was about keeping her mouth shut. But apparently Karin wasn't. Maybe it was time to see just how much information she was willing to part with. "That's an—"

The door to the exam room slammed open. Reese glanced up as the topic of discussion stalked in, her ball cap pulled low on her forehead, the corners of her mouth drawn just as low. That couldn't possibly be worry, could it?

About *him?*

No way.

Karin glanced up from her stitching. "Hello, Jade. Yet

another customer from your division. What a surprise, huh?''

"Very funny, Doc. How's the patient?"

She took another stitch. ''Fine. Just practicing my sewing. Have a seat, be done in a minute.''

Reese noted the relief in Jade's eyes as she crossed the deck and stared down at his arm. He tried to stifle the spurt of pleasure—and failed.

''I never should have agreed to this.'' The mutter was so low, he almost missed it.

He grinned up at her. ''Aw, sweetheart, I didn't know you cared.''

Her answering smile dripped with saccharine. ''Don't get your hopes up, Macbeth. Just covering my rear. I'd hate to have you sue the Navy for ruining that pretty face of yours.''

He felt his grin deepen. ''Make you a deal. You keep focusing on my pretty face and I'll cover your hind end.''

Her smile didn't budge, but he knew he'd gotten her back. The proof was in the pink splotches darkening her cheeks.

Karin tied off a stitch and glanced up. ''Knock it off, you two. You're not allowed to bring the battle into Medical— we settled that one back at the Geneva Convention.''

''DCA, you there?'' The raspy, disembodied voice hinted at a solid nicotine addiction—her chief's voice.

Jade tugged the walkie-talkie off her khaki belt. ''What's up, Chief?''

''Finished that scenario for tonight's fire drill. Got a minute?''

Jade glanced back at Karin as she headed across the tilting deck. ''Mind if I use the phone in your office?''

Karin nodded as she clipped off the ends of the last stitch. ''No problem.''

Caving into temptation, Reese tracked the tight rear in question as it taunted him all the way across the tilting deck. He turned back as the exam room door snapped shut.

Karin laughed as she peeled the backing off an oversize

bandage and sealed it over his stitches. "Taking your offer seriously, huh?"

He smiled. "It'd be a shame to leave that rear end uncovered for a second."

"Uh-huh. Which reminds me. You never did answer my question about the club."

Reese leaned back in his chair, rolling down the sleeve to his coveralls as she pitched the scraps from her surgical tray. "How about a trade? I'll tell you what happened after you left the club and you tell me who gave Jade that necklace she wears."

Karin's hand jerked and she dropped the vial of anesthetic, wincing as it hit the deck. She scooped it up and carefully laid it back on the tray. "Which—oh, *that* necklace. I'm not sure. I think it was a gift."

She snatched the anesthetic off the tray and made a beeline for the door. "Reese, would you excuse me for a minute? I need to return this to the drug locker." She was gone before he could answer.

What the heck was that all about? He'd just been making conversation—trying to establish a rapport. Okay, so he did want to know who'd given Jade something she cared enough about to wear even in uniform. All right, so he was more than curious. He was becoming downright obsessed.

After he'd torn himself away from the hottest kiss in his life—with barely enough wits to salvage his plan—he'd stumbled back to his own stateroom and fallen into his painfully narrow rack. And there he'd lain.

Trying to ignore the sensation of silky blue-black hair twined around his fingers. Trying not to picture a pair of white lace panties sliding slowly up that pair of dusky legs. Trying not to envy a chunk of cold, green stone. And most of all, desperately trying to forget the sight of it nestled between those perfect creamy breasts.

All night long.

* * *

Jade hung up the phone as the door to Karin's office smacked open. She stepped back from the desk as the doctor plowed around it, slapping a vial on the desk before plunking down into her chair.

"All right, woman, start at the beginning, don't quit till the end—and you'd better not leave anything out."

She blinked. "I beg your pardon?"

Karin leaned back in her chair and stared up at her. "I asked you about Reese this morning and you told me nothing happened."

Damn. She glanced at the door, then back at Karin before demanding, "Just what did he tell you?"

"Not a darn thing—all he did was ask me about your lovely *necklace.*" Hurt flooded her face. "You know, I thought we were friends. You didn't have to lie, all you had to do was tell me to butt out."

Jade slumped down into the chair next to the desk, regret stabbing into her. "I didn't lie—exactly. I just left a few things out." She met Karin's steady gaze slowly, latching on to the thread of compassion in it. Even though she didn't deserve it. "It was just a kiss."

"*Just* a kiss?" Disbelief took over. "The man saw a necklace that up until that moment three people on this earth have seen you wear, and you want me to believe it was *just* a kiss? Honey, I got an island off the Florida Keys I'd like to sell you."

Jade glared at her. "Cute."

"No, I'm adorable." Karin cocked her head toward the door. "*He's* cute. Now, you'd better start spilling your guts, or tell me to butt the hell out, before I strangle you."

She stared back at her best friend, wanting more than anything to tell Karin the truth—if she only knew what it was. She wavered for a full minute before her resolve cracked on a ragged breath. "Remember when I told you about my apology to Reese?"

"Yeah, you said he'd let you know this morning."

"Well, he decided to accept my offer early. He showed up in my stateroom last Friday night after I'd showered and—"

"Wait a minute—*shower?* As in, you were wearing that silk kimono I bought you last time we were in Japan?"

Jade sighed. "I knew I should have left that thing at home."

Karin clapped her hands together and grinned. Jade was half-afraid she was going to hug her. "Are you kidding? That's the best decision you've made all week!" She leaned forward and propped her chin onto her hands. "So?"

"So what?"

"The kiss, you idiot! How does the man *kiss?* Scale of one to ten—and you'd better spot him a few points since you're out of practice."

Jade lowered her voice to a near whisper. "Twenty."

She needn't have bothered, they'd probably heard Karin's squeal all the way down in after-steering. "*Twenty?* Good God, woman, grab on to the man and do *not* let go."

"Will you *please* quiet down!" Jade slumped back into the chair and stared up at the pipes, vents and cables criss-crossing along the overhead, using the slow, steady rock of the ship to soothe her nerves and calm her stomach. For once it didn't work. Her breath came out in one long, depressed hiss.

"What?"

She ignored Karin as she picked out an electrical cable and traced the line across the space.

"He's not Jeff, you know."

Jade glanced down long enough to glare at her.

"Well, he's not, so relax. Reese isn't going to—"

She jackknifed up in the chair, cutting Karin off with a scowl. "You're right. He's not—because I'm not going to give him the chance."

"May I help you, Mr. Reese?"

Reese clamped down on his instincts, shifting his attention from Karin's door to the young hospital corpsman staring at him earnestly. She couldn't be more than nineteen.

He conjured up his most distracting smile and casually pushed off the edge of the door frame. "Nope. Just waiting for the doc. I'll stop in and catch her later. Bye."

He didn't wait for an answer as he turned and sauntered down the passageway. He snapped the door to Medical shut behind him and concentrated on accommodating for the pitch and roll of the ship as he headed back to Jade's shops, struggling all the way to catalog the information he'd just gleaned.

The plan was working!

He grinned and practically laughed aloud as he headed down the midships ladder. In fact, it was working better than he'd dared to hope if that score was any indication. *A twenty, huh?*

His grin faded as he reached the bottom of the ladder. Who the hell was Jeff? And what had he done to her? Had *he* given that necklace to Jade? If so, why was she still wearing it? The only reason that came to mind stopped him cold. Nope, that particular reason did not bode well for his plans.

Not well at all.

"Steaming course one-eight-zero for the rest of the night, speed—fifteen knots. Winds at zero-two-zero, no contacts visible on the horizon, steering drills to be conducted during the watch at my discretion." Jade nodded as she finished repeating the spiel to the off-going Officer of the Deck and saluted. "Very well, Lieutenant Shale, I have the Deck."

The lieutenant returned her salute and announced the changing of the watch to the bridge in general. "Attention on Deck. This is Lieutenant Shale. Lieutenant Parker has the Deck."

She completed the turnover as Shale headed for the chart

table to sign the ship's log, "This is Lieutenant Parker, I have the Deck."

The navigator passed the ship's log to Greg for his signature and glanced over. "Quartermaster, aye."

"Boatswain's mate, aye."

Jacobs looked up from the ship's wheel. "Helmsman, aye. Steering one-eight-zero."

"Very well." Jade motioned Reese over from the back of the bridge. She slung the strap to her binoculars around her neck and sighed as the familiar weight dropped to her chest.

Reese cocked a brow as he approached. "Heavy?"

She shook her head, smiling. "More like heaven."

For the first time in a week, he looked truly baffled.

She snagged an extra pair of binoculars off the chart table and held them out, laughing as he stared at them as if she held a spoonful of cough syrup. "Come on, they don't bite." She pointed to the open watertight door off their right. "Head out on the starboard bridge wing. I'll meet you in a couple of minutes."

He finally took them, looping them around his neck as he passed through the skin of the ship.

Jade turned back to the bridge, verifying the *Baddager*'s course and speed and glancing at the radar before she headed out onto the port bridge wing. She sighed as she lifted her binoculars to study the horizon. On a clear day, you could see over twenty deep blue miles in every direction. Today was clear—warm, too.

She pulled off her cover, tucking the bill into her waistband at the small of her back as she embraced the salty air. *This* was what being a sailor was all about. The sun in your face, the sea in your lungs, the waves crashing in your ears. Land two hundred miles astern and more than a thousand ahead. All you had to do was stand still, feel the deck roll beneath your feet and look around to know the one absolute truth in life.

God was a sailor.

She drew another deep breath, filling her lungs to the brim, and then sighed. Yeah, this was heaven all right. And the best part was heaven knew no rank. It was here for anyone who wanted it—captain, lieutenant, chief, right down to the most junior seaman aboard. Even civilians.

But would Reese?

And would he understand? Could he move past all the electronics, the computers and the weapons to feel the true call of the sea? Would he embrace it? Would he feel it down in his soul? Because only then would he have a chance at conveying a real sailor on some TV show.

Jade donned her ball cap and turned back to the bridge, suddenly anxious to find out. She stopped in the center of the row of windows spanning the eighty-foot width, checking the radar and scanning the darkening horizon again before she joined Reese.

He was against the rail, his back to her as he stared off at the sunset beyond.

"How's the arm?" She sucked in her breath, gripping the binoculars tightly as he turned and smiled, the blue in his eyes somewhere between the sky and the darker ocean below.

"Fine."

"I *am* sorry."

He glanced at the bandage covering his stitches. "Don't be. Doesn't even hurt anymore."

She doubted that, but returned his smile, anyway. "Not the gash—though I did speak to Vega about taking better care of you." She sighed, forcing her way past the lump of shame in her throat. "I'm sorry for treating you the way I did. I know—we agreed to let it drop. I just want you to know I'm doing it right this time." She lifted the binoculars to study this side of the horizon.

Yes! Reese grinned as victory flooded him. He'd done it. He'd finally managed to bridge Jade's trust. Yes, she'd made the same promise in her stateroom. But that one was coerced—this one was not.

And that made all the difference.

By next week, those keys would be his. He could feel it. He closed his fist, almost feeling *them*. All he had to do now was find a way to get the codes off Lieutenant Coffey. And even that might not be as difficult as it seemed. If he was lucky, he'd get another crack at that keypad when they picked up the mutilated dummy for Jade's birthday. If not? Well, then it was back to courting her favor.

And frankly, that wasn't such a bad place to be—even if it was on a damn ship. His gut tightened in wholehearted agreement as he watched her stare out at the ocean. The sun was setting behind her now, the fiery sky defining her profile in colors more vivid than the scarlet cap on her head.

The tightening in his gut moved lower, turning painful as she dropped the binoculars to her chest, tipping her face into the breeze, inhaling slowly, deeply—her sigh more at home in a coil of steamy, tangled sheets than on the deck of some blasted ship.

He almost groaned as she turned to him, sighing again. Oh, God, that smile definitely belonged in a bed—*his* bed. He wrapped his fingers around the ship's safety rail, holding on for dear life as he ripped the image from his mind.

The means to an end, buddy.

"I need to make rounds and talk to the Boatswain Mate. Back in a few."

Reese stared after her as she entered the bridge and checked the radars, losing sight of her as she exited the opposite side, no doubt to scan the horizon. It was his turn to sigh as he leaned over the rail of the bridge wing, staring into the bottomless water below, hating it.

The ocean.

He wasn't fooled by the beauty beneath him. It was nothing more than a watery mirage. One that masked more than barren emptiness—it masked a monster. A cold, heartless creature that clawed its way into a man's heart, hooking into him so tightly he never knew it until it was too late.

He turned his gaze away, staring at the swaths of gold, orange and red as the sun slipped down to the horizon, wondering if Jade had already been snared. Wondering if there was still time to save *her.*

"You know, if you're very quiet and the sea is very calm, you can hear the sun sizzle as it touches the water and sinks below."

Reese turned his head and froze—unable to move, unable to speak.

Unable to breathe.

And not from that husky voice. It wasn't even the slender hand resting on his arm. It was the hair. Her hair.

It was bare.

Yes, it was still twisted into that thick braid, the long tail still tucked under at the base of her neck. But what he *could* see was shimmering in the receding light, the final rays of day catching it, igniting the blue flame within. He dug his fingers into the rail as the breeze picked up, swirling the wispy bangs into her eyes. He stared at her fingers, hypnotized as she caught and smoothed them back.

And then he nearly screamed as she brought that damn red hat up from behind and butchered his view.

He turned away sharply, hiding the breath that came out in a blistering rush. *The means to an end.*

He took a shallow breath and turned back. "So tell me why you joined the Navy."

There.

That should do it. If any topic could bring his raging desire to heel, that one would. He took another breath, praying she wouldn't give him the answer he dreaded. Praying like crazy the only thing she had in common with his insidious ghost was the uniform.

She blinked—and then shook her head as she smiled. "You of all people should know the answer to that."

For a split second, he thought she'd read his mind and he panicked. Then he calmed as she lifted her palms and turned slowly around.

"Look around you, Macbeth. What do you see?"

Water. And a helluva lot of it. More than he cared to see in this lifetime, anyway.

She completed her circle and pointed up. "Now, look at the sky. Pretty soon it will be black—pitch-black. I'm talking so dark and pollution-free you could count every star and pluck them with your bare hands if you had the time. Do you know how many people *pay* to be where you and I are, right here and right now?"

Her blinding smile lowered the tip of the stake until it pierced his chest. But it was her next words that drove it home. "I didn't choose the Navy, Reese—it chose me." She sighed. "Can you understand that?"

Yeah, he understood. More than she knew. Thirty years of frustration and abandonment clamored for restitution as yet another disciple prostrated herself before that damn, *selfish* idol. He understood all right.

His father had made sure of it.

He shifted slightly, escaping her gaze as he glared out at the sea. The Navy had provided dear old Dad with all this grandeur as well—and more. But look what it demanded in return.

His soul.

Oh, it started out slowly enough. So slowly, the man never saw it coming. A promotion here, another ship there. By the time he'd figured it out, he no longer seemed to care. Or maybe he'd just forgotten he even had a life off the boat. Because he certainly couldn't remember he had a home. A wife.

Kids.

He turned back to Jade, more determined than ever to solve the case and get off the ship as quickly as he could. Because there was no way in hell he was starring in a remake of that particular nightmare. And he was prepared to do what it took to make sure of it.

Whatever it took.

"DCA! Number two fire pump is off-line—firemain is ninety-five psi and falling!"

Reese glanced over the heads of the ten-odd sailors separating him from Jade, trying to gauge her reaction to the stress in the kid's voice. He caught a glimpse of the back of her steel helmet, marked DCA, just before another sailor off her right cupped a hand to his sound-powered earphones and called out another update.

"Repair Three reports the fire in Lieutenant Wynne's stateroom has spread to the adjacent space."

And then another voice joined the fray. "Electrical power has been secured in the machine shop. Repair Five fire teams are preparing to access the space."

Jade finally stepped back from the set of huge shipwide schematics attached to the far wall of Damage Control Central. Still staring at the charts, she fired off a round of acknowledgments. "Very well. Decker, have Engineering bring number three fire pump on-line. Advise me when firemain is up and rising. Sanders, tell Repair Five not to crack the seal on that watertight door until firemain is above 125 psi. Smith, get Dannon down to pump room two and *fix that pump*."

"Aye, aye, ma'am." The three Petty Officers responded in unison and turned to carry out her orders.

"DCA, Captain's on line two."

Jade nodded and held out a hand. "Thanks, Smith. Sanders, inform Repair Two I'm shifting my assets. I want their primary hose team sent to Repair Three."

A couple of sailors played pass-the-phone until the receiver reached her. "DCA here. Captain, I need the Officer of the Deck to alter course. Topside scouts report our present one is trapping smoke inside the ship." She paused, apparently listening to the other end.

"DCA, number three fire pump is on-line. Firemain's at 132 psi."

Jade sent a thumbs-up over her shoulder, then turned and caught Reese's eye, waving him to her side, the phone still at her ear. "Aye, aye, Captain. DCA out."

She passed the receiver back as he wove his way through the bodies, curious to see what she could possibly need from him. The Captain wasn't kidding when he'd said he'd assigned Jade as his running mate because she was the best officer in the command. She was.

Jade smiled up at him beneath her battle helmet as he reached her side. "Confused?"

He readjusted his own as he grinned back, answering honestly, "Yup."

Her husky laugh carved a crater into the center of his gut. "Then listen up, I've probably got ten seconds before the next crisis hits."

She was taking time out from this shouting madhouse to explain it to him? He hoped to hell the grin on his face wasn't as big as it felt. Just three days at sea, and he was well on his way to gaining her complete trust. At this rate, he might even have the keys before the week was out.

Luckily, she'd already turned back to the laminated charts. "These plates depict every inch of the *Baddager* to scale. As you already know, the ship is divided into three sections, from the weather decks right down to the keel. Repair Two is responsible for the bow, Repair Three for amidships, and Repair Five the aft end."

She pointed to the line of black grease pencil she'd added to the diagram, extending out from the midsection of the plate marked *USS Baddager, AD-52:* Deck 01. "These are called damage control symbols. They help me track the various fires and flooding—drill or real—as they occur throughout the ship. See? This one tells me the missile entered the port side of the ship here.''

She traced the box she'd drawn around several compartments. ''We lost these four outer staterooms in the initial explosion. This part of the diagram tracks the actual damage control progress.'' One by one, she pointed to the symbols. ''Fire and smoke boundaries have been established. Electrical power has been secured in the area and hose teams have entered the space and have the fire under control. However—'' she tapped her finger on the next square ''—due to extreme heat, we sparked another fire in this adjacent stateroom.''

''DCA, Repair Five hose team has accessed the watertight door and entered the machine shop.''

''Very well, Sanders.'' Jade didn't look up as she flipped the plate back to reveal another chart, this one marked Deck Three. She added a symbol with her grease pencil and then continued the brief.

''The second missile impacted here in the machine shop. Again, fire and smoke boundaries have been set, electrical power secured, and—as you just heard—our hose team has accessed the space and begun battling the blaze. Due to the extent of damage reports in my possession, I've concluded that this second warhead did not explode.''

Reese whistled. ''Not bad for two hours' work.''

She laughed and glanced around the room. ''In reality, this would take a whole lot more—all day. But why put everyone through it for that long if we don't have to?''

He definitely agreed. The sooner this drill ended and the ventilation kicked back on, the happier and cooler they'd all be—her included. He hadn't missed the way she'd been rubbing the perspiration from beneath her helmet every now and then. But he wasn't surprised she didn't complain.

He hadn't heard her grumble once in the past three days. Not about the sleep he knew she hadn't slept, the meals she hadn't eaten, or the free time she plainly did not have. He was beginning to think the woman existed on coffee alone. And it wasn't healthy.

He ought to know.

"Excuse me, DCA?"

They both turned to face the guy with tattooed thighs for arms. The one who'd been manning the phones and repeating each stage of the drill's progression over the ship's loudspeaker—or 1MC, as Jade called it. "What do you need, Smith?"

Reese caught the pointed glance the guy shot in his direction—and Jade's responding, almost imperceptible nod.

"Go ahead, Smith."

"It's Repair Two, DCA. They still haven't sent that fire team you requested to Repair Three."

Reese also caught the streak of pure fury in her gray eyes before she conquered it. The serene smile she replaced it with didn't fool him for a second. "Petty Officer Smith, do me a favor and contact the Repair Two Locker Officer over the phone. Tell him if he doesn't cough up that hose team soon, I'm going to pay him a visit and pull it out of his hind end *personally*."

Smith grinned, obviously relishing the task. "I take it I can quote you on that, ma'am?"

She nodded solemnly. "You may."

Reese stared down at her as Smith spun around to do her bidding. "Let me guess, Lieutenant Dillon's the Repair Two Locker Officer."

Jade's lips twisted into the semblance of a real smile. "Macbeth, you must have ESP."

He noted the new tension in her shoulders as she turned back to the charts. No, but he sure as hell wished he did.

"DCA, Repair Five reports the fire in the machine shop is under control."

"Very well, Decker. Sanders, ask Lieutenant Shale if he needs any more firefighters beyond what he's been sent. Smith, have Ensign Turner send fifteen extra sailors from the pool on the mess decks to Repair Three to suit up, just in case.''

''Aye, aye, ma'am.''

Reese clenched his hands together as she rolled her shoulders, swamped by the ever-increasing urge to lift his hands and rub the tension out himself.

''DCA, Repair Five reports the fire in the machine shop is now out!''

Her sigh was almost inaudible as she closed her eyes. ''One down, two to go.''

''Desmoking and overhaul of the fire is in progress in the machine shop.''

She stepped up to the charts and added another symbol.

''DCA, Repair Three reports the fires in Lieutenant Wynne's stateroom *and* the adjacent space are now out!''

That elicited an honest-to-God smile. ''Petty Officer Smith, pass the word over the 1MC to the crew—all fires throughout the ship are now out.'' Then she turned around to address the sailors still clustered around. ''Relax battle dress in Damage Control Central.''

A collective sigh ripped through them as they yanked off steel helmets, unhooked the gas masks dangling from their hips and rolled up their sleeves as far as possible. Reese could have sworn he heard the blessed sound of ventilation kicking on as Smith broke the seal on the heavy watertight door to the space.

The tension even seemed to seep from Jade's shoulders as she pulled off her helmet and tucked a wisp back into her tight French braid. ''What do you say, Macbeth. Can I interest you in a cup of coffee while we wait for the debrief?''

He swallowed his disappointment as she pulled that damn red hat from the back of her waistband and capped her hair. ''Lead the way, DCA, lead the way.''

Jade kicked her boots up onto the edge of her desk and leaned back in her chair, sighing as Reese poured a cup of coffee from the steaming pot at the other end of the space. "You're a prince, Macbeth."

He tossed her that heart-stopping grin—the one she'd been trying to ignore for over a week—as he balanced the mug so the swells hitting the ship didn't end up sloshing it over the rim. "Yeah, I bet you say that to all the guys who bring you caffeine. Besides, Macbeth was a king."

She nodded as he reached her desk. "You're right—on both accounts. But that doesn't—"

She glanced up as the watertight door to her office undogged and opened. It figured. She bit back a groan as she claimed her mug.

"Well, well. Isn't this the picture of domestic bliss. She got you fetching slippers yet, Mack?"

Reese stiffened. "Shut up, Dillon."

Shut up? Weren't they supposed to be pals? Okay, so she hadn't actually seen them together since that night outside the NSF, but it was a big ship. At any rate, she didn't need Reese defending her from this moron. She'd handled him quite nicely for three years by herself.

She refused to give him the courtesy of standing as he closed the door and strolled in. "What jarred you out of your coffin, Mike? We've still got a couple hours of sunlight left."

For some reason, Dillon didn't rise to the bait, he just smiled as he meandered around Reese and hooked his hip on the corner of her desk, inches from tainting the soles of her boots. He crossed his arms and glanced over at the mountain of work covering her desk. "Got an extra report chit somewhere in that mess?"

Her gaze narrowed instinctively. "If you have a point to make, make it."

Dillon flicked up the cover to the latest revision of the Nuclear, Biological, Chemical Warfare Doctrine and pretended to study it. Pretended, because she knew reading was at the bottom of his favorite activities—unless the material was about himself.

She kicked her feet off the desk and slapped her mug onto the NBC Doctrine, cutting him off from his stalling tactic. "You've got exactly two seconds of my time, Dillon. It's been a long day and I'd like to finish my coffee in peace. Before the sight of your face curdles it."

Apparently, that was enough to force him to get the point, because he shot off her desk and loomed over her. "Where the hell do you get off ordering an enlisted guy to dress me down in the middle of a drill?"

Oh, he wanted to play rough today, did he?

Fine.

She'd taken just about all the crap she could handle from him. Drawing herself up on pure fury, she met him nose to chin—three nights' sleep deprivation more than made up the rest of the difference. "I'll tell you where I get off, buster. On your head. If I *ever* have to send down a multiple request for backup to your locker again, you *will* regret it."

Dillon took a step back and sneered down at her. "Don't get your panties in a wad, honey. You weren't desperate. I heard you send for help from the mess decks' pool."

She felt more than saw Reese rise up over Dillon's shoulder. She cut him off with a sharp jerk of her chin, closing in on Dillon herself, hunting him down until she was breathing up his neck.

"You arrogant *ass*. The safety of this ship should never have to depend on a group of inexperienced sailors who've never worked together before when I have an expert hose team at my disposal."

She stabbed a finger into his chest. "And while we're on the subject, *honey,* let me explain something to your feeble, radioactive little brain. This ship doesn't play at damage control and neither do I. If today's scenario had been real, that stunt you pulled could have cost lives. If you don't believe me, just ask the crew of the *USS Iowa* or the *Stark.*

Or maybe, you should just ask Petty Officer Erickson. Have I made myself perfectly clear?''

His curt nod was almost nonexistent—but she took it.

''Good. Because if I'm *ever* tempted to have this discussion again, I'll haul your butt up to the Captain's cabin and pound it into your skull right then and there. Now, *get out of my office.*''

Dillon stabbed her with an unholy glare just before he spun around and stalked out.

A full minute later, blood was still roaring in her ears and she was still seething, viewing the world through a haze of red.

A hand came down on her shoulder and squeezed gently.

What the—? She jumped back, trying to douse her fury long enough to figure out where it had come from.

''You okay?''

Reese?

She nearly groaned aloud. Oh, God, how could she have forgotten *he* was here? Great. So much for maintaining a healthy professional defense—uh, distance—from the man. Taking a deep breath, she sank into her chair. ''Just peachy.''

He didn't look convinced.

She faked a better smile. ''I guess I'm going to have to tell Karin that Dillon skipped his Prozac again.''

He didn't laugh.

Damn, why the hell did he have to look as if he could see right through her? Way down deep. Right down to the part of her that wasn't smiling.

He crossed his arms and kept on staring. ''So, you want to tell me what's really going on between you two?''

Chapter 6

Reese studied Jade as she seized her cup of coffee with both hands. One by one, he noted the telltale signs as her tension returned. First, the steady stare. Next, the blink. And then…yup, there it was—the clincher. The way the side of her cheek tucked in, as if she was biting down. Hard.

Whatever was between Jade and Dillon was personal. Any idiot who took the time to look, listen and think could tell that. He should know. He'd already spent far too much time there himself.

But how personal? *That* he didn't know—and he wasn't sure he wanted to, either. Unfortunately, it was necessary.

He pulled up a chair beside her and sat down. "How long did you two date?"

"*What?*" Coffee sloshed onto her desk.

Okay, so that wasn't it. He grabbed the mug before she dumped out the rest, mopping up the spill with a couple of blank papers as she slumped back in her chair. He mopped up the relief seeping into him as well before it got any ideas. "Sorry, my mistake."

Her gaze came back to his, dark and solemn.

Then again, maybe it *wasn't* a mistake. He sucked in his breath, holding it until his lungs began to blister, only releasing it when she sighed.

"Don't apologize. You weren't far off."

Damn.

"We never dated, but it wasn't because he didn't try."

He welcomed the relief as it swamped him again—for a moment. Then he shoved it aside. "What happened?" He waited for her to continue.

But she didn't.

"Jade—"

"Look, Macbeth. I admit we've gotten along pretty well lately, but let's not push it, okay? I'm not searching for a father confessor, and even if I was, you don't seem the type."

So much for the direct approach.

He was already reexamining his options when she closed her eyes and groaned. "I did it again, didn't I?" She peered over at him. "That was out of line, wasn't it?"

Surely she didn't expect an answer?

"Sorry." She sighed again, and this time it seemed to come from deep inside her. "Don't take this the wrong way. But frankly, you wouldn't understand."

"Because I'm a man?"

She shook her head.

So it wasn't a case of smoldering sexual attraction—on her part, anyway. There it was, that damn relief again. Only this time, it was choked off by a noose of dread. "Because I'm not Navy?"

Her gaze focused in on his sharply—too sharply, and he covered with a quick smile. He held his breath as she studied him, releasing it only when she shook her head.

"You know, sometimes I get the feeling you *are* Navy."

Holy sh—

"I know it's insane, but sometimes you have the lingo and the moves down a little *too* well."

He gripped the mug in his hands tightly and forced his smile to deepen. "Thanks, glad you noticed. I've been working pretty hard on my characterization."

"No, it's more than that. Like your cover." She leaned over, her fingers, smooth and warm, touching him where his blue cap met his temple. "I've spent years trying to retrain my guys how to wear it and they still cock it back like they're out on the baseball diamond. But the second you don yours, it's *there*. As if by instinct."

He laughed.

But she didn't—and the noose cinched in a little tighter as she continued, "Then there's the way you say bulkhead, overhead and deck—consistently. Almost as if the words had been drilled into you."

They had. But there was no way in hell he was telling her that. He met her steely gaze and held it. "Isn't that what they're called?"

"Yes, but I've never met a civilian who doesn't say walls, ceilings and floors."

She was good—really good. She ought to be working in his outfit; they could certainly use her. He leaned back in the chair as casually as he could, fighting the urge to rip his cover off. "Well, you'd never met *me*. Besides, I thought we were talking about Dillon."

He had to bite back a smile as she blinked. It worked; he had her back on the defensive. "I told you, you wouldn't understand. How could you? You're an actor. Everyone you meet thrives on what you do, hangs on to your every word. How could you possibly understand what it's like to have someone condemn you simply because of what you do?"

The noose snuck up and wrapped itself around his heart, nearly strangling it altogether. Damn, that was close—*too* close. Every nerve in his body warned him to change the subject. But he couldn't. It was a connection he could use. And he *would* use it—until he got to her.

He leaned over, picked up the mug of coffee and took a sip of what was left, then another—not even caring it was cold. "Actually, I do understand."

Yup, he'd snagged her interest now.

He managed a shallow breath. He could do this. All he had to do was reel her in—carefully. "My father."

"Your *father?* You mean he doesn't approve of your career?"

He gripped the mug tighter and took another sip. "You could say that. He spent years trying to turn me into something I didn't want to be—*couldn't* be." Eighteen years, to be exact.

She stared at him steadily for a minute and then startled him by laying her hand on his free one and squeezing it. "I'm sorry."

"Why?"

"Because it hurts."

He stared down at her fingers, warm, gentle—and somehow, now linked with his. He tried to stop his hand from shaking as the truth socked into him. Jade was right. It did hurt. Even after all this time.

"Do you want to tell me about it?"

"There's not much to tell." He shrugged. "My father wanted me to follow him into the…family business. I didn't want anything to do with it."

"You hated it."

How…? He stared into her eyes—and swore she could see into his soul. "How could you know that?"

Then he caught her rueful smile. "Because you're crushing my hand."

"Oh, sh—sorry." He tried releasing her fingers, but she held on to him and laughed.

"Hey, I'm tough, I can take it." She sobered. "Can you?"

He should have made a joke then, he had a hundred of them elbowing their way up his throat. But before he could choose, the truth slipped quietly past. "I don't know. Maybe I was hoping this particular job would bring him around."

He froze. Good God, how could he have *said* that? And how did he get the words back without calling attention to them? He opened his mouth, but she beat him to it.

"I don't get it, how can portraying a sailor bring your dad around?"

A joke, buddy. Crack a joke.

To his horror, he couldn't think of one.

She glanced down at her khakis and chuckled. "Hey, this gorgeous uniform may stop hearts on the street, but I don't think it can work miracles." Seriousness returned. "Have you tried sitting down lately and just talking to him?"

Get off this topic. Now. "What about Dillon? Have you tried talking to him?"

She blinked, and then smiled. "Okay, I'll back off—for now."

He squeezed her hand gently—doing his damnedest to ignore how right it felt in his—as he nudged her again. "Turnabout's fair play, you know. *Have* you tried talking to Dillon?"

"Once. And believe me, it was enough." For a moment, he thought she was going to continue. But she just shook her head. "Anyway, it doesn't matter. I can handle Dillon."

He wasn't so sure. If Dillon was running heroin, there was a chance *he* might have difficulty handling him. "Jade, the guy sounds like he's out to get you."

"Yeah, I know. It's weird, he's never gone this far before." She shook her head. "But even so, Mike wouldn't really endanger me or the ship. At least not deliberately."

"What do you mean, not deliberately?"

"Nothing. Forget it."

Reese was tempted, *very* tempted, to give her an extremely compelling reason to talk. But it was too soon. Both

Coffey and Dillon had the necessary clearances and opportunity to run the heroin in. But even with his gut leaning toward Dillon, he still couldn't cut her in the loop.

Because he didn't have proof. Without it, he was on his own awhile longer. At least until he'd had a chance to clear Coffey and the rest of the sailors who worked in the NSF. No, he'd have to find another way to get to the bottom of this.

He squeezed her hand again. "So the guy hates you because you wouldn't go out with him, huh?"

Her husky chuckle swirled around him. "I think you misunderstood. Mike asked me out *once,* shortly after I came aboard. That's it. Trust me, this is not the face that launched a thousand ships."

He disagreed. The few times she'd taken off that damn hat, it sure as heck had launched his. He shoved his lust back in line and reviewed his mental notes—ah, there it was. "So who's Petty Officer Erickson?"

Her hand twitched in his. A split second later, he knew he was on the right track when her gaze narrowed. "Who told you about that?"

"You did."

It narrowed even farther as disbelief entered her eyes. "I beg your pardon?"

"Right now—or rather when Dillon was in here. You told him to ask Erickson if his delay could cost lives."

"What, you have a photographic memory or something?"

He grinned. "As a matter of fact, yeah. It comes in handy in my line of work." For a moment, he basked in the respect in her eyes—it didn't come along too often. And then he pressed her again. "So who is he? And why does the mere mention of his name rout the pit bull and send him scurrying off with his tail tucked between his legs?"

She laughed. "Nice analogy. But I'm not sure your buddy would appreciate it."

"Buddy? Not on your life." He squeezed her hand. "Now, answer the question."

"Now look who's the pit bull."

He squeezed it again—harder.

She took a deep breath, then sighed heavily. "Oh, what the heck. I'm surprised you haven't already been filled in on the whole tawdry story. Erickson was an electrician. Two weeks after I checked aboard, I stumbled upon him shocking the hell out of himself while working on a transformer. I started CPR and managed to keep him with us until Karin arrived with her bag of magic. She did the rest to save him."

"What?"

She shrugged. "Believe me, no one was more surprised than me—except Dillon. He—uh—froze."

"What?"

This time, she squeezed his hand. "You're repeating yourself."

He recovered enough to let out a long, low whistle. She'd saved a guy's life while Dillon stood by with his thumb up his rear? Hell, that explained a *lot*. But not quite enough. "Okay, I see why the guy might feel a bit put out in your presence. But there seems to be more going on here than a mild case of embarrassment."

"There is. Apparently, Erickson's eighteen-year-old assistant was cowering in the corner when I arrived. Frankly, I don't remember. I was slightly occupied with breathing for Erickson and trying to get Dillon out of his trance long enough to alert Karin while I whaled on the guy's heart. By the time I got out of Medical, the seaman had recovered from his own shock and spread the tale all over the ship."

Now, *that* explained everything. "So he's been trying to make you pay for his mistake ever since?"

"That's what I always figured. Except about a week ago, things changed. Before that, he'd limited himself to a derogatory name every now and then, and some mild harassment. Only once did he step over the line. He involved someone who worked for me. But I slammed into him so hard, he never forgot the lesson.''

''So what happened last week?''

''Heck if I know. Maybe he was ticked he didn't get assigned as your running mate—I know he wanted the job. But whatever it was, he just snapped.''

He'd arrived last week. The realization stopped him cold. But did that mean Dillon was the *one* and was now suspicious, maybe even on to him? Is that why Dillon wanted the job—to keep an eye on him? Or was it just jealousy over the fact that he'd been assigned to Jade?

''Okay, Macbeth. I let you into Rumor Control, now it's time to pay admission.''

This time he blinked.

''Coffee.'' She pulled her hand from his and pointed to the empty mug on the desk. ''I need coffee—and you drank mine.''

Jade stared at her cheeseburger and fries as her plate slid six inches to the right. A moment later, like the pendulum of a clock, the plate reversed its tack and slid back over to the left.

''You should see sick bay. We've got gear all over the place.''

She glanced up, almost laughing as Karin attempted to navigate her way across the wardroom. She looked like a drunk trying to walk the line on a traffic stop—and she was having about as much success, too. Karin finally made it to the table and collapsed into the vinyl chair across from her.

''That was a blast. How long before we ride this one out?''

Jade grabbed the ketchup bottle as it slid back within reach. ''We should be through the storm in a few hours. So what did you do with Macbeth?''

''Stripped him down and left him tied spread-eagled on

my rack. Wanna stop by and make sure he's secured for sea?''

Jade opened her mouth—and then closed it. She was not falling for it. Not this time. She shrugged and concentrated on squirting ketchup over her fries. ''Maybe later.''

Karin laughed. ''Not bad. Just watch the blush and you might get away with it next time.'' She leaned forward. ''As long as we're on the subject of stripping, has Reese gotten another look at your necklace this past week?''

She tried to follow Karin's advice on her blush—and failed. She snatched up her water and downed the entire glass, praying it would help. ''Isn't there someone in sick bay you can bug?''

''Nope. Finished removing Reese's stitches about twenty minutes ago. No one else stopped by, so I split while the getting was good.'' She grinned. ''So, are you going to answer my question?''

''Do I have to?''

Karin laughed. ''You have to ask?''

Not really. If she didn't, she'd just hound her until she cracked. The woman was wasted in medicine—her skills would have been more useful in the Inquisition. ''I told you, Reese and I agreed it was a mistake. We've managed to put it behind us, why can't you?''

''*It? The man lays a twenty* on your lips and you call it an *it?*'' She grabbed Jade's fork before it slid onto the deck and waved it at her. ''Are you nuts?''

''Is who nuts?''

Jade glanced up to see Lieutenant Coffey and Reese zigzagging their way across the space. Thank God.

Reese eyed her burger as he claimed the chair next to hers. ''You're not really going to eat that, are you? I think we used one of those to patch a steam line this morning.''

She swallowed the lump of gristle. ''I'm desperate.''

Coffey laughed from across the table. ''You should have said something sooner. I just gave Mack my last Power

Bar.'' He grinned from her to Reese and winked. "But I bet if you bat your lashes real nice, he'll share."

Karin laughed. "I bet he'd share more than—*ouch!*"

Jade smiled as her boot struck home.

"Did we miss something?"

Replacing her smile with pure innocence, she turned to Reese. "Not a thing." She glanced down at the granola bar he'd slid over to her and pushed it back. "No, thanks. I'll just grab a cup of coffee and I'll be fine." He ignored her and shoved it back.

Coffey laughed. "Don't worry, Mack. She's serious. I watched her suck down cup after cup of caffeine for seventy-two hours straight during our navigation final in ROTC."

Jade laughed. "Ha! How would *you* know? You were sound asleep at your drafting table half the time."

"True, but I didn't have anyone running a constant line of coffee to me, either. I had to fend for myself along with the rest of the class."

"You guys went to school together?"

Startled, Jade glanced back at the disbelief in Reese's gaze, following it down to the granola bar that was now too squashed for either of them to enjoy. "Is there something wrong with that?"

Evidently Coffey read a bit more into Reese's expression. "Hey, buddy. We just went to school together. We didn't date. Heck, once she laid eyes on Jeff, no one else had a chance."

Reese released the flattened remains of the Power Bar, leaving it next to her half-eaten cheeseburger as he pinned her with a stare. "Who's Jeff?"

"DCA, you there?"

If Chief Haas had been standing in front of her, Jade would have kissed his weathered cheeks. She settled for ripping her walkie-talkie off her belt as she evaded that steel-blue gaze. "What's up, Chief?" Please, God, let it require her personal attention.

"Sorry to bother you, ma'am, but we've got ourselves a small problem out on the second deck fantail."

"How small?"

"Well, it seems several of Supply's forklifts have broken loose from their chains. They're playing tag with some of the guys as we speak."

"On my way." Jade hooked the walkie-talkie back on her belt and stood. "Catch ya later, guys." She shook her head at Reese, who'd stood along with her. "Sorry, Macbeth, this is the real thing. I can't afford to have you underfoot." She rounded the table and leaned down to whisper in Coffey's ear before she left the wardroom. "Thanks a lot, pal. Next time your office is on fire—I'm gonna let it *burn.*"

Using a jerky run-walk, she managed to cross the compartment without falling flat on her face as the *Baddager* rode out several increasingly severe swells. Coffey's chuckle dogged her the entire way.

She left the wardroom and grabbed her ball cap off the row of hooks outside the door as she passed. She shoved it on her head and turned to brace her hands on the ladder two feet away. Hooking her legs over the metal railing, she pushed off, sliding down to land at the bottom of the next deck with a solid thump. Then she was off and running again.

Two minutes later, feeling a lot like a battered pinball, she reached the aft end of the ship and stopped short—only to have something hard and muscular barrel into her from behind. She swung about and glared up at Reese. "I thought I told you to stay put."

He shrugged. "So I don't follow orders well. Sue me." He jerked his head toward the watertight door. "Are we going to stand here and argue or are we going to help?"

"*We* aren't doing anything. *I* am. You stay here—and

that's one order you better learn to follow." She didn't bother waiting for an answer, but turned back and undogged the door and shoved it open.

Son of a—

She severed her shock and quickly assessed the situation. Though the darkness and driving rain, she could tell three of the four forklifts had broken loose. Two were still rolling amok around the deck as if driven by invisible demons. Chief Haas and several members of the Flying Squad had captured the third one and were straining to hold it steady while Petty Officer Smith reattached its flailing chains to the deck.

She quickly set out to join the smaller of the two groups converging on the other lifts. It wasn't until she and two other sailors surrounded and latched on to it that she realized Reese was still with her. She lost her chance to yell as the lift dragged all four of them across the deck. They managed to stop it just before it slammed back into the fantail's safety rail.

"Macbeth!" Her bellow barely rose above the howling wind and other shouts. "See if you can grab that chain!"

Reese nodded and managed to twist around the back end of the machine, snaking out a long, muscular arm while maintaining his iron grip with the other. "Got it!"

She inhaled a mouthful of stinging sea spray before shouting over the blast of wind that engulfed them. "There's a padeye behind you—looks like half a doughnut upside down! Can you reach it?"

"I think so!"

Petty Officer Vega wrenched a new hook out of his pocket to replace the one lost when the chain snapped and passed it over. Reese snapped it on and then bent into the gale and pounding rain. His biceps strained and bulged beneath the rolled sleeves of his coveralls as he tugged the heavy chain over to the padeye welded to the deck. Jade winced as his knuckles scraped the rough, nonskid coating on the deck—he had to have lost a few layers of skin on that pass.

"Got it!"

All four of them let out a collective sigh. But it wasn't over. They still had three chains to go, and two were too short. They'd have to be replaced or welded first.

Jade realized she was the closest to the one chain that might be long enough to reach the padeye on her left. "Hand me a hook! I've got this one!"

She grabbed the hook and shimmied around the slick metal, cursing the rain as she strained to maintain her grip along with Reese and the other two men. The ship took another steep roll, and she grunted as it sent the end of the chain lashing back at her—smack into her stomach. She threw her free arm over it, clutching it to her. Her fingers were stiff as she fumbled her way down the links. But she finally reached the last one and moved away from the fork-lift, dragging the chain over to the padeye.

"Hold on tight!" She bent to reattach the new hook.

"DCA!"

Shock punched the breath from her lungs as she shot up. The fourth forklift had succumbed to the surging ship. Its chains lashing out behind, the runaway machine screamed across the deck, aided by the force of the swells pounding the hull. But a second before she was to greet four thousand pounds of rolling steel, someone shoved her out of the way.

She blistered the side of the safety rail with a string of purple curses as she smashed into the steel pole instead, the agony splitting into her temple offset by the realization that she would've been crushed if someone hadn't pushed her. She turned back, barely making out Reese's face amid the fog closing in on her.

"Oh, God, Jade. Are you okay?"

She nodded, clearing her head enough to manage a shaky smile as she brushed off his hands. "Fine. Thanks. Now, let's get this job wrapped up."

He looked ready to argue, but she didn't give him the chance. Adrenaline kicked back in and she turned to join the group. Thankfully, it had grown in her absence—the remainder of the Flying Squad had mustered while she was dazed.

Between the rest of them, they managed to trap the remaining lifts and hold them steady while Smith and Vega welded them in place. The sea started mellowing out of sub-hurricane conditions as they worked, and even the rain slacked off. Apparently, the course correction the captain had set was doing its job.

Jade let out a heavy sigh as the last chain locked into place, finally reaching up to rub the welt at her temple. She hadn't realized she'd gasped out loud until Reese turned back.

He tipped up her head and pulled off her cap, frowning as he smoothed his fingers along her forehead. "Dammit, woman. You said you were fine."

She jerked her chin from his palm and snatched her cover back, more embarrassed at the fuzzy feelings his fingers generated than from being touched in front of her division. "I am."

His frown deepened to a scowl. "Jade, you're bleeding."

That's it? It felt like half her forehead was missing. She glanced at his raw knuckles. "So are you. I don't hear you whining."

He took a deep breath. *"Jade—"*

She waved him off. "Don't worry, I'll stop by Medical and pick up a Band-Aid when we're done."

"DCA!"

She whipped her head toward her chief's voice—and instantly regretted it, grateful Reese didn't smirk as he grabbed her arms and steadied her. "Thanks."

"I'm taking you for that Band-Aid. Now."

The ship swam in front of her eyes again, and suddenly,

she wasn't in the mood to argue. "Okay. Just let me see what Chief Haas needs."

"Jade—"

She ignored the warning as she headed back to the watertight door. "Wait here." Through intense concentration, she made it without fainting. "What's up, Chief?"

He motioned her closer. "Take a look at this."

Jade struggled to focus on the link he'd placed in her palm. She moved it in closer and that seemed to help.

What?

She turned the link over in her palm and stared at it from the other side.

Good God!

She raised her eyes, a chill sliding down her spine as she saw the confirmation in her chief's gaze.

"No, you're not seeing things. I checked two other links and they look the same. They've all been deliberately cut."

Chapter 7

Jade grabbed the frame of the watertight door and held on for dear life. The wave of nausea passed and she blinked up at her chief. "I don't get it. Why would someone cut the chains deliberately?"

Chief Haas scratched the back of his neck. "Damned if I know. There are better ways to sabotage a ship than this."

"You're telling me. Unless—" she clenched her fingers harder over the steel frame as his face wavered in front of her eyes "—they just wanted to take out the Flying Squad. But even then, a fire would have been a better choice."

"You okay, Lieutenant?"

She didn't trust herself to nod, but knew she had to hurry—she saw Reese approaching out of the corner of her eye. She slipped the incriminating link into her pocket. "Fine. Look, I need to see the doc about a Band-Aid. I want you to check into this while I'm in Medical. Don't breathe a word of this to *anyone* until we've talked. Understand?"

"You got it." Haas pulled a handkerchief from his pocket and she winced as he pressed it against her head. "You're bleeding pretty bad. Let me get you to Medical before I get started.''

She shook her head—it was a mistake.

Reese grabbed on to her as he reached the door and pulled her close. ''I've got her, Chief. I'll make sure she gets there in one piece.''

She fixed the steadiest stare she could muster on Haas. ''It's okay. I need you to finish that write-up before this turns cold.''

He nodded. ''Aye, aye, ma'am.''

Reese led her through the doorway as Haas left. ''Before what turns cold?''

She clutched his forearm and used it to combat the swells hitting the ship as well as the fog in her brain. ''The scene, standard procedure. Didn't you promise to get me to Medical?''

''You want me to carry you?''

Which one? The one staring down at her intently or the other one—the one who wouldn't stop weaving in and around the first? She dug her fingers into his skin. ''Not if you value your life, Macbeth. Just don't move your arm and I'll be fine.''

''Jade—''

''Hush, I'm concentrating.''

She made her way down the darkened passageway at a drunken crawl. Thank God it was after taps. With most of the crew in their racks and the rest on watch, there was no one about to witness her weakened condition firsthand— except Reese. But by now, she was pretty sure he knew better than to open his mouth.

She swallowed a groan as they reached the ladder leading up to Medical. Peachy. She'd forgotten about this particular hurdle. How was she going to climb the steps without stumbling? She stuck out a boot and almost fell flat on her face.

Reese grabbed her by the waist and flipped her up into his arms.

Giving into the fog, she slumped against him as he took the steps two at a time. ''Thanks.''

His husky chuckle rumbled beneath her cheek, and the last thing she remembered before the fog closed in around her altogether was his seductive scent wafting over her.

Reese stared down at the jagged cut marring Jade's temple, trying to get the image of her smashing into the ship's safety rail out of his head. He willed her eyes to open for the countless time—his breath catching as they finally did.

''What happened?''

''You fainted.''

''What?'' He pinned his arm across her chest as she tried to scramble off the examination table. ''I did not.''

He grinned. ''You did, too. If I hadn't peeled you off the deck and slung you over my shoulder, you'd still be a trip hazard.''

Okay, so it wasn't exactly the truth. But he was trying too hard to forget how soft and vulnerable she'd felt in his arms to discuss what really happened. Besides, he was still ticked to discover she'd gone through ROTC with Coffey. It added a whole new facet to his case he'd rather not consider right now.

Instead, he focused on the look that had passed between Jade and her chief before he'd approached them. But that only left him wondering what she'd slipped into her pocket. Whatever it was, neither of them seemed anxious for anyone else to find it. And he would have found it, if the hospital corpsman hadn't interrupted his search in the nick of time.

Damn.

The door to the exam room slammed open, admitting one worried-looking doctor. She snapped on a pair of gloves and hurried over to the table, frowning as she probed the gash on Jade's temple. ''How many times do I have to tell you to duck?''

''I feel fine, Doc. Thanks for asking.''

Karin glared down at Jade. "Shut up." She glanced at Reese. "What happened?"

Jade tried to sit, and this time Karin joined him in pushing her back down. "Lie there and be quiet before I give you a shot of Seconal and knock you out."

Reese swallowed a chuckle as Jade's bottom lip puckered. "Yes, ma'am."

He turned back to Karin. "I shoved her out of the way of a forklift and into the safety rail by mistake. She made it to the ladder outside your office and then fainted."

"I did *not!*"

He and Karin both arched brows as they turned to stare down at her.

Jade flushed, bringing a bit more color back into her cheeks. "Sorry."

His breath caught, and he quickly turned to Karin to cover it. "What do you need me to do?"

She cocked her head toward the door. "Go see my chief, she's waiting in the next exam room to take a look at you."

Reese stared down at his scraped hands. Until then, he'd forgotten about the stinging. "You sure you don't need help?"

Karin smiled as she swiped a sterile pad around Jade's temple, cleaning the excess blood. "She'll be fine—go."

"W-wait."

He turned back to Jade, his heart taking up a deafening cadence at the falter in her voice.

"My ball cap—where is it?"

What? She'd just about split her head open and she was worried about that damn hat? He snatched it off the seat next to the table and thrust it at her—but she didn't take it.

Instead, she smiled. A beautiful, honest-to-God, *I like you* smile that reached straight into his gut and pulled him inside out. "It's yours, Macbeth—you earned it."

Somehow, he managed to smile back. Then he turned and

stumbled from the room, still clutching that stupid scrap of scarlet like a two-year-old gripping his blankie.

He'd *earned* it?

The door snapped shut, and in one fell swoop, his mantra crumbled to the deck. He'd known all along Jade wasn't capable of running drugs or even turning a blind eye—and now it was time to act like it.

He leaned against the door, letting his head drop back against it, his grin turning downright painful as he felt the force of Jade's scowl through the steel.

"What are you smiling at, Doc? Just stitch up my head—I've got work to do."

Reese wedged his gauze-covered fist into the pocket of his coveralls and pulled out the key to his stateroom. He glanced at Jade's door before unlocking his own and entering. Then he dropped the keys to his desk and stared down at the ball cap she'd given him.

Her cap.

Her *cover*.

It still had the officer's emblem—a gold eagle brandishing a silver shield—pinned beneath the ship's name. He trailed his fingers along the scarlet edge, battling the temptation to don it. Because of Jade, the urge damn near won.

Hell, wouldn't Dad laugh his ass off if he could see him now?

He flung the cap onto his rack, wishing he could rid himself of what it represented as easily. No matter what Dillon said, no matter how much she loved the sea, Jade was *not* like his father. And maybe when this case was over, he'd set about proving it. Until then, he had to get his mind back on the job.

Somehow.

He had a lot to figure out tonight, like how he was going to get Jade to tell him what really happened to those forklifts. He had to. Because his gut was still doing a dance that could only mean one thing.

Something was wrong. And from the surprise on Jade's face when she'd spoken with her chief, he had a pretty good idea what it was. Some*one* had caused that accident. But who?

Dillon?

Coffey?

But the most pressing question of all was *why?* And why now? He crossed over to the trash can underneath the sink and unwrapped the bulky gauze from his hands before dumping it into the trash.

What the—?

The hair on the back of his neck snapped to attention as he stared at the contents of the garbage can. Someone had gone through his garbage!

He spun around to the door, his ears straining for the slightest sound out of the ordinary—but if there was one, he couldn't make it out. All he heard was the constant whir of air passing through the ventilation ducting overhead and the rhythmic creaking of metal as the ship pitched and rolled smoothly with each successively less powerful wave. Beyond that, nothing.

But his gut was still on alert.

He crept across the compartment and released the catch on his modular wall unit, peering inside as he lowered the flap to form the temporary desk.

Crap.

He'd left the combination on seven and a half—and now it was on seven. Someone *had* been in here. Not only had they rifled through his garbage, they'd tampered with his safe.

He spun the dial back and forth several times and popped the catch. Relief flooded him as he stared inside. Everything was exactly where he'd left it—including the tiny speck of lint on top. He removed the contents and slipped them into his boots. His cover story might have survived this particular attempt, but he wasn't taking a chance on another.

Once he'd locked the safe, he turned and executed a systematic search of his quarters. Suspicion gnawed a hole into certainty as he worked his way around the room. Whoever had violated his stateroom had taken their sweet time, because everything he owned had been handled, then carefully replaced, in almost exactly the same spot.

He'd test for prints, even though he doubted he'd come up with any. Anyone who'd taken this much time to toss his room would be smart enough to wear gloves. But that realization led him to another. Whoever had rifled through his gear knew he *had* time.

Like Lieutenant Coffey.

He glanced over at the mutilated dummy Coffey had dumped on his rack—just before the guy suggested they join Jade and the doctor in the wardroom. Yup, Coffey definitely had opportunity. Especially if he managed to create a diversion with a time delay factored in. Then again, maybe he was just pissed the guy had dropped the dummy off instead of letting him accompany him to the NSF. The missed opportunity still burned him.

Reese jerked his head up as he heard Karin whispering in the passageway.

"I mean it, Jade. You're not allowed to stand watch tonight."

"But I feel *fine*. Though I have to admit, I'd feel better if you gave me *something* for the pain."

He heard Karin's muffled sigh as Jade's key slid into the lock. "I wish I could, but I can't take the chance of it masking symptoms of latent brain swelling. Besides, even if I did give you something, you still couldn't stand watch. You're not supposed to operate heavy equipment on painkillers—and, honey, this ship *definitely* qualifies. Especially when I'm on it."

He missed Jade's response as her door closed, but chuckled, anyway. It didn't take much imagination to figure it out. He squelched a smile and pondered the upcoming minefield as he headed next door. As much as he hated pushing Jade after what had happened, he had to talk to her.

Now.

The more time that elapsed, the greater the risk of her forgetting something seemingly insignificant, but potentially vital. He also needed to question her about Coffey—carefully.

He rapped the knuckles of his good hand on Jade's door, wishing he knew up front if the relationship he'd just discovered between Coffey and Jade was going to work for or against him.

Jade glanced at Karin as someone thumped the outside of her door.

Chief Haas?

If it was, as much as she wanted to confide in Karin, she had to get rid of her. She yawned and stretched. "I'm pooped. How 'bout I check in with you in the morning?"

Karin nodded as she headed for the door. "Sounds good. Remember, lie on your back. I don't want to have to redo my handiwork." She opened the door and chuckled. "Well, well, fancy meeting you here."

Damn. She needed to see Haas, not Reese. Jade suppressed a wince and smiled. "Hey, Macbeth. How's the hand?"

He held up a set of raw knuckles. "Fine. How's the head?"

"Fine."

Liar, liar, pants on fire. Her head throbbed out an accompaniment to the taunting litany.

She tried to ignore the concern creasing his brow. It was dangerous—that same concern almost had her crumpling into his arms to sniff and whine until the pain passed on the fantail.

"Bet it hurts like hell."

"It's been better." She took a deep breath as he entered her room uninvited.

Karin traded places with him, turning back as she reached the door. "Well, I'm off to hit my rack. You seem okay, but I'll check back in an hour to see how you're doing."

Reese shook his head. "Get some sleep, Doc. I'll take the first shift."

Karin stared at him intently for a few moments and then nodded. "Okay, but call me if you don't see the whites of her eyes or she doesn't respond when you call her name."

"You got it."

Jade considered murdering Karin as she smiled that secret smile of hers. The door snicked shut before she could execute her plans, leaving her standing in the middle of the room staring across the silence at Reese.

He cracked the tension with a grin. "Guess we've come full circle—seems the baby-sitter's become the baby-sittee."

Humor was such an ugly concept at this hour. She frowned, regretting the motion a split second later.

The concern slid back into place as he moved closer. She didn't know which hurt worse, the pain in her skull or the piercing blue in his gentle gaze. "That bad, huh?"

She sighed as he guided her around and began rubbing her neck and shoulders. "Worse."

Reese chuckled and she leaned back, against her will, into the soothing sound, into his magic hands. The more he rubbed, the more the pain in her head ebbed.

Yeah, his hands were magic all right. Black magic. Because her defenses were weakening. Not only that, she couldn't find the strength to move. Before she knew it, she'd sunk back even farther, stopping only when she reached his chest.

He wrapped his arms around her and pulled her close. And there they stood, for what seemed like an eternity. If she died right now, she'd die content. Because then she wouldn't have to tear herself from this warm, musky cocoon.

And she *did* have to. Soon.

But not now.

Right now she just wanted to stand here and fill her lungs with Reese's scent, feel his strength, draw on it—and pretend nothing else existed. For just a moment, she wanted to forget the lesson Jeff had carved into her heart. A lesson she'd learned so well that it now ruled her life.

"I didn't know you went to school with Lieutenant Coffey."

The spell broke.

She tried to pull away, but Reese wouldn't let go. He tucked her head beneath his chin and rubbed his jaw lightly over the top of her hair, luring her back under.

She sighed, closing her eyes as she followed. "I went to school with a lot of guys—the Navy's kinda funny that way. First in Austin, and then a whole other set when I transferred back to San Diego the end of my junior year."

He cupped his palms over her arms and soothed them up and down her bare skin, igniting fires she had no desire to douse. His lips whispered against her uninjured temple. "Why did you transfer?"

She followed the warm breath, snuggling closer as his arms came to rest on top of hers. "My mom had a heart attack." She lifted her fingers and threaded them into his as he tensed slightly. "It's okay. She's fine now. It was a warning and she heeded it. My parents hired a manager for their restaurant and learned how to take it easy."

"Good."

His arms relaxed, but his fingers continued winding in and out of hers, weaving a string of desire through her heart and knotting it deep inside her. Deep inside places she'd gotten extremely good at ignoring.

Until now.

She sighed as she realized he'd made her forget about her head for a few minutes. She really should move—while she still could.

"So who's Jeff?"

This time she tensed. "Just a guy I knew."

"Did he give you the necklace?"

Was that jealousy she heard? If it was, it was a pretty heady note. She smiled. "Why do you want to know?"

His fingers stopped, trapping hers. "Did he?"

"No. It was a commissioning gift from my mother." That was mostly true. He didn't need to know the rest.

Jade drew a deep breath as he released her fingers and resumed the heavenly torment along her arms. Another few minutes of his touch and she'd be tossing her principles overboard. And then where would she be? Turning around in his arms and pressing her lips into his, that's where.

Suddenly the phone rang, giving her just enough strength to escape him.

"Hello?" She frowned at the husky voice that came out of her mouth. Damn, why did she feel so cold and bereft?

"DCA, that you?"

She turned away from Reese, hoping it would clear her voice—and her head. "What's up, Chief?"

"Near as I can figure, three of the four chains on each lift were tampered with. The links were cut clean through on one side. The remaining chain was left whole—probably to buy time."

She cupped the phone and lowered her voice to a near whisper. "How much lead time are we talking?"

"The way we were rocking and rolling? Not much. Half hour, maybe an hour, tops. You got someone listening in?"

She returned her voice to its normal pitch. "I understand. Who do you want to take the watch?"

"Gotcha. No other leads yet. Have no idea who could have done it, but I'm not done asking around, either."

She forced a light laugh. "Better wake him gently. You know how he gets."

"I hear ya. I'll be careful. How's your head?"

She touched it automatically. "Fine." Oddly enough, it did feel better.

"Good. I'll call you if I get more tonight. Otherwise, see you at quarters in the morning."

"Great. Thanks, Chief."

Reese studied Jade as she hung up the phone, relieved the massage had helped. It had to have—because she wasn't favoring the eye below the cut anymore.

That cut.

Just the sight of it made his blood run cold. If he found out someone was behind this, he was going to pay. And it was going to hurt.

But first he needed answers. And who better to give them than the one woman who seemed to have her finger on the pulse of the ship? "So, are you going to tell me what happened tonight?"

He focused on her eyes. The second she decided to misconstrue his words, it was there—smack in the middle of those dark gray depths.

She smiled. "Oh, that. Just a problem with a sick sailor. Chief Haas needed to run it by me."

He crossed his arms. "Tonight?"

"Hmm. The guy was supposed to be on watch already." She unhooked her keys from her belt and stared at them.

"Jade?"

She glanced up. "Yeah?"

"Why are you lying to me?"

The keys jangled in her hands. "What are you talking about?"

Reese squared his feet on the deck as another swell hit the ship. He stood his ground, cutting her off before she could argue. "I've been following you around for two weeks now. And if there's one thing I've learned about you, it's that you expect your people to pull their weight. Whether or not you're around to watch.''

He approached her slowly, taking the keys out of her hand and carefully setting them on the desk. ''Now, I'm not saying you don't have a problem with your watch bill. What I am saying is there's no way in hell Chief Haas would call you up in the middle of the night with a correction—especially after what you've been through. He would have handled it himself.''

''Listen—''

He cupped her chin and tipped it, gaining better access to that telling smoky gaze. ''No, *you* listen. Something happened to those forklifts and I want to know what.''

She blinked.

He closed in. ''Jade, you trusted me enough to let me in this past week. You even trusted me enough to give me your ball cap. Trust me now—when it really matters. When I can do something to help. *Please.*''

She stared up at him for a few long moments and then cleared her throat softly. ''Let's—uh—just say the lifts might not have snapped the chains by themselves. They might have had a little help.''

Damn.

It was what he expected, but it was not what he wanted to hear. He traced his fingers across her cheek, wanting more than anything to smooth those tiny, neat stitches and that jarring cut from her temple.

But he couldn't. And he couldn't get them to stop blaring the truth at him, either.

He'd done this to her.

Not Dillon, not Coffey, but him. He'd gotten her involved even after he knew she wasn't the one. He'd used her. He'd used her until he'd gained her trust and gained access into this tight little world called the Navy. He'd used her until he'd gained the attention of whoever he was really after.

Dillon, Coffey—right now it didn't even matter which

one. What did matter was that Jade finally learned the truth. And that she heard it from him. He'd spent the last hour examining the ramifications of what he was about to do. And he'd come to the conclusion that he'd be better off working *with* Jade than around her.

He just hoped to hell she felt the same way.

Jade swallowed and tugged her chin from his hand, making him realize he hadn't responded to her revelation. She stepped back, almost as if she was embarrassed.

He reached for her, but came up empty as she took another step.

"Look, Macbeth, forget what I said. Blame it on my head. Even if it's true, it's probably just a simple case of vandalism. Heck, you and I both know this isn't Hollywood. We're not talking danger and intrigue on the high seas here."

It was time.

He dragged her chair from the desk and hiked his boot up onto it. Reaching inside, he fished out the one piece of evidence that would change everything Jade thought she knew about him. He leaned over his knee and carefully laid it on the desk between them, anticipating the blink before it came.

"W-what…?"

"It's a Glock. Nine millimeter, semiautomatic. Carries seventeen rounds in the magazine, no safety—"

"I know *that*."

He'd suspected as much—war *was* her profession. But it was his, too—he just fought a little closer to home. He glanced down at the gun, then back at her. "It's loaded."

Her gaze narrowed and her hands twitched at her sides, as if instinctively. He linked his hands together on his propped leg, making damn sure she noticed them. His gut warned him if he so much as breathed toward his weapon right now, she'd fight him for it.

And she wouldn't stop until she won.

"Might I ask what you plan on doing with it?" The churning shadows in her gaze belied that cool, steady voice.

He let out a sigh and slowly reached into his boot again, allowing himself one last glimpse of the now-crumbling trust he'd worked so damn hard to build before he pulled his real wallet out and flipped it over to her.

She caught it neatly.

He held his breath as she opened the leather and glanced down at his badge. The moment the last of her trust vanished, he felt the answering void suck into him. She raised her eyes then, her icy gaze carving what was left of him in two.

"Who *are* you and just what the *hell* is going on here?"

Chapter 8

Jade stared at Reese, slicing into the inside of her cheek as she tried to absorb the blow. She hadn't been this dazed when she'd smashed her skull into the side of the ship a few hours ago. And she certainly hadn't been this ticked.

God, how he must have been *laughing* at her!

She shoved the bulk of her anger and betrayal deep into her box and studied the Glock. Then she stared at its owner. He wasn't going to shoot her. That much she knew. Because if that was his intention, he'd have done it already. Besides, he wouldn't have saved her life on the fantail just to shoot her now. But of course, that only meant one thing.

The ID was real.

He cocked his head toward his badge. "It's real. But if you can get to a cell phone, I can have it confirmed."

"I know. But I'll take the confirmation just the same." She glanced down at the badge again. She needn't have bothered—the words were already branded into her brain. "It says here you're Special Agent C. Reese Garrick with the Drug Enforcement Agency." She managed a cool smile.

"Well, Mr. Garrick, would you like to explain to me how you ended up on my ship posing as some Hollywood bimbo?"

She'd offended him.

Good.

"Bimbo? I don't think a man can be referred to as a bimbo."

"Mr. Garrick—"

He was standing in front of her—his fingers pressed to her lips—before she'd even realized he'd moved. He shook his head, tsking gently. "Honey, *please,* you bandy that name around much louder and you're liable to get me killed."

She jerked away from his hand and glared up at him. "Thanks—I'll remember that."

"Ouch."

"I'm waiting."

He plowed his fingers through his hair and sighed. "It's a long story."

"Since I'm not allowed on the bridge tonight, I seem to have some free time on my hands. Start talking." He didn't have a choice—because she didn't plan on giving him one.

Reese motioned for her to have a seat on her rack and turned to lock the door. Then he slipped his weapon back into what was probably a holster in his boot and flipped on her CD player. He dragged her desk chair over to the bed and sat down as a sultry sax moaned softly around them.

His eyes flared and deepened to cobalt. "I had no idea you were into jazz."

She bit down on her cheek again. He had no right smiling at her like that. And she sure as heck shouldn't be responding to it—not after what she'd just learned. She leaned back against the bulkhead, strangling his wallet as she tucked her legs under her chin. "Yeah, well it's nice to know I've still got a few secrets left from you, too."

"Jade—"

She glowered at his outstretched palm. "Spare me the apologies, Macbe—Reese—and skip to the explanation."

He pulled his hand back and nodded as he crossed his arms. "Several weeks ago a heroin dealer showed up—"

"*Heroin?* You think someone on this ship is running *heroin?*" She would have slapped her head if it didn't already hurt. Of course he did—or he wouldn't *be* here.

"I'm sorry. This is just one more shock on top of a really long day."

Ah, damn, there was that compassion again. She didn't want to see it. She couldn't handle it. Not right now.

"Are you okay? Do you want to get some sleep and finish this in the morning?"

"No. Really—I'm fine." There was no way she could sleep. The accident and hour be damned—she was wide-awake now. "Please, continue."

He stared at her intently for a few moments, as if trying to determine if she really was up to it. He'd apparently decided in her favor, because he sighed and nodded. "Okay. But if you need to rest, you let me—"

"Just *tell* me."

He leaned back in the chair. "As I was saying, I was brought in on the case after a known drug dealer showed up in the burn unit of San Diego General. He had several unusual burns to his hands and his…ah…genital area."

Jade blinked. His *what?* How could he burn just his hands and his—well—*there?* She swallowed the question. "How unusual were these burns?"

"They were caused by radiation."

"*What?*" Good Lord!

"That's what I thought. Obviously, the bastard didn't know the outside of the package was radioactive when he handled it and shoved it in his pants."

"Obviously. But I still don't see how that led you to us. When it comes to radiation, the Navy's not the only game in town anymore."

"It is when it also involves a repair ship."

Jade snorted. "Right. And you're going to take the word of a drug dealer? Come on, you know better than I do, they're not exactly pillars of honesty."

He grinned at that. "You're right, they're not. But this one I believe." His grin twisted into a wince. "I was there when the doctor informed him his other—ah—*appendage* might blacken and fall off. He sang louder than a gospel choir. Unfortunately, he didn't know all the notes. I didn't get much out of him except the date he'd received his last shipment. He'd always met his contact at night, so he couldn't ID the guy from the collection of official Navy photos we obtained."

Something clicked. She pulled her legs from under her chin, crossing them Indian-style as she leaned forward. "Wait a minute, you said you had the date. Who was in port?"

Reese nodded. "You and the *Durante*."

That's it, then. "It's us." She slumped back against the bulkhead.

"You sound pretty sure, though it *is* starting to look that way. We've got a guy on there, too, and he's turned up even less than I have."

She sighed and explained her instinct. "The *Durante*'s a sub tender—which means she services submarines, not surface ships. Security is just too damn tight on one of those to let a supply of heroin slip through for long. That *is* how the drugs are getting aboard, right? Through another ship—a nuclear-capable one?"

"I don't know."

"You don't *know?*"

He dropped his elbows to his knees and leaned forward. "That's the problem. I haven't been able to get into the NSF long enough to find out."

Jade stared at Reese, trying to reconcile the happy-go-lucky, almost obnoxious man she'd come to know these past two weeks with the serious DEA agent seated eighteen inches away, staring at her intently. It disturbed her that she couldn't.

Until she realized why.

Mack Reese didn't exist. He was a creation. Reese Garrick was the real thing. She'd seen a hundred telling signs over the last couple of weeks, but she'd ignored them—because she'd wanted to. She'd wanted to believe he was just an airhead who'd do his time and then just float away when it was over. Because if she believed that, she'd be safe.

From herself.

She took a deep breath and decided to rent that movie of his the moment they pulled back in port. Apparently Reese was a better actor than she'd thought.

But for now, it was time to put the actor aside and deal with the agent. "You won't be able to get into the NSF on your own—not without arousing suspicion, anyway. Not with TPI in effect."

Confusion furrowed his brow. "TPI? That's one acronym I haven't run across yet."

"Two Person Integrity. It's a safeguard that means there must be at least two sailors present whenever classified material is involved."

"Damn." He stared down at the deck and rubbed the back of his neck.

She was tempted to take over and provide him with the same relief he'd given her. But she had the feeling he'd prefer another service instead. "I can get around it. Of course, it'll take some thought and some planning, but I can get you in."

He raised his head, hope spreading like fire across his face as he stared at her.

And then the phone rang.

His eyes narrowed and his hands tensed.

"Relax, it's probably Karin checking up on me."

He reached over and pushed the silver button on the side of the receiver. The handset popped off and he passed it to her.

"DCA here."

"The news is good and bad."

She glanced at Reese, her eyes locking with his deep blue gaze. "What have you got, Chief?"

"Flushed out two lovebirds who make a habit out of nesting near the forklifts whenever the ship's underway."

She closed her eyes briefly and rubbed a finger between her brows. She was better off not knowing this part. "What did they see?"

"Not much, thought it was already occupied."

He was going to make her ask. "And?"

"Whoever it was—it was Khaki."

Her head began to throb, and it had nothing to do with her stitches. Khaki—officer, chief. Mike Dillon. Greg Coffey. Oh, God! Reese was after *Greg!*

"I know. Talk to you in the morning, DCA."

She thrust the phone back at Reese, blindly.

"Jade, what is it?"

She recovered long enough to remember his arms around her not more than a half hour ago. Her teeth tore into the side of her cheek as the betrayal struck. Hell, that black *magic* wasn't an accident. It was Reese. He'd lured her under his spell—slowly, carefully, *deliberately*. Then he'd asked her about Greg. He'd been leading her on, using her, so he could arrest one of her best friends!

The control she'd managed to hold on to when she'd discovered his identity finally snapped as the extent of his deception smacked into her. She clenched her fist around his wallet and launched it at him. He ducked just in time. It whizzed past his head and smacked into the closet behind him.

He had the bloody nerve to look surprised. "You want to tell me what that was all about?"

She followed the wallet with a blistering glare. "You *used* me."

Reese sucked in his breath as the black loathing in Jade's gaze slammed into him. It was over.

She *knew*.

She'd figured out he'd been leading her on to get to Dillon and Coffey. To get into the NSF. This woman was just too damn smart for his tricks. He wished to heck that didn't please him—but it did.

He leaned over, shoving the discovery deep inside as he retrieved his wallet. But he couldn't push down the realization that she hadn't lost her cool until she thought he didn't care. Nor the hope that it meant *she* cared. "Jade, please. I—"

"Don't bother denying it. I've had just about all the lies I can stomach for one night."

He gripped his wallet, biting back every filthy curse in the book—and then a few more. "I won't deny it."

He watched as the last flicker of hope died and extinguished from her eyes. She stared down at her hands—talking more to herself than to him. "*You set me up.* Probably from the beginning. All the smoldering looks. The dance. That *kiss*."

She raised her head and focused on him with deadly precision. "It was all part of the plan, wasn't it? To get me to trust you. To get you in."

He'd have given anything to deny it.

But he couldn't.

He clenched his fingers around his wallet, crushing it. "Yes, it was." At first.

Her eyes grew even colder until they were barren. Then the chill spread out beyond her, clawing into him as well. She nodded slowly, her whisper slicing into his gut. "Well, congratulations. You're *in*."

So why had he just felt a steel door slam in his face?

''I have one more question for you, Mr. C. Reese Garrick.''

His name had been on her lips quite a bit in his dreams these past few weeks, but it had never dripped with that particular note before. At least she was still whispering.

''*Why* are you trusting me now? What makes you so sure I'm not going to get up off this rack and march straight through that door, climb two sets of ladders, knock on the Captain's cabin and *blow your cover from here to Kingdom Come?*''

''Your file.'' And his gut.

He may as well have slapped her. ''You've *read* my record?''

That solved one question—the chill wasn't going to stay in her eyes forever. He just wished the heat replacing it would stop before it blew the top off the thermometer.

''No wonder you seemed surprised to discover I'd gone to school with Greg.'' Her lips twisted bitterly. ''I take it my transfer isn't listed.''

''Nope. Just you graduating with honors from San Diego, your follow-on military schools and, of course, your officer fitness evaluations.''

''Those are *private*.''

''I know. But yours are stellar, so why the huff?''

Bad choice of words.

''Well, hell, why not snoop into my background investigation as well? That would take you back to grade school. Then you'd know all my dirty little secrets.''

He opted for bald honesty. ''Didn't have the time. I had forty officers to investigate in twenty-four hours, and you didn't work in the NSF. All I needed to know was you'd been granted your Top Secret clearance.'' But he wished he had. It probably mentioned Jeff. ''Look, I know it doesn't help, but I'm sorry. I didn't even read it until the night I'd been assigned to you. I didn't mean to pry. I was doing my job.''

She ignored him.

He practically ripped his wallet in two. "Jade—"

"Someone saw a khaki uniform near the forklifts earlier this evening."

Yes!

He refused to feel guilty as the rush hit. In fact, she was right to change the subject. He was here to do a job. When it over, he'd find a way to breach the pain he'd caused. But right now, he had to find out who was running that heroin.

Before they got a crack at the other side of Jade's head. "Who was it?"

She dug her fingers into her braid. "We don't know." Sighing heavily, she pulled three large bobby pins from her hair and laid them on the bed between them in a neat row. "So who do you think it is? Dillon or Coffey?"

Reese swallowed as the thick braid fell over her shoulder all the way down to her thigh. "I don't know. Who do you think it is?" His lungs slowed as she pulled the brown rubber band from the bottom and threaded her fingers up into the rope, separating the strands.

He glanced at her face, trying to ignore the inky curtain spilling into her lap—and almost laughed at her expression.

"You really have to ask which one *I* think is behind it?"

He had to smile. "No. But I need proof." His lungs nearly stopped altogether as she plowed her fingers into her scalp, sending a shimmer of midnight blue through the black.

Ah, damn, not *now*.

Not while she hated him.

But it was too late. He was already hard. He swallowed a groan, cursing his fetish as it ripped into him. He'd *never* had trouble controlling it.

Until Jade.

He shifted in the chair, reviewing the multiplication tables as she continued to slide her fingers through her glistening hair. He moved on to division, but that didn't help, either.

Maybe he should get up and leave. He could come back later. He would.

If he could stand.

He cleared his throat, louder than he'd expected. "Tell me about Lieutenant Coffey." He sighed, breathing easier as her hands dropped into her lap. There was a God after all.

She shrugged. "There's not much to tell. Greg's a friend. Actually, he's more than that. He was my frat brother in college. He's been there for me through some pretty tough times."

"Like Jeff?"

He'd gone too far.

"Jeff is *none* of your business."

The hell he wasn't. He nodded, anyway. "Okay."

She sighed. "Let's just stick to the case. Besides, we can't be sure what happened tonight is even connected to the heroin. What would be the point?"

"To search my quarters."

"Did you just say what I think you did?"

He nodded. "Someone searched my quarters while we were out playing dodge-the-forklift." He leaned back in the chair, slipping his wallet down into his boot and patting it. "I imagine they were looking for these."

"You think he's on to you?"

He smiled at her shock. For someone who was great at waging war, she was fairly naive when it came down to the dirty, underhanded battles in life. But then, most honest people were. "Maybe, maybe not. I'm not taking any chances."

He never did.

Whoever he was after was smart enough to watch his own six. Yeah, the forklifts were connected. He didn't need physical proof to know that. He could feel it.

"Oh, my *God*." She went deathly pale, and for a second, he thought she was going to throw up.

He leaned forward and grabbed her arms. "What is it? Your head?"

She didn't answer.

He clamped down on her hands, squeezing tightly as fear really gripped him. "Jade, what's *wrong?*"

Still looking dazed, she finally focused. "The watch bill."

What? "Honey, what does your sick sailor have to do with this?"

"Not the enlisted watch bill. The officer's. Coffey and I are in the same section—I'm on the bridge, he's in radar. But the point is, we rotate together."

Understanding dawned. "You mean when you're on watch, he's on watch?"

She nodded.

It made sense. A lot of it. He'd spent the entire week practically glued to Jade's side. Wherever she went, he went. If Coffey couldn't search his quarters when they were on the bridge because he was also on watch, he'd have to create a diversion—a little damage control diversion—to get him out of the way.

He linked his fingers into hers. "What about Dillon?"

She shook her head. "He's in section three. Greg, you and I are in section two." She must not have noticed their hands. Because if she had, there was no way she'd keep smoothing the pads of her fingers on his. Bittersweet longing coursed through him as she rubbed them over his palm.

Maybe this wasn't such a good idea.

"I still don't believe Greg could do this. I know him, he doesn't even drink. Besides he'd have a hell of a time pulling one over on Dillon *once,* let alone on a regular basis."

He must not have hidden his surprise well enough, because she squeezed his fingers and laughed.

"What, you think because Dillon's slime he's not smart?" She shook her head. "I thought you big, bad undercover guys knew better than that."

He squeezed her hand right back. "Lady, you have no problem hitting below the belt, do you? No, I've got the same concern. I'm just amazed to hear you defend the guy, that's all."

"Trust me, I'm not defending him. It's just a reality check. Dillon is the senior lieutenant in the NSF—he's the division officer. And he's a type A, micro-manager to boot. *Nothing* comes out of that compartment that doesn't go through him first."

Damn. "That leads us back to square one then, doesn't it? Which guy am I after?"

She smiled that tiny, naughty smile of hers. The one he'd seen her use when she'd gotten Dillon good—when she thought no one was watching.

He liked it.

She slipped her hand from his and leaned back against the bulkhead. "Well, there's only one way to find out if the drugs are there for sure. We'll just have to get you behind the second door."

Yup, he liked it a lot.

Chapter 9

"I was wondering if you were going to show up."

Jade waited for Karin to close the medical chart on her desk before she entered her office. "Don't you start in on me, too."

Her day must have shown on her face, because Karin tsked softly and swatted the chair next to her desk. "Park it and tell Dr. Scott all about it."

Jade sighed as she slid into the chair, wishing she could do just that. How *did* you go about telling your best friend and fellow officer you'd spent the afternoon hammering out a covert plan to break the ship's resident pretty boy—who was not who he appeared to be—into the nuclear spaces so you could figure out which one of your fellow officers was really spending his days running heroin on and off the ship?

You just didn't.

She sighed again.

"Bad day, huh?"

"You could say that."

"Cheer up, it can only get better."

Wanna bet?

Karin leaned close and studied her stitches for a few moments, whistling as she settled back. "Damn, I'm *good*."

"Modest, too."

She stuck out her tongue. "Just for that, I'm not going to fork over your gift."

Gift? Jade perked up. That's right. It *was* her birthday. How could she have forgotten? Maybe today wasn't going to be a bust after all. She stuck out her hand and smiled. "Too late, you owe me. I just spent the last twenty minutes listening to Dillon whine about how he had to pull my watch last night because *you* wouldn't let me on the bridge."

Her hopes rose as Karin pulled a package that looked a lot like a CD box out of her center drawer and slid it across the desk. "Will it help if I tell you part two of the gift is dinner when we get back in port?"

"Yup." She straightened, smiling at the neon pink bow. "If that's what I think it is, I'm going to have to kiss you."

Karin laughed. "I think you'd better hang on to your kisses. Someone else might want to claim them later."

Jade didn't have the heart to tell her how far off course she was. Even if she wasn't, there was no way she was falling for that man's tricks again. At least Jeff had the decency to be aboveboard about everything.

She still couldn't believe she'd been so stupid.

Step one, get on board. Step two, get close to Jade. Step three— *"Don't hold your breath."*

She hadn't realized she'd said the words aloud until Karin shook her head. "I don't know, Reese seemed awfully eager to usurp my bedside duties last night."

True. But it was all just part of the master plan, wasn't it? And it still smarted. "What's your point?"

"My, my, we're awfully testy today. What's wrong? Didn't get enough sleep last night?"

As a matter of fact, no.

"What happened?"

"Nothing." Nothing she could talk about, anyway.

Jade started as Karin reached over and pressed her fingers into her wrist and glanced at her watch, obviously taking her pulse. "What are you doing?"

She grinned. "Just verifying your story. Last time you said nothing happened, he laid a twenty on you."

Jade flushed and tugged her wrist away. She snatched up the present, making a point of staring at it while she untied the bow and peeled off the paper.

Karin laughed. "Chicken."

She wadded up the wrapping paper and pelted it at her. "Vulture."

She laughed harder. "At least I'm moving up on the evolutionary scale. Last night, I was a vampire."

"Yeah, well, you were a bit too ghoulish stitching me up. So, am I cleared to stand the bridge watch tonight?"

"I don't know. I think you could use another full night's sleep."

Jade gripped the jazz CD and kept her voice light. "Afraid it's not gonna happen. I've got a drill I need to run later tonight."

"Postpone it."

She shrugged lightly. "Can't. Tonight's the last night I can run it before we head back into port." Another lie.

"So, do it during the day tomorrow."

"Karin, *please?*"

Her blue eyes narrowed. "All right, what's going on?"

Trust me, you don't want to know. She strove for innocence. "What makes you think anything's going on?"

"Gee, dunno. Maybe it's the fact that you just turned down an offer for sleep when you're so tired you can barely sit up straight—or maybe it's that you're holding the very CD in your hands you've been waiting for months to be released and you haven't even said thanks."

She flushed. "Thanks."

"You're welcome. Now, do I get the rest?"

Jade stared her down, not trusting herself to open her mouth. Karin was right, she was bushed—and her nerves were shot to boot. Not to mention the throbbing ache that had taken up residence beneath the stitches again following Reese's confession. She kept her mouth shut. There was no telling what might come out.

"Guess not." Karin drummed her fingers on the desk. "Can you honestly tell me you're up to driving the ship tonight?"

"If I take a nap." At least *that* was the truth.

Karin sighed. "Okay. If you take a nap now, I'll let the captain give you the keys to the ship and you can stay out late."

"Thanks!" She shot up out of the chair and headed for the door before her friend could change her mind, catching Karin's response just before it closed behind her.

"Now *that* was the reaction I wanted from the CD."

"Hey, Mack, wait up!"

Reese glanced down the passageway outside the wardroom. He'd know that shock of strawberry blond anywhere. He stopped and waited for Lieutenant Coffey to catch up.

"Where're you going?"

Reese jerked his head toward the ladder. "To catch a little shut-eye. Why?"

Coffey grinned and palmed him something. "Great. You'll need this. Tonight's the night."

Damn! In light of everything that had happened last night—and the fact that he hadn't gotten more than an hour's sleep—he'd forgotten all about the mutilated dummy. Which meant he'd also forgotten the date.

Jade's birthday.

He glanced down at the contents of his palm and stiffened. A key? He forced himself to relax as he slipped it into his coverall pocket. "Where'd you come by this?"

Greg grinned. "Dillon. But don't tell Jade, she'll blow a gasket."

The heck with her, *he* was going to blow one. Dillon had a *key* to Jade's stateroom? And perhaps his as well? Motive, means *and* opportunity? He wasn't sure he'd have the patience to wait until tonight to get into the NSF—he wanted in *now*.

Reese headed down the passageway, hoping to draw Coffey along for a little one-on-one interrogation disguised as conversation. He kept his voice light, "So, Jade tells me you two go way back."

Greg laughed and crossed his index fingers as if warding off evil spirits. "Oh, no, Jade already ripped me a new one for *mentioning* Jeff. You want to know the details, ask her."

That wasn't the information he was after. But as long as they were on the topic, he might as well delve into it.

Purely for professional reasons, of course.

Jade *had* agreed to be his link to the NSF. It stood to reason he should learn all he could about her. Any allusion to a budding relationship between them could only solidify his cover. He waited until they'd climbed the ladder and headed down the narrow corridor to Coffey's stateroom. "I understand. But can you at least tell me how serious they were?"

Coffey stopped at his door and shook his head. "Sorry, buddy, not even that." He held up a hand. "Don't get me wrong. I like you—but Jade? She's more than my frat sister, she was my *pledge* sister. We joined the Praetorian Guard together. And we saved each other's hide more than a few times during the years that followed. Understand?"

Yeah, he understood. He was jealous as hell, but he understood. "I got it."

Coffey unlocked his door and then turned back. "Good. There's just one more thing. Jade likes you. You know it and I know it. But what you may not know is that if you hurt her, I'm gonna hunt you down and feed you to the fishes." He smiled. "In pieces."

Reese grinned back. "What makes you so sure *she's* not going to hurt *me?*"

Coffey laughed at that. "True enough. I could tell you stories that would—"

The shrill whistle proceeding every underway announcement piped over the 1MC. "Lieutenant Coffey, please dial seven, zero, zero, zero" followed it.

Coffey groaned. "The Captain. There goes *my* nap." He snapped his door shut and relocked it. "See ya later."

Reese returned the wave and headed down to his own room. He didn't need access to Coffey's cabin tonight. He'd already taken it upon himself to pick the lock twice already. Unfortunately, he hadn't turned up anything.

In Dillon's, either.

Jade stared up at Reese, her knuckles still in mid-knock as he opened his door and ushered her inside.

"You're late."

"Sorry, Mom, I got held up." She knew something was wrong when he frowned. Usually *he* was flip. "What is it?"

He pulled a key from his pocket and held it up for her inspection. "It's a gift from Coffey."

She tugged her new ball cap off and laid it on his desk, rubbing the skin above her stitches as she glanced back at the distinctive metal scroll on the head of the key. "I don't get it, why would Greg give you the key to his stateroom?"

"It doesn't open his door, it opens yours."

An uneasy shiver swept through her. "Karin doesn't even have my key."

He slapped it on the desk beside the red cap. "Well, Dillon did. Apparently, Coffey got it off him."

Dillon had her key? The chill reached her chest and rattled against it. "I'm going to kill that SOB."

"Stand in line. First, tonight—is it a go?"

She nodded, a yawn smacking into her as she switched gears. She stifled the tail end of it and rubbed the back of her neck. Filling Reese in could take a while. She'd better sit down before she fell down.

She turned to his rack—and burst out laughing. The NSF dummy corpse was laid out on the green blanket, propped up against the pillow, its errant eye flopping down its cheek. Someone had pulled the blackened, shredded hands together and secured them around a bunch of silk daffodils.

Daffodils?

She turned back to Reese, still chuckling.

The side of his mouth quirked at her sick humor. "Glad you like it. I was supposed to stash it in your rack tonight. Coffey's idea of a present."

She glanced back at the dummy. That explained the daffodils—she had a feeling her personnel record wasn't that detailed.

Reese cupped her chin and drew her attention back to him. "By the way, happy birthday. Twenty-six, right?"

She nodded, willing herself to ignore the heat in his palm and in his eyes. "Thanks."

"I'd like to take you out to celebrate when we pull in."

She tugged her chin from his grasp and smiled brightly. "Sure. Karin just said the same thing. We can all go."

He reclaimed her chin, this time stroking a thumb across her bottom lip as he leaned down. "I offered to take *you*—not Karin. *Just you.*"

The words hovered between them, suspended by the unmistakable meaning burning in his gaze. She wanted to move, but she couldn't. She wanted to glance away, but she didn't. She wanted him to kiss her, but she shouldn't. Surely Reese knew he didn't have to pretend anymore? That she'd help him without the lies and the subterfuge?

Obviously not. Or maybe he didn't believe it. In either case, his gaze didn't waver so she finally answered. "Maybe."

She clenched her fingers as he lowered his head the rest of the way and softly pressed his lips to hers. But before she had a chance to think, to argue, or even to close her eyes—he pulled back, his gaze deepening to cobalt as he withdrew. She wanted desperately to believe desire caused it.

And then she knew it had as he slid his thumb back over her bottom lip, his finger not quite steady this time. Neither was his voice as he whispered, *"Happy birthday."*

Oh, God, she could *not* handle this. She couldn't handle the feelings slamming against the dam she'd painstakingly built around her heart. Once again, Reese had her thinking of things that could never be—making her want them, dream about them. And it wasn't fair. It wouldn't work.

It couldn't. She blinked, trying to clear her head. Damn, where was her father's advice when she *really* needed it?

Sorry, Missy. You're on your own. Your mother would kill me if I interfered now.

She hadn't realized her hand had slipped up to her neck until her fingers dipped beneath her khaki uniform. She snagged the chain beneath her T-shirt and held on for dear life. She did not want this. She *couldn't.* She'd cut those desires out of her heart and mind a long time ago.

She nearly jumped out of her boots when Reese closed his hand over hers and pulled the necklace out the rest of the way. The jade pendant dangled between them, her swirling emotions still tangled and meshed with the chain, along with her fingers.

Reese stared into Jade's smoky gaze as he cupped the heart with his free hand. He smoothed his fingers over it, wishing he could erase the fear and uncertainty from her eyes. He was certain that's what he saw—fear.

And it baffled him.

It also had him curious as hell. What could possibly put that look in this woman's eyes? The same woman who faced fires and four-thousand-pound screaming forklifts with cool control and iron confidence? "There's a story behind this, isn't there?"

There was.

Maybe it was the cornered look that joined the fear. Or maybe it was the knowledge that, as obviously cherished as the necklace was, it was not meant for public display. He gently disengaged the chain from her fingers and looped it around his own, deliberately staking his claim. She was trapped, inches from him—whether she wanted to be there or not. "Why do you keep it hidden?"

She blinked, and then recovered. "I'm in uniform."

The excuse was a little too pat. And he wasn't falling for it. She *wasn't* his father. He knew that now. "So why hide it when you're not?"

Her eyes narrowed slightly.

Careful.

"How would you know that? You've only seen me in my uniform." She flushed and corrected herself before he could. "And my robe."

Her hoarse admission stoked the sizzling memory, held at bay but never dormant. Desire flared with it. He choked back a groan as both threatened to incinerate him on the spot.

No.

Now was *not* the time for that. He took a deep breath and, somehow, managed to douse the inferno within him. "Lucky guess." He tugged the chain gently. "Continue."

He didn't think she would, but then she shrugged, almost defiantly. "It's no secret. The necklace was my mother's. I guess you could call it my namesake. It was a gift from my father when they were dating."

No, it was more than that. He could tell by the way she jerked it from his hand and shoved it back inside her uniform. By the way she picked up her ball cap and wrapped her fingers around the scarlet fabric—tightly—as she edged away. The way she couldn't quite meet his eyes.

And that bothered him most of all.

He wasn't proud of it, but it made him press. "If it's just a necklace, why hide it?"

She slumped down onto his rack, shoving the dummy aside to make room. "You wouldn't understand."

"Ah, the *Navy* again." Damn, that came out stronger than he'd intended. He slapped the irritation back. Now wasn't the time for *that,* either.

"No." She stared at him for a few moments, obviously wrestling with the denial in her eyes and on her lips. And then she sighed. "Maybe." She massaged the spot between her brows. "All right, it was more than a gift." Reaching over, she plucked the yellow flowers from the dummy's hands and leaned back against the bulkhead. "It's a long story."

He dragged his desk chair to the bed backward and sat down, resting his arms and chin on the back. "I've got time."

He wasn't fooled by that tiny smile—she was still tugging at the flowers. "My mother was nineteen and still living at home when my parents met. To hear Dad tell it, he strolled into my grandparent's restaurant one night with a couple of guys off the ship and it was love at first sight. But my grandfather didn't trust sailors."

He smiled back at her. "So how'd he convince your grandfather he was serious?"

"He didn't." She laughed at his surprise.

The pure, husky sound nipped a hole through his stomach and began gnawing his resolve. He multiplied out his twelves and took another deep breath. He was safe. As long as she kept her fingers on those damn flowers and out of her hair.

"Well, not at first, anyway. Dad returned the next night without his buddies and took a table at the entrance so he could watch my mother work. She was the hostess. But that didn't work, either."

He lifted a brow.

She smiled. "Granddaddy was stubborn." Another smile. "But so was Dad. He just came back again the following weekend. And then again and again. For six months he dined at that table, every Saturday night, except when he had duty—and then he came on Friday. But that *still* didn't work."

"You're kidding." He hoped her father wasn't that tough. Damn, where did *that* come from?

"But then one Saturday he came in and told my mom in front of her parents that his ship was deploying. He asked them to save his table—he'd be back. Six months later, he was." She tugged the necklace out over her uniform and held up the jade heart. "And he brought this. He gave it to Mom in front of Granddaddy and asked her out again."

"And this time he said yes."

She chuckled. "He had to. My mother and grandmother were ready to kill him. Anyway, they married six months later."

Reese smiled even as the envy seized him. What he wouldn't give for a story like that in his background. To know with certainty that his father loved his mother more than some lousy chunk of iron and steel, than the damn gold braid on his uniform. Didn't she realize how lucky she was? She couldn't possibly—or she wouldn't keep the necklace hidden.

Or maybe there was more here than she was letting on? She'd told him it was a commissioning present. Was Mom sending her very serious daughter a message? Was it connected to Jeff?

He reached out and cradled the heart, still warm from her skin. "That's a wonderful story. But it still doesn't explain why you hide it."

Her gaze shuttered and she tugged the pendant back, concealing it beneath her uniform. He didn't need an answer. Her actions told him everything he needed to know. That

necklace was more to her than just a gift from her mother—
and it was more than a symbol of her parents' relationship.

It represented love.

The all-consuming kind. The kind that made you eager
to leave the ship at the end of the day. Maybe even the kind
that made you not want to step aboard in the first place. He
rested his chin atop his arms. That's what it represented, all
right. Only this time, he didn't feel it in his gut, he knew it
in his heart.

The only problem was, Jade wasn't comfortable with
what *that* heart represented. But the fact that she wore it
gave him hope. And that hope terrified him. Because it also
made him realize that somehow, somewhere along the way,
he'd gone from needing to use Jade to simply *needing* her.

*"Fire, fire, fire. Fire in compartment 4-126-0-R, the
NSF."*

Jade shook off the effects of her nap, pulled on her boots
and headed out of her cabin before the Damage Control
Central Watch could repeat the announcement over the
ship's 1MC system. She passed Reese's stateroom and
glanced at her watch as she headed down to Central.

Zero three hundred hours.

By now Chief Haas already had Reese suited up in a
Kevlar firefighter's ensemble, complete with a helmet, face
shield and a breathing device. With a little help from the
ship's glycerin smoke generators, he'd be able to walk up
to his own mother and she'd fail to recognize him.

Which was exactly the way they wanted it.

Jade slid down the midships ladder and turned to undog
the door to Central. Petty Officer Smith cupped the tele-
phone receiver to his chest as she entered and announced,
"DCA's in Central!"

She nodded a greeting to the three phone talkers already
plugging headsets into the *Baddager*'s sound-powered

phone system as she flipped the ship's laminated schematic back to reveal the forth deck.

"Well, well. If it isn't Wonder Woman in the flesh at 3:00 a.m. Where's your boy toy, DCA? Still curled up, snoring in your rack?"

Jade stiffened. She should have *begged* Karin for a couple of pain pills—because a massive headache just walked in.

She rounded on Dillon, still rumpled from sleep and mindless of his audience as he unzipped his pants and tucked the tail to his khaki shirt inside.

"You're late."

"And Mack must not be any good, because you're on time."

Jade bit the inside of her cheek as Petty Officer Smith pantomimed snapping Dillon's neck behind his back. Dillon wouldn't have caught on, either, if one of the phone talkers hadn't let out a giggle. Smith jerked his arms into a yawning stretch and then winked at her over Dillon's shoulder as he turned back.

"So where *is* Mr. Hollywood?"

You'd spit uranium if I told you.

She took the first set of messages from her incoming phone talker and shrugged as she flipped through them. "Like you said, probably still snoring."

Turning her back on Dillon, she drew a black grease line out from the NSF on the charts, then scratched out a couple of symbols above it to track the progress of the drill. Electrical power was secured, fire and smoke boundaries set.

And any moment now, Chief Haas would break the first cipher lock and lead Reese through the second.

Even though she trusted Haas with her life, it'd taken a bit of convincing to get Reese to confide in him. But in the end, he had to—mainly because the plan wouldn't work without her chief. TPI stood for *Two* Person Integrity, not one. With her in Central, they were one body short.

Dillon skirted the phone talkers and leaned his forearm

over the charts, obstructing her view. "You know, I could have sworn Mack would want to be here for this one."

Jade forced her hand to remain steady as she scratched out an order on the message blank and handed it to the outgoing phone talker. "Why is that?"

"Mack didn't tell you?" He laughed, grinning his cheesy grin. "It seems Mr. Hollywood has a thing for the cloak-and-dagger side of the Fleet."

Somehow, she managed to keep writing.

"Then again, maybe he's just bored." He paused for effect, as if waiting for her to look up.

Like an idiot, she did.

"But then, I guess you already know that. It's not like it's the first time you've had a problem keeping someone interested, now, is it?"

Jade shoved Dillon's arm out of the way, grinding her teeth as she updated the chart. One of these days she was going to hunt Jeff's big mouth down and seal it—permanently.

By the time she'd scratched out the symbols, she'd recovered enough to smile at Dillon. "I know it's standard procedure for you to show up when the NSF is on fire, but do you have to talk? You're using enough air as it is."

Smith mutated his guffaw into a hacking cough, and the phone talkers suddenly bowed their heads to study their notes.

"Very funny—"

"DCA, the hose team has accessed the NSF and has the fire under control."

Jade nodded to the phone talker and added another symbol to the chart, wishing Dillon would get tired of harassing her and head to the Chief Engineer's office to camp out for the remainder of the drill like he usually did.

"You know what else I wonder?"

No such luck. She rubbed her fingers above her stitches.

"Believe it or not, Mike, I *never* lose sleep over what goes on in your head."

He wasn't fazed. "I wonder how a guy who's supposed to have all the right connections ends up on a woman's ship?"

It was just too damn late for this.

She made a point to step into Dillon's personal space as she leveled him with a cool stare. "Gee, I don't know. You tell me. Just how *does* a smart officer with all his stuff together end up on a noncombatant and not on—oh, say— a nuclear-powered cruiser?"

She could tell by his scowl, he hadn't thought that one through, or at least hadn't arrived at an answer that satisfied himself. That was his problem. She glanced at her waist. Hers was her silent walkie-talkie.

What the heck was taking so long? Why hadn't Haas given the all clear? Did the delay mean Reese had found something?

She jerked her attention back to Dillon as he yawned. If she could just get him into the Engineer's office, she might be able to call down for an update.

"Well, DCA, you may get your jollies off sleep deprivation, but I don't. I'm outta here."

That was easy enough. But she couldn't afford to look too eager. She let her gaze narrow. "You're supposed to stay until the fire is overhauled. It's not even out."

"So what? I've got to stop by my office, anyway. If your guys are any good, by the time I leave the NSF, it will be." He had the audacity to grin as he dropped the bombshell at her feet. Then he shoved the door to Central open and stepped over the lip.

She waited for the door to close and counted to ten before ripping her walkie-talkie off her belt.

Slow down and think!

"You there, Chief?"

Several agonizing seconds later, his gravelly voice crackled back. "Right here, DCA. What can I do you for?"

She turned back to the charts, pretending to study them intently. "Just wondering what the holdup was. You guys are taking so long Lieutenant Dillon decided to abandon ship."

She knew Haas's chuckle well enough to know that one was forced. "Can't have that, can we? Guess we'd better wrap—"

A loud crash, followed by an equally loud curse, drowned out the rest of his sentence.

Reese's curse.

"Gotta go, DCA." And then there was nothing.

Not even static.

Chapter 10

"Son of a—" Reese bit off the rest and ignored the metal boxes and cylinders crashing down around his feet. So much for Dillon and Coffey securing the storage cabinets in the NSF for sea.

"You okay?"

Reese nodded as Haas herded several canisters together on the deck and slapped them back up on the shelf, then braced himself against the next wave hitting the ship as he worked the lock in his hands. One more twist and he'd have it—there. He popped the lock and peered inside the metal box.

Once again, *nothing*.

He'd been at this for the better part of an hour now and he still hadn't found a shred of evidence to connect either guy to drugs. By the time he'd finished tossing the second room, he was beyond regretting that he'd started in there. He was royally pissed. Unfortunately, he didn't have time to vent. So he'd just sucked it up and moved back to the office and started on the cabinets in there.

Reese closed the box and reached for another, picking that padlock as well. Dillon was on the level about one thing, that second room was the most incredibly boring classified spot he'd ever searched. And he'd had the opportunity to search more than a few over the years. As far as he was concerned, Jade's job was a whole lot more exciting.

Again, not a damn thing.

He reset the lock and pulled up yet another box as Haas shoved several more canisters up onto the shelf.

"That was the DCA, we've got to wrap it up. Lieutenant Dillon's on his way."

Reese nodded as his pick struck home. One quick twist and the lock was off. He jerked the lid up and stared inside. *Damn.* But something seemed different—almost off—about this one. Maybe it was his gut or maybe just his nerves. But to be sure, he reached inside and tapped the bottom.

Yes! He quickly trailed his fingers along the inside, locating the small metal tab and lifting up the false bottom. And there it was.

Heroin.

Still uncut, too, from the splotches of dark brown mixed within the lighter areas. Jeez, there had to be four units in here alone.

"Son, we've got to go. *Now.*"

He held up a hand. "Another minute. I need—"

Too late. A loud, grating voice cut through the bulkhead. "I don't *believe* it. You idiots did it again!"

Dillon.

Reese shoved the false bottom back in place and snapped the lock on before sliding the box to the rear of the shelf.

"If I find one *drop* of water on this deck when I come out, there'll be hell to pay!"

Haas was a step ahead of Reese as he spun around, motioning him beneath Coffey's desk and waiting until he was wedged into the hole before he crammed a swivel chair into his face. Reese grabbed it and held it in place with his left hand as he tried to reach his boot with his right.

He froze as the cipher lock buzzed, admitting a scuffed set of black boots.

"Ah, damn, Chief. Not in here, too. Can't you guys *ever* run a drill without trashing a space?"

Reese could practically feel Haas's shrug. "Accidents happen, Lieutenant."

"Accident, my ass. The DCA put you up to this, didn't she?"

Haas ignored him as his hand came down to retrieve several more canisters.

"Whose gear is that on my desk?"

Crap! Reese closed his eyes, resisting the urge to bang his head on the legs of the chair. Dillon had to be referring to the fireman's helmet and gloves he'd left on the desk.

His gear.

There was no way Haas could pass it off as his own. Because Haas wasn't wearing the bulky Kevlar coveralls that went with it—*he* was.

Reese twisted his head down a bit to the right, down again, and then to the left. When he finished, his face was lower than his knees, with his left cheek and shoulder welded to the deck. The pretzel position was uncomfortable as hell, but at least he wasn't blind anymore. By staring just so, he could see out through the slit of daylight under the desk.

Haas grabbed the helmet off the other desk, stared at it, then slammed it back down in disgust. "Vega's. That boy would leave his pants down around his ankles if someone wasn't there to pull them up in the morning. Gonna have to have a talk with him again. Soon."

"Well, get rid of it—and the rest of that crap out in the passageway, too."

The deck pitched again—a bit too far forward this time—as another wave hit the ship.

Nice and slow, buddy. Breathe nice and slow. Now was not the time to turn green.

Damn! Reese clenched his fingers as one of the remaining canisters took off with the swell, rolling straight toward his hiding place under the desk. He stared the cylinder down, willing it to stop.

But it didn't.

It *kept* coming.

Five feet. Four. Three, two, one—

A split second before it slid under, Haas snagged it, lifting it away.

To *hell* with this. Reese let out a slow, painful breath. He hadn't felt this naked in years. Gritting his teeth, he practically dislocated his wrist as he shoved it up under the leg of the firefighter's ensemble and down into his boot, sweet success flooding him as his palm slipped around the familiar butt of his Glock.

Now he was dressed.

He eased the pistol from his boot as Haas ambled back across the space and shoved the canister into the cabinet.

Good thinking. Take your time. Maybe Dillon would get tired of waiting and leave.

"Ah, the hell with it, Chief. *I'll* clean up the mess. I'd like to see my rack before the Second Coming."

Then again, maybe not.

Haas ignored him and his hand came back down to the deck for another canister. "Don't let me stop you, Lieutenant. Go ahead, I'll have this cleaned up in a minute."

Evidently Dillon didn't have a minute. "I said *out*. That's an order."

Reese ignored the painful crick developing in his neck as Dillon tossed the helmet and gloves to Haas and then escorted him to the door. The cipher lock buzzed and he bit back a curse as Dillon nudged the guy out, none too gently.

He ran through his options again as the lock reengaged. Unfortunately, they were few and far between. In fact, the list was so damn short—it began and ended in the same spot.

He was trapped.

And hot. Between the firefighter's ensemble and the desk, he was beginning to feel like a pig in a blanket. One that was still in the oven. Sweat trickled down his shoulders and pooled where his arm crushed the deck.

Ah, damn!

He ground his teeth as yet another canister succumbed to the rolling ship and beat a path to his hiding spot. If he didn't know any better, he'd swear the blasted things were in cahoots, determined to flush him out.

Here we go again.

Five, four, three, two, one—

He sent up another round of thanks as Dillon grabbed the cylinder and slammed it onto the desk above him. Then promptly retracted it as he heard it wobble, staring in horror as it careered back down and smacked onto the deck right next to him. The damn thing executed a flawless, mesmerizing performance of spin the bottle, twirling smoothly around, coming to rest a fraction of an inch from his head— fingering him straight between the eyes.

Reese drew a deep breath, tightening his grip on the Glock as he took careful aim at the hand that made the mistake of following the canister beneath the desk.

Jade didn't bother cleaning the ship's schematics before she slammed them shut and flicked the latch. "That's a wrap, Central. Restow your gear and hit your racks."

Because I'm outta here.

"You okay, ma'am?"

No, she was *not*. She waved off Petty Officer Smith's concern as she passed. "Just tired. See you in a few hours." With that, she headed out of Central and made a beeline for the repair locker.

What the hell was going on?

It had been fifteen minutes since she'd lost communications with Chief Haas, but it felt more like fifty. He'd better have a damn good excuse for shaving a year off her life when she found him—or she'd leave him counting his seconds.

She rounded the corner and ran smack into her senior Petty Officer. "Vega, where's Chief Haas?"

His dark eyes widened. "I thought he was with you, ma'am. He never showed back up at the scene. I couldn't hail him on the walkie-talkie, so I debriefed the guys on station and had them restow the gear."

Haas was missing?

What about Reese? She glanced over at the locker; most of the gear was already back in place. Where *was* he?

He was *really* late. Unfortunately, she couldn't ask Vega about him because her Petty Officer wasn't supposed to know Reese was there. According to the plan, he should have skated into Central at the last minute, looking ruffled and apologetic—as if he'd overslept and missed the drill. But of course, he hadn't.

Cool, Missy, stay cool. They're around somewhere.

She forced a smile. "I must have just missed him. If you see him, tell him I need to talk to him, okay?"

"Will do."

She headed for the locker, dodging a stack of helmets and a rack of firefighters' ensembles as she closed the door and grabbed the phone. Four calls later, full-blown panic had set in. They weren't in the chief's lounge, Haas's office, his stateroom, *or* Reese's.

So where the hell were they?

Well, she couldn't sit around here and wait, that was for sure. She was already going nuts. But where? Of course, *her* stateroom. With the drill over, it was probably the first place they'd check. In fact, they were probably already on their way there.

Her panic down to dull roar, she left the repair locker and

repeated the rationale all the way through the ship. By the time she reached officer's country above the main deck, she was feeling her way along the passageway. She'd moved too quickly to acclimate her eyes from the bright repair locker on deck three to the dimly lit decks above. As she rounded the last corner, her hope faded and panic flared again.

Empty.

She stopped in front of Reese's stateroom, praying silently as she checked for the telltale strip of light beneath the door.

Nothing.

For some reason she couldn't explain, she decided to wait for Reese in his stateroom. Okay, so she *could* explain it, she just didn't want to. Not to herself *or* Reese. She didn't know what she'd tell him when he found her, but it sure as heck wouldn't be the truth. There was no *way* she was admitting she felt more comfortable in his stateroom than her own.

She jiggled the handle, but it was locked—just as she'd expected. Unhooking her keys from her waist, she located the DCA master key and inserted it.

Please, God, don't let Reese see this as a violation.

Because she really needed it. She nudged the door open and slipped inside.

What the—

Jade stiffened as a hand clamped down over her mouth, yanking her back so hard she almost lost her balance. She managed to right herself long enough to twist around and jab her knee up.

Unfortunately, her attacker anticipated her. He shoved her knee down between his legs and locked his thighs around hers. She stared blindly into the dark, cursing her still-nonexistent night vision as she tried desperately to catch a glimpse of the guy as she clawed at his face.

But she couldn't—it was just too damn dark.

She didn't know who the hell this was, but it didn't matter. Who*ever* he was, he was not getting the best of her. She had a few dirty tricks up her sleeve as well. And he was about to take notes.

She tightened her grip on her keys, splaying them wide on the ring as she crammed them into her attacker's waist. She dug them in deeper, remembering to twist them sharply for added effect. And it *did* have an effect.

A hoarse grunt filled the dark cabin, followed by a hiss as she ripped the keys down his abdomen. But she wasn't finished yet. She was going for the groin. His hand left her mouth, turning to iron as he realized her intent, clamping down on her wrist a split second before she gelded him. But before she could let out a scream that would alert the ship from bow to stern, a harsh whisper tore into her.

"*Good God*, woman, it's *me.*"

Jade froze—her hand still millimeters from the source of his future children. *"Reese?"*

"In the flesh. Now, would you please *move those keys?*"

She jerked her hand open and they clattered to the deck.

A soft whoosh filled the air as his pent-up breath blew out over her cheeks. "Thank you." His grip loosened.

Her night vision *finally* adjusted, sharpening enough for her to make out the shadowy outline of a face and body.

Reese.

Maybe that's what did it. Or maybe it was the overwhelming wave of relief crashing into her as she realized he was safe and not trussed up somewhere in the bowels of the ship—or worse, gutted and tossed overboard. But even if it wasn't, she didn't care.

All she cared about was him.

She launched herself at him, wrapping her arms around his neck, pressing herself into his solid chest as she rained kiss after thankful kiss along his whiskered jaw.

He was safe.

But she was not.

She realized that as he growled and lashed his arms around her as well. But she didn't care. All she cared about was that *finally* she was in the one place she'd wanted to be—*fantasized* about being—each and every day of the past two weeks.

In Reese's arms.

And for once, she wasn't going to think about the consequences. She wasn't going to think about who she was and how she was supposed to act. She wasn't going to think about where she wanted to go.

No, for once, she was just going to *feel.*

And she wanted to make *him* feel.

Reese groaned as Jade blistered a wet, needy path up his jaw. His gut smelted to a pool of hunger by the time she reached his earlobe. He shuddered as she tugged it into her mouth, nipping and sucking at it frantically, mimicking a baser act with such searing precision he was afraid he'd lose it right then and there.

Enough!

He could take no more.

He grabbed her jaw and dragged her mouth beneath his— knowing full well the stubble on his face was tearing at her lips. But he didn't stop. He couldn't.

Hell, he couldn't stop touching her any more than he could slow his pummeling heart. He battered past her lips, razing them in his greed. He drove his tongue inside— spurred on as she tightened her arms around his neck, nearly strangling him as she welcomed him home.

And oh, God, how she felt like home.

That alone should scare the hell out of him. And tomorrow it probably would. But tonight, he wasn't going to think about it. No, the only thing he was going to think about now was right here and right now.

Tomorrow would take care of itself.

He scraped his hands down her back, cupping her rear

and sealing her close—so close even her uniform couldn't disguise the goddess beneath. And then he devoured her.

Jade shuddered as Reese swept his way deep into her mouth. She needed no words to know how he'd spent his night.

She knew.

It was all there.

Right there, as she tasted bitter agonizing fear, the sweet rush of adrenaline, and finally, the spice of undiluted victory. And then she was filled with the savage taste of hunger.

For her.

The answering ache searing through her should have had her running for cover. But it didn't. Instead, she was straining up into him, clutching him, feeding on him—losing herself in his white-hot heat as she pleaded for more.

But even as he gave it, it wasn't enough. She wanted even *more*. She shoved her hands beneath his sweatshirt and kneaded a path up his back—now damp with sweat—digging her fingers into the slabs of sinew stretched across his shoulders.

It still wasn't enough.

She shoved the sweatshirt higher, and before she realized it, it was gone, hurled across the space to God-knew-where. And then all that existed were the naked, slick ridges, the hard nipples, his corded, straining arms. She touched them all—almost all at once. Her hands and fingers were everywhere—smoothing, scraping, kneading.

But it *still* wasn't enough.

So she followed with her mouth. Tasting the places her fingers had been, and a host of new ones as well. She followed the salty crater down the center of his chest, licking and consuming a torturous path to his stomach—stopping to swirl her tongue deep into his navel. She was determined to taste every inch of him along the way down—but it was taking too long.

And not long enough.

She was nearly overcome with the sheer *want*.

Of Reese.

And then, finally, she was *there*. Even in the pitch-black of the room, she knew exactly where she was. She didn't need to see the shadowy sweats hanging low on his hips. Didn't need to see the solid evidence of his need pulsing mere inches from her lips. She could hear it, smell it.

But she couldn't taste it.

Yet.

She reached out and hooked her finger into the drawstring loop. But before she could yank them down, steel slapped around her wrist for the second time that night. This time it tugged her up, trapping both her hands behind her with just one band of his.

Firmly.

And then he leaned down, inches from her face as his breath battered into hers.

"Not just yet."

She shuddered as the ragged words grated against her nerves, scouring them into a bundle of raw need. No matter what he wanted, she would not deny him.

She could not.

Reese clenched his teeth and slugged back his surging hunger with an iron fist. *God,* how he wanted to strip that uniform from Jade. Wanted to strip the *lieutenant* right off her. Until all that was left was the woman beneath.

And he would.

Because Dillon was wrong—Jade *was* a woman.

All woman.

Yeah, he was going to strip her, all right. But not yet. Not until he completed the one task that had carved itself into his gut with such brutal finesse that it sliced at him daily, nightly, hourly. And every second in between.

Her hair.

He dug his fingers into her braid, finding the pins and

ripping them out, searching for the rubber band as he followed the rope down her back. He found it. And then her hair—that thick, glorious silk—was unraveling.

He shoved his fingers into it, not stopping until every last strand was separate and flowing. Only *then* did he pause—for a moment—sucking in his breath as he savored the searing relief. Her hair was free.

And it was *his*.

He yanked the mass over her shoulder and buried his face into it—inhaling the sweetest fragrance he'd ever known. He had absolutely no idea what it was, but he knew without a doubt he'd be smelling it until the day he died.

And beyond.

Suddenly his hunger ripped free, slamming back into him with such force he shuddered from the blow. He was mindless with want, desperate with need, and *still* the craving tore at him, possessing him until he knew he'd never find relief until he possessed *her*.

He jerked his hand from her wrists and grabbed the upper edges of her uniform, ripping them down and apart in one clean rent. Buttons flew off, hurling across the darkness, plinking into the metal wall unit and bulkheads surrounding them. He shoved the shirt halfway down her arms and then stopped, not even taking the time to complete the job.

Instead, he swept his gaze back to the snowy T-shirt he couldn't really see. The one that taunted him daily from the vee formed by her uniform. The one that was now in the way.

And then it wasn't.

How in the hell he'd thought that puny mantra would be enough to keep him from Jade, he'd never know. All he knew was he didn't deserve this. He didn't deserve to feel this good. He didn't deserve *her*. He also knew there was no use in torturing himself with forever.

Forever was impossible.

Especially with Jade.

But as long as she was offering him tonight—he was taking it. For as long as it lasted. He just wished to God the lights were on as he found the front clasp to her bra and wrenched it open. The sight before him had to be magnificent. But it would have to wait for another moment, another time. For now all he could do was touch, smell and taste.

And then he did.

Jade moaned as Reese covered her with his hands, kneading her breasts with such force she thought she'd die. He scraped the tips with his palms, rolled them beneath his greedy fingers, pinching and pulling and tugging at them until they were nothing but hard, aching nubs. And then— when his hands abandoned her—she *did* die.

Until he knelt and returned with his mouth.

She shuddered as he crushed his face to her breasts, groaning as he began to lick and suck. He explored every inch of flesh he could find. Seeking, demanding, taking. And then he finally settled on her nipples, flicking his tongue at them relentlessly, stabbing them over and over until they were standing at perfect, painful attention.

Perspiration slicked her skin and passion drenched her core as she dug her fingers into his hair and pulled him up.

It was time.

This time, she didn't even bother with the drawstring loop. She just hooked her fingers into the sweats and yanked them down in one smooth sweep. She gasped as he sprang out rigid and hot against her belly, and then *he* gasped as she wrapped her fingers around him.

Good Lord, he was *huge*.

His hoarse grunt filled the dark as she squeezed him firmly, savoring the hard, stiff satin. And then his voice broke. "Honey, I—"

Three loud whacks on her stateroom next door cut him off. "Hey, DCA, open up!"

It was Dillon.

Chapter 11

Damn!

Somehow, Reese managed not to roar and bash his head into the wall unit as Jade ripped herself from his arms. She was across the stateroom in two seconds flat. He knew, because he could hear her ragged breath through the dark.

It matched his own.

From the fumbling sounds that followed, she was jerking at her uniform, trying to get it back together. But it was no use. Without buttons on that top, she wasn't going anywhere.

Which meant he had to. And that was going to be a difficult task given his state of distended arousal. Perhaps insurmountable. Then again, maybe he wouldn't have to leave. Maybe Dillon would go away.

He slid his sweats over his throbbing erection, praying the guy would do just that as he started in on his multiplication.

Three more thumps followed. "Come on, Jade, I know you're in there. I talked to Central."

Think, buddy, think.

Think? Hell, he was lucky he could still *breathe.*

He felt more than heard Jade slip past him and reach for the knob.

He had to do something—now. Before she sacrificed her reputation on the slim chance that whatever Dillon wanted was actually important. He closed a hand over hers and pressed his lips to her ear, whispering, "Trust me."

She nodded shakily and moved back to the corner.

Good. That's where he wanted her, out of view and safe from Dillon's nasty mind.

He slipped across the stateroom and flipped down the shelf. Once the temporary desk was formed, he reached inside and snapped on the tiny reading light before turning to Jade.

Big mistake.

She stood next to his rack, holding the edges of her shirt together, her eyes wide, her cheeks flushed, her inky hair so disheveled, he was nearly overcome. He wanted to dig his hands back into it, wrap it around himself—wrap *her* around himself—and finish what they'd started. But she trusted him enough to get her out of this.

And he would.

He spun around and headed for the tiny sink at the foot of his rack. He went straight for the cold, shoving his face under and welcoming the freezing flood as it gushed over his face and hair. He ran through another line of division, praying it would be enough. He turned off the water and glanced down.

It wasn't.

He cursed inwardly as he dried his hair, hooking the towel around his neck as Dillon thumped her door again. With the nearby staterooms vacant, the guy could keep it up all night if he wanted to.

He glanced down at the front of his sweats again. Damn. He needed to go *down.* Right now.

"DCA, I don't care if you're dressed or not, get your butt out here."

That did the trick. He smiled grimly as he headed for the door, closing it firmly as he entered the dim passageway. "Hey, Mike, you got a reason for waking the ship at this hour?"

Dillon spun around. "Where is she?"

He cocked his head toward her door. "Obviously not in there. She's probably still in Central—she had a drill to run tonight."

"*That,* I know. The Flying Squad left their squalor all over my spaces. Bunch of pigs if you ask me. Anyway, she's not there, I just checked."

Reese smiled openly. Pigs his ass, the mess was his. And right now, he was damn proud of it. His smile faded. But was the heroin Dillon's? Now, there was a question worth asking. Unfortunately, short of smashing the bastard up against the side of the bulkhead, he wasn't likely to get the answer he was looking for.

At least not tonight.

He shrugged. "So find her in the morning. Surely you can wait until then." After all, one interrupted, painful wait deserved another.

"Why should I care if she gets her beauty rest? She didn't care if I got mine."

That's it. He'd heard enough. Reese advanced on him with deadly calm. "How about the fact that the woman is still sporting a brand new gash and a head full of stitches?"

Dillon sneered up at him. "So what? What's it to you, anyway? Unless…" His words trailed as his black gaze settled on the scratches Jade's keys had left in his abdomen.

Damn! Reese kicked himself for forgetting to don his sweatshirt. He paid for the oversight a hundred times over as the lecherous twist to the guy's mind became apparent.

The bastard grinned slyly as he jerked his head from Jade's door back to his. "Unless the *real* reason she's not in there is because she's in with you giving a little one-on-one first aid.''

Reese grabbed the ends of the towel, pulverizing them. ''If you've got a point to make, make it.''

Dillon's laugh was as short and ugly as he was. ''My point is, someone seems to have forgotten to tell Little Miss Perfect that sex on a naval vessel is against the Uniform Code of Military Justice. Why, she could even be court-martialed.''

Pure, cold fury stabbed into Reese. He whittled the distance between them down to a hair's width—and then leaned closer. ''If you so much as *think* that thought in the company of anyone on or connected to this ship again, I'll crush it right out of your brain. And I won't care if I have to go through your skull to get it. You got that?''

Dillon's humor backfired, the knob in his neck revving as he swallowed and screeched, ''Got it.''

Reese touched his ear. ''I don't think I caught that.''

He swallowed again, managing more volume. ''Got it.''

''Good.'' Reese smiled as he straightened. ''Now, when I see the DCA at quarters in the morning, I'll be sure to let her know you're looking for her, okay?''

Another quick nod.

''Say good-night, Gracie.''

'''Night.''

Reese stared down the dimly lit corridor, waiting until Dillon slunk out of sight. And then he waited some more. Only when the boot steps rounded the corner and he heard the watertight door open and close, did he turn back to his room.

He wasn't fooled by Dillon's easy capitulation for a second. Not only had he burned a major bridge tonight, he'd also left one hell of an enemy seething on the other side.

Way to go, buddy.

Jade jerked away from the door as she heard Dillon's steps trail off, moving as far away as she could get. She retreated all the way onto Reese's rack, tugging the fire-fighter's ensemble into her lap as she tried to disguise her gaping shirt. Short of clutching the bulky coveralls beneath her chin, it didn't do much good.

She still couldn't believe what they'd nearly done. Hell, who was she kidding, what she *had* done. Humiliation seared her from her head to her toes. Twice he'd kissed her, both times igniting a raging, rutting inferno inside her. Even now, it could reflash in a second. She closed her eyes and wilted against the bulkhead. Lifelong goals be damned, she *wanted* him.

And that terrified her.

"Got any sage advice now, Dad?"

A deep chuckle resonated through her brain. *Oh, no, I don't think you want my advice on this one, Missy. But I will tell you this—try and keep it on the beach.* It took a bit for his chuckle to die out.

Yeah, Dad was a sailor, all right. She jolted upright, digging her fingers into the firefighter's suit as the doorknob clicked and turned.

Reese reentered the room. The lights were still dim, but she could make out his face clearly enough as he leaned back against the wall unit. He nodded to the coveralls in her lap. "Didn't know what to do with them after the plan fell through, so I changed in here."

She nodded, wishing the towel looped at the base of his neck covered more of his chest. His torso glistened in the low light, reminding her again all too vividly of what they'd done.

"Jade?"

She evaded the concern in his gaze and voice, tugging the coveralls closer as she stared down at his feet. They were naked as well, long and lean, with a sharp, masculine slant to his toes. Oh, God, even his *feet* were sexy.

She yanked her gaze back to her lap, focusing on the

yellow reflective tape stitched onto the coveralls as he walked over and hunkered down in front of her.

"Honey?" He tipped her chin up and forced her to stare into his liquid blue gaze. "Talk to me."

She closed her eyes and sighed, opening them when she found her nerve. "I *should* be brought up on charges."

Reese raked a hand through his wet hair. "You heard."

"I was listening." She paused, nearly choking on the irony before admitting it out loud. "Dillon's right, you know."

He released her chin, only to capture her hand. "No, he *isn't*. Nothing happened."

Nothing? Guilt cooked off her top layer of skin as the memory came snapping back. *Nothing?*

Reese chuckled, the fire in his eyes not at all related to embarrassment as he squeezed her hand. "Okay, a hell of a lot just happened. And for the record, it was *not* part of some nefarious plan of mine. *But*—for lack of a more polite word—*penetration* did not occur."

Another layer went up in flames.

He pressed on, trapping her chin once again. "And it won't, now that I know the rules."

She tugged away, but he brought her right back.

"Not *here*."

He couldn't possibly mean—

"That's exactly what I mean. I swear to you, I won't touch you as long as we're on this ship." He dropped his hands to either side of her, using them as leverage until his lips were buried in her hair, pressed to her ear, his growl low, his breath hot, "But, honey, you'd better watch out, because the *second* your foot hits the pier, *you're mine*."

And then he was gone.

She drew a shaky breath. Just *how* was she supposed to respond to that? Agree? Argue? Maybe she shouldn't do either. They still had another night underway. Maybe she should take the reprieve and think long and hard about

Karin's advice. Having sex didn't mean they were headed down the road to marriage. Look at Jeff.

But she'd have to keep it light this time. She'd have to keep her heart out of it. Because if she didn't, she had a feeling Reese would leave her razed to the ground when *he* left.

By the time she found her composure and looked up, he was across the space, yanking open a drawer in the wall unit.

He pulled out a set of worn gray sweats matching the ones he had on and tossed them at her before turning away. "Now, get dressed, woman. We have to talk, and I can't concentrate with your shirt hanging open."

He knotted his fingers over the towel at the base of his neck and sighed. "You might want to do something with your hair as well."

What? Stunned, she stared at his naked back. He expected her to just strip down to her underwear and change while he just *stood there?*

"Don't worry, I won't look."

Undercover agent. Photographic memory. Did he read minds, too?

"Just yours."

Now that *was* a lucky guess. It had to be. She started to stick out her tongue, but thought better of it. Just in case. She flushed again as she kicked the coveralls to the deck and hopped off the rack. It was a good thing she looked good in red. She had a feeling she'd be wearing it for a while.

She was changed in under thirty seconds, but loitered for another thirty as she cinched the drawstring around her waist and cuffed the sleeves, all the while savoring the feel of snuggling deep in Reese's sweats. If she was only imagining they still carried his musky scent, she didn't want to know.

"Okay, done." She gasped as he turned around. With the

desk light inches from his thighs, she made out the angry scratches across his abdomen. "Oh, God, I am *so* sorry."

Reese froze. For a split second, panic gripped him. Blessed relief followed as he realized Jade was referring to the scratches on his stomach. For a moment, he thought she'd actually apologized for initiating the best sex he'd ever had—and that was saying a hell of a lot, since they hadn't done it *all*.

He smiled ruefully as she headed for the sink and soaked his washcloth before ringing it out. "Don't worry, the sting's already gone. The second you kissed me, a much lower ache took over."

He chuckled as she blushed, then choked back a groan as she pressed the cloth against his stomach. Damn, that felt *good*. Too good.

"Well, it's your own fault. Why didn't you tell me it was you when I opened the door, anyway?" She washed off the streaks of blood and rinsed the rag.

He held his breath as she pressed the cloth to him again, tracing the scratches down to his groin. "At first I thought you were Dillon or Coffey." He pointed to his Glock on the desk as he tried like crazy to ignore her hands. "By the time I realized it was you, I was trying to ditch that while dodging knees and keys."

He bit back another groan as the cloth flirted with the edge of his sweats. That rag was doing a hell of a lot more to enflame his lust than it could ever do to cool the scratches. If she didn't get her hands out of his pants soon, his promise was going to shatter into a million pieces. Personally, he was all for it. He didn't give a rat's ass about the Navy's rules.

But she did.

And that was enough for him.

He grabbed her wrist as it made another achingly low pass. "Honey, you keep that up and you're not going to make it to the pier. It's going to happen right here, right now."

She jerked her hand away, looking everywhere *but* his rapidly tenting sweats. She finally turned away altogether, laying the damp cloth over the edge of the sink and fingering it nervously. "Sorry."

She cleared her throat and turned back. "You—ah—said we had to talk. Did you find out anything?"

He took pity on her. There'd be time enough to torture her later. When they were truly alone. Besides, right now he needed information. And much as he knew she wouldn't want to hear his questions, he was hoping she'd have the answers.

He guided her back to the bunk, flipping on his Walkman with its tiny speaker for cover noise as she settled in, cross-legged. Then he dragged his desk chair across the cabin and straddled it backward. He took her hand, wishing he could delay the inevitable.

For once, he didn't *want* to say it. Because once he did, she'd know Coffey was officially a suspect.

Surprisingly, it was her hand that squeezed his. "Just tell me."

He sighed. "I found it."

She blinked. "It? I don't understand. What exactly did you find? *Oh, my God*—you found *it.*"

He nodded.

The confusion and disbelief gave way to horror. "You really found *heroin?* In the NSF?"

He nodded again, waiting for it to sink in before he pushed it further. But he didn't have to, she was right there with him. He wasn't surprised—she was sharp. It was one of the things he admired most about her.

"Oh, God, you found it in the office, didn't you?"

"In a storage cabinet across from their desks."

She was perfectly motionless—for about ten seconds. Then she laced her fingers and began twisting them back and forth, her knuckles white. "I see. Do you think they could be in on it together?"

That was pretty much the sixty-four-thousand-dollar question, wasn't it? And he wished to hell he had the answer. He shrugged. "At this point, I honestly don't know. The container was locked and looked like one of about fifty others I searched. It's possible one of them could be doing it alone."

"Describe it."

Huh? What was the point? He knew heroin when he saw it. But this was Jade, so he humored her. "Brown, uncut. I saw four units—about three kilos—but there could be more—"

She shook her head. "Not the heroin, the *container*."

Aah. He spread his hands two feet apart. "About this big—a square silver box with a lid. It looked like anodized steel to me."

She leaned forward, tightening her grip on his hand. "Was the outside marked in any way? Was there an orange symbol on it? Something that resembled a ship's propeller— a large dot with three blades radiating out?"

So that's what that was. "Yeah, as a matter of fact it did. I was going to ask you about it."

"Oh, my God." She stiffened, staring at him, but not *at* him.

"What?" He squeezed her hand, then eased off, afraid he was crushing her fingers. "Jade, what is it?"

She finally focused on him. But the horror was still there in the swirling gray depths. "Reese, you just described a ship-to-ship transport container."

"A ship-*to*-ship—?" *Holy Mother of—*

She nodded. "We're not the only one involved. You may have found your heroin—but you found something else as well. There's a least one more ship in the loop."

Son of a bi—

"Did you see anything else on the outside? A label? A

name or a set of letters followed by a number? Most likely written on something temporary, like masking tape.''

"No. I didn't get a chance to really look at the box before Dillon showed up, but I don't think so.''

"*Dillon* showed up? Why didn't he say anything in the passageway?''

He chuckled as she crushed his fingers. "Relax. He never even knew I was there. Though you're probably going to take some grief for the mess I left.''

She waved his warning off. "Don't worry about it. At least he'll have something legitimate to whine about for a change.''

True. "Anyway, I do know this batch wasn't radioactive. Your chief tested the shelves before I began.''

She slumped back against the bulkhead. "That's a relief. So now what? Are you going to confiscate it as evidence?''

"Not yet.''

"But—''

Guilt swamped him as she tried to stifle a yawn—and failed. He was going to have to make sure she got a decent night's sleep when they finally hit port. "It's okay, the stuff's not going anywhere. I think the reason it's still there is because the regular guy is out of commission thanks to radiation burns. Whoever put it in that container is too smart to move it now. He won't make a move until he has someone to hand it off to. And when he does, I'll be ready.''

"But in the meantime—wait a minute…'' Her gaze narrowed to steel gray. The same shade he'd seen it turn on several occasions when she'd grasped the problem at hand and hooked the solution.

He liked that color.

"When did you say the last deal went down—exactly?''

He checked the date on his watch. "Five weeks to the day. Why?''

"Because not only do I go to PB4T, I take notes.'' She leaned forward and reached for the khaki pants crumpled at the bottom of the rack. "Could you hand me those? I need my wheel book."

PB4T? Wheel book? And he thought his father was bad. He handed over the trousers, waiting patiently as she pulled a small green tablet she and about every officer on the ship carried. Okay, so that was the wheel book, but that still didn't explain PB4T.

"Yup, here it is." She stopped to cover another yawn and then continued, "Five weeks ago we were working on six nukes."

Man, her yawns were contagious. He suppressed one of his own and then held up a hand. "Whoa, you want to try that again—this time in English? And start with the PB4T."

"Sorry." She grinned. "I forgot you don't speak Navalese. PB4T—Planning Board for Training. All the department heads attend once a week to hammer out and fine-tune the ship's schedule. I'm there because of the Damage Control drills. Anyway, the point is the *Repair Officer* attends."

Now it made sense. He smiled. "Coffey and Dillon's boss."

"You got it, Sherlock. But what you don't have are the *names* of the ships the *Baddager* was servicing five weeks ago. I do."

"So what are you waiting for?" He reached for the wheel book, but she snatched it away and laughed.

"A trade." She glanced down to the mini-refrigerator at the head of the bed next to him. The one she'd coolly informed him was purchased and installed especially for his pampered butt just before he arrived. The Captain even had it stocked.

He grinned, leaning over to whip it open. "What's your poison?"

"Anything—as long as it has plenty of caffeine."

He pulled out a cola, cracked the seal for her and handed it over before taking one for himself. "Now, talk."

He dropped his can to the back of his chair, no longer

needing it as she took a long swallow from hers. The husky sigh that escaped her as she lapped the bubbles from her upper lip packed one hell of a jolt—more than caffeine ever could.

He was awake now.

"Talk." But his voice was hoarse.

She took another sip and then pointed to a list of names in her wheel book. "I'd start with these bottom three."

He glanced at them as he polished off his soda. "Why?"

"Because the *level* of contamination that produced those blisters on your informant most likely came from contact exposure to the primary power supply in a propulsion plant. That leaves the bottom three ships—because they have nuclear power plants on board." She smiled as he rubbed the back of his neck and continued, "Let me put that in layman's terms."

"Please do."

"Somehow, that heroin—directly or indirectly—touched the uranium core."

He crushed the empty can.

"Exactly."

He hooked the can across the room, nailing the trash in mid-basket, his gut doing the dance of the *Titanic* as he turned back. "You're telling me there's no way the heroin could simply have been packed next to a contaminated machine part while it was in the NSF, aren't you?"

"It *is* possible, but highly unlikely. I think your best bet is one of those ships. In fact, I'd lay money one of them had a core breach. If the ship was run out of specs—kinda like running an economy car at a hundred and twenty miles an hour for a while—*that* would contaminate the containment water surrounding and insulating the uranium core."

She took another sip. "I'd lay odds the heroin was packed in one of the valves that control the flow of that coolant water." She handed the wheel book over. "Reese, you find out which ship ran out of specs—and you'll know where the heroin came from."

Chapter 12

Jade ignored the taunting chuckle inside her mind as she yanked the sweatshirt down over her head.

Reese's sweatshirt.

So she'd held on to it for a day. If she wanted to wear it one more time before they headed into port in the morning, there was nothing wrong with that. Besides, she'd have to wash his sweats before she returned them, anyway, right?

Who you trying to convince, Missy? You or me?

She stuck out her tongue as the laughter died out, then glanced at her watch. Rats. She still had fifteen minutes to kill before she headed to Karin's stateroom for the movie. Reese's movie. Somehow, Karin had bribed a copy from a sailor—probably threatened him with an extra battery of shots.

Sorority Rush.

The title said it all. She'd lay odds at least twenty minutes of footage was filled with screaming debutantes running bare-breasted through the night. But she was curious. Karin *did* rave over it. Then again, Siskel and Ebert Karin wasn't.

She thought Freddy Krueger was a gas. Maybe it was the doctor in her. All you had to do was give her a little blood and guts and she was yours for life.

She sighed as she tugged the bobby pins from her hair, pulling the French braid over her shoulder. Somehow, she'd suffer through.

The laughter picked up again.

Okay, so her curiosity had a bit more to do with the movie's male co-star than she wanted to admit.

Thump, thump, thump.

Jade froze, her fingers threaded halfway up her braid. Speaking of co-stars...

Please, God, don't let that be Reese.

She didn't know *what* she'd say if he caught her in his sweats.

She forced herself to relax. It couldn't be him. Reese said he'd be tied up in paperwork for the next two hours at least. Besides, even if it was him, she didn't have time to change.

The door thumped again, this time impatiently.

She took a deep breath, praying Reese hadn't decided on a break, and opened the door.

Karin stood in the passageway, grinning like the village idiot as she brandished a VCR tape and a steaming bag of microwave popcorn. "Got it!"

Jade slapped a hand around her wrist and yanked her inside. She snapped the door shut and leaned back against it, her ears straining for the slightest sound of Reese stirring next door. Whew! The coast was clear. She sighed and pulled away from the door.

Karin arched a brow. "My, my, *someone's* anxious to see Macbeth in action after all."

"Do you think you could be a little louder next time? Reese is *in* his stateroom." Unease swamped her as Karin plopped down on the rack, obviously settling in for the long haul. "What are you doing here, anyway? I thought we were supposed to meet in your room."

''We were, but my VCR just broke. Sorry.'' She shrugged and popped a piece of popcorn into her mouth.

Sorry?

''Relax—you have one. We'll just watch it here.''

''No!''

Karin tossed the tape onto the mattress, her gaze narrowing suspiciously. ''Why not?''

The question seemed simple enough. On the surface. Unfortunately, the answer wasn't. Jade shifted beneath that steady stare, finally looking away altogether, studying the carpet intently. ''Because.''

''Because…?''

She couldn't look her in the eye. ''Just because.'' Because what if Reese caught her? What if she couldn't hide her feelings? What if he figured out he'd really gotten to her?

What if he figured out she cared?

Would he use it against her? Would he push her into a physical relationship she wasn't sure she was ready for— let alone able to handle? Not now, anyway. Maybe not ever.

''Jade?''

She glanced back at Karin, into blue eyes that were compassionate—and far too knowing.

''You want to talk about it?''

Yes—no.

Not yet, anyway. ''I—I need some time.''

Karin nodded. ''Okay. Sure you're up to a movie?''

Not by a long shot. But this wasn't just any movie. It was *his.* Maybe it would help. Maybe staring at Reese for two hours without him really staring back might help make up her mind. Anything was possible. Besides, what else was she supposed to do before watch tonight?

Sleep?

She stared at the bulkhead behind Karin. The one separating her rack from his by a quarter-inch of gray steel. How could anyone sleep knowing Reese Garrick was that close? *She* certainly couldn't. The last two weeks had proved that.

Jade snagged the movie from the bed and opened the center doors of the wall unit, revealing her small television. She sighed as she slid the tape in and punched Play.

Karin reached over and squeezed her hand briefly as she settled down on the rack. "Just give it time. You'll see—it'll work out."

Jade nodded, then jerked her pillow into her lap, balling it up tight as the opening credits rolled across the screen. That was the problem. She wasn't sure she wanted it to work.

Hell, who was she kidding? The real problem was she *did* want it to work. For the first time in her life, she really wanted it to work.

And it terrified her.

Her phone rang, mercifully postponing another panic session. She shook her head at Karin, silently telling her to let the movie run as she reached for the receiver. "DCA here."

It was Medical. She handed it to Karin and turned back to a wide-angle shot of a sorority party in full swing.

"You're kidding." Karin sighed. "Okay, I'll be right there." She vaulted from the rack, turning back as she shoved the receiver back in place. "Can you believe it? Twelve hours from port and some sailor falls down a ladder and breaks his leg." She shook her head as she headed for the door. "No—don't bother stopping the movie. It doesn't get really good until twenty minutes in. I should be back by then."

Jade pitched the remote back on the bed as the door closed. At least now she knew when to expect the serious gore. She snagged Karin's bag of popcorn, propping it on top of her pillow as she settled in for the count.

Fifteen minutes later, she'd won her own bet. At least ten women were gyrating on the makeshift dance floor. Every last one of them so top-heavy they'd be a stability nightmare in a lifeboat. And—surprise, surprise—every last one of them was already well on her way to getting undressed with a little help from her date. But where was Reese? His name had co-billing with Brandee Lane—you'd think he'd have shown up by now.

The camera pulled back from the drunken revelry to pan the front door of the sorority house and the couple arguing on the steps.

Aah, *there* he was....

The camera closed in on Reese and his date—who was having a heck of a time convincing him to join the debauchery. Smart man. Then the close-up switched from Brandee to Reese.

Jade dropped the bag of popcorn and dug her fingers into her pillow as the shock waves rolled over her. Damn.

He looked *good.*

No, scratch that. Better than good. He looked great, fantastic, incredible. And it didn't have a damn thing to do with makeup or wardrobe or whatever else they enhanced actors with.

It was him.

Looks, charm, charisma—whatever Hollywood called it, Reese had it. It sizzled off him. Hell, he was hotter than the steel deck of a ship on a blistering day at sea.

Sex appeal.

That's what it was. It was sex, pure and simple. All you had to do was look into those blue eyes and you were hooked. He had you for the rest of the movie. Script, plot, action be damned. You were there for him.

And she was.

Another thump on her door jolted her out of her trance. She tore her gaze from the screen. Damn, Karin locked it behind her. She grabbed the remote, pausing the movie in the middle of the camera's affair with Reese's biceps. Karin or no Karin, she was *not* going to miss this.

She twisted the lock, yelling as she yanked the door open, "About time. Hurry up, it's starting to get good."

"Didn't know I was late." That was *not* Karin's chuckle.

Jade dropped the remote—and her jaw. The remote smacked down on the deck and bounced twice, landing right side up alongside a pair of brown boots.

Cowboy boots.

She looked up slowly, knowing she was beyond red and well into purple as she gazed past the tight jeans, the empty belt loops, the snug white T-shirt, right up to that incredibly sexy smile.

Oh, God, that smile. She sucked in her breath and held it. Yup, that smile packed a much bigger punch in person than it did on the screen.

"Hi." She choked on the annoying squeak that followed.

Reese grinned, his gaze never leaving hers as he hunkered down for the remote, snagged it and lifted it up. "Hi, yourself."

Her fingers grazed his as she took the remote. She shifted her gaze to avoid the smoldering offer that came with it.

"Well?"

Steeling herself, she looked back, praying the grin had left by now.

It hadn't. "Can I come in?"

Jade bit into her cheek as panic struck. How on earth was she going to get rid of Reese without being rude? Because there was *no way* she was letting him in. Not with his movie on. She cleared her throat. "I'm—ah—not sure it would be a good idea."

His grin deepened, spiriting away yet another piece of her heart. "Why not? I can keep my hands to myself."

Yeah, but could she?

Damn, why had he changed out of his coveralls? At least when he *looked* Navy, there was a visible warning beacon keeping her on course.

"Well?"

Against her will, her gaze slid back to that *smile*. She jerked it back up. She needed an excuse—a good one. Before the pause on her VCR expired and the movie kicked back in—

Too late.

His brows rose as the movie's distinctively campy soundtrack floated out between them. "Is that what I think it is?"

She nodded—and to her astonishment, a crimson tide rose up *his* neck, flooding every inch of his face.

Special Agent C. Reese Garrick was *blushing?* Her nerves bounced back with zeal. Well, heck, this was definitely worth capitalizing on. She glanced over to the television and smiled. "Care to join me?"

His throat worked as he obviously searched for an excuse.

She tried to keep her smile from splitting into a grin while she battled the urge to rub her hands together in glee. By God, he really *was* embarrassed. Over his movie, no less. *What* a turnabout. She recognized the moment for what it was. An occurrence more rare than a sincere compliment from Dillon. Oh, this was going to be such *fun*.

She swung the door wide. "You coming in or not?"

Reese stared at Jade's wide grin. Half of him was ecstatic to find her in his sweats watching his movie. The other half was mortified. Not about the sweats. Finding her in his clothes because she wanted to be there fell under a one hundred percent *life couldn't get any better than this* moment—and he didn't care who knew it. Because it meant something.

Something good.

Something promising.

But that *stupid* movie? He swallowed a groan. The one he'd been forced to audition for to bust a drug ring? The same humiliating movie he'd been ordered to participate in day in and day out while he laid his trap for the film's director, producer and half the cast? The movie that was *so bad* his own mother had trouble finding something good to say about it? Not to mention the ribbing he'd taken—was *still* taking—from his partner, TJ, and the rest of the guys at the agency?

Hell, the only good thing about that movie was the solid cover it provided him for this assignment. Maybe there was a way he could sabotage the VCR while Jade wasn't looking? A single shot from his Glock oughta do it. He stared into the laughter lurking in her smoky gaze and decided to wimp his way out. He just didn't think he could handle watching it again.

Not with her.

"Sorry, not tonight. Fresh out of popcorn. I can't seem to enjoy a movie without it. I'll just stop by later."

Unfortunately, he'd forgotten she didn't know how to take no for an answer. Her smile turned wicked as she hooked a finger into his waistband and tugged him inside. "Right there on the bed, Macbeth. Have at it."

The groan he'd been holding back escaped as he grabbed the bag of popcorn. "*Macbeth?* Didn't we get beyond that?"

She hopped up on the rack, patting the spot next to her. "That was before I checked out your cinematic talents."

He winced as he joined her. "That bad, huh?"

She smiled. "Not really, but I wouldn't recommend quitting your day job."

"Hey! I got some pretty good reviews out of that thing." He had. He just wished one or two of them had mentioned his acting ability—in a favorable light, anyway. He reached out and tucked a strand of hair behind her ear.

Not a smart move.

His fingers slipped into the mass against his will—or maybe with it. He wasn't sure anymore. He wrapped the silk around his fingers, rubbing it gently as she rolled her eyes.

"Oh, I'm sure you did. Your talents are quite obvious. So are Brandee's."

"Jealous?" He smiled, hopeful as hell.

"Of *her?* Of course not."

He used her hair to tug her in close. *"Liar."* His heart thudded painfully as her eyes darkened with the truth.

"Maybe a little." She paused as she eyed the screen, then admitted softly, "Okay, maybe a lot."

Reese glanced up to find Brandee shoving her overly healthy assets into his chest as they joined the rest of the cast on the dance floor. Yeah, he remembered that particular scene. Especially the tireless attempts at seduction that followed. Brandee refused to believe he preferred women without surgical enhancement.

Women like Jade.

He could still feel her perfectly formed breasts in his palms. He could still smell them and taste them. *Damn.* He jerked his mind from those moments of darkened bliss before he was forced to move from division to square roots and cupped her jaw. "Brandee Lane has nothing on you."

For one thing, he'd never, ever, seen Brandee blush. It wouldn't have suited her. But it *did* suit Jade.

And it turned him on.

He trailed his fingers down her throat, following the flush. If someone had told him a month ago he'd be this jealous of his own ratty sweats, he'd have turned them in for a psych evaluation. But he was.

He was also lost.

He knew that the moment her lips parted. He stared at them, mesmerized as he slipped a finger into the collar of the sweats and caressed the soft flesh beneath. He found the chain, winding it around his fingers as he dipped his head.

"Reese, *please.*"

Somehow, with less than a millimeter to spare, he managed to turn. He buried his face in her hair, his breath scorching them both as he groaned, "I know, honey—I know."

She was right.

If he kissed her, he wasn't going to stop. He swallowed another groan, pulling her to his chest as he leaned back against the bulkhead. He tucked her head firmly beneath his chin and stared at the television screen, slowly regaining control of his breathing. Just in time to catch the close-up of the butcher knife—and the carving lesson that followed.

"Oh, *please. No one* has that much blood in them."

He tightened his arms around her and smiled. "That's nothing. Just wait until Brandee gets it."

She twisted slightly, her eyes wide as she stared up at him. "*Brandee* gets it? I didn't think co-stars were supposed to die."

He chuckled. "She does if her co-star is the killer."

"*You're* the killer?" She threw up her hands. "Thanks a lot. What's the point of watching if I know the ending?"

Actually, that *was* the point. He bit back a grin as she grabbed the remote and killed the movie. "Sorry."

She tossed the remote down before threading her fingers into his hair. "I'll just bet you are. Did spoiling the ending work on your mom and dad, too?"

He shook his head, not bothering to deny it. "Nope, my mother went to see it, anyway. But not for lack of me trying to dissuade her." He held his breath, praying she'd let the rest drop.

She didn't. "What about your dad?"

He reached up, taking her hand in his, twining their fingers together as he measured his words carefully. "I haven't seen him in a while. But I heard he wasn't impressed." That much was true. Other than a strained phone call the day he checked aboard the ship, he *hadn't* spoken to his father. Face-to-face, anyway.

She squeezed his hand gently. "You know, I don't get it. I might understand your father's concern if you actually were an actor. But you're not. How can arresting scum be bad?"

Damn. She was treading into dangerous water—and he

had to get her out. Now. Before she figured out the rest. The tiniest slip on his part and she'd realize not only what, but *who* his father was. She was too smart not to.

Yup, diversion was his best defense. Even if it was painful. "It's gone beyond that. I think my father would have forgiven me for choosing a different path if I hadn't taken my mother's side in their divorce a few years back."

"Oh, Reese." Her hand slipped out of his, back up to his jaw. "I'm so sorry."

"Yeah, me, too. I guess I got tired of him popping in on her every once in a while, jacking up her hopes, then kicking them away again. What was left of our relationship fell apart when I told him what I really thought."

"Your dad wasn't around much?"

"Nope. Even when he was—he wasn't. Know what I mean?"

She shook her head. "Not really. I mean, I know what you mean about the separations. But the reunions?" His gut constricted as her smile turned downright dreamy. "Ours were wonderful. My mom used to meet my dad at the ship when it pulled in. They'd spend the night in a hotel while my grandmother and I baked a cake and decorated the house. The next day, we'd start a party that lasted all week. Every day, I'd get a different present—dolls, toys, whatever he'd picked up from the ports he visited." She sighed. "I still have my dolls."

Reese shoved the green monster down. *His* reunions had been the exact opposite. He could count his presents on one hand—from his entire childhood. And hotel rooms? By the time he was ten, he'd known those were reserved for anyone *but* his mother. Yeah, he'd supported his mother during the divorce. He still did. And she was happier than she'd been in years.

Jade shifted in his arms. "So, what does your father do?"

He tensed, despite the fact that he'd been anticipating— even dreading—the question for days. Ever since he'd confided his cover to her. He'd never had a problem lying before. It was all part of the job.

Until now.

Now the lie he'd been ordered to prepare stuck in his throat, the irony of it nearly choking him altogether. Unfortunately, he didn't have a choice. He'd have to pray she understood when she learned the truth.

"Reese?"

Just spit it out. "Sorry, lost in thought. Dad's a—" He bit off the rest as the phone rang, tipping his head back against the bulkhead in relief. *Thank God.*

Jade groaned out loud as she pulled herself from Reese's arms. She stood reluctantly, her body arguing all the way to the phone. *This had better be good.* "DCA here."

"Came across some interesting information in the chief's lounge this evening."

She wrapped her free hand around the coiled cord and turned back to Reese. "What's that, Chief?"

Reese read her expression correctly because he stiffened.

"Senior Chief Canton ran a surprise audit on the wardroom today. Two keys were missing—yours and our guest's."

She lifted her hand, rubbing the itchy skin above her stitches. "Great. Any idea how long they've been missing?"

"Couple days, a week at the outside. I asked him to keep it to himself."

"Thanks, Chief. Let me know if they turn up."

"Will do. Catch you in the morning."

By the time she'd replaced the receiver and turned around, Reese was at her side. He reached out and cupped her chin. "What is it?"

She sighed. "Dillon must have gotten my key off the extra panel in the mess cooks' office—those are the guys in charge of cleaning the staterooms. Yours is missing, too."

"Damn." The hand rubbing his neck froze. "Wait a minute. How long ago?"

"The senior chief in charge thinks days—a week, max."

His eyes narrowed. "Then it's possible Coffey *was* telling the truth about your key. I'll search their rooms again in the morning while you guys are driving the ship into port. Maybe something will turn up."

"*Again?* As in, you've searched them *before?*" A chill slithered down her spine as he nodded. Did that mean…? She was almost afraid to ask. "Did you—" She took a breath. "Did you search mine, too?"

He didn't even have the decency to look embarrassed as he nodded. "Why do you think I was surprised about the jazz?"

Jazz? Oh, right, he did seem startled at that. Probably because the compact discs were in the player, the covers at home.

But that wasn't the point.

"You *searched* my room." She backed away, crossing her arms as she leaned against her wall unit. "Why? I thought I wasn't a suspect." Not to mention she'd spent the entire day agonizing over whether or not to have an affair with a man who trusted her enough to snoop through her belongings.

"It's not what you think. For the record, I'm not proud of rifling through your underwear." He closed the distance between them, until he was inches away. "Frankly, I'd rather see you *in* it. So I can take you *out* of it."

She flushed.

He dropped a hand to her desk, then pulled it back up, dangling her keys between them. "I was looking for these. I thought I'd need them to get into the NSF."

She blinked, more disturbed by the heat radiating along his body than his confession. "But I never let those out of my sight."

He raised his other arm, resting it on the wall unit above her head, trapping her. She stifled a moan as he stroked a key down her cheek.

"*Now* I know that. But I didn't when I came aboard, did I?" His voice was much too low and much too vibrant for her peace of mind. A wave of goose bumps rippled down her arms as he traced her lips with the tip of the key.

"I—I suppose not."

He smoothed the cold metal down her jaw, using it to sculpt her neck. She shivered as he reached the hollow at the base, gently carving it anew. "Besides, I've already paid in spades for invading your privacy."

"How s-so?"

He leaned closer, his breath fanning her cheeks as he slipped the keys beneath her collar. She sucked in her breath as they slid lower, closer and closer to her aching breasts. "Because every time I close my eyes, I can see exactly what's beneath these sweats—in heavenly, *excruciating* detail."

The keys reached the edge of her bra, and he scraped the tips of the keys back and forth, again and again until she was suffocating with longing. His breath was caressing her neck now, setting a torch to her tenuous control. She was so aroused she wanted to scream. But other than the keys, he wasn't touching her at all.

Yet she was pinned.

Just as surely as if he'd shackled her.

His gaze darkened, piercing into her, forcing her eyes to stay open, to stare straight into his. "Are you wearing the white or the pink today?"

"Pink." She heard a groan, but wasn't sure if it was hers or his.

"The satin, or the lace one?" It might have been his, because his voice was hoarse now.

"Satin." But so was hers. She bit down on her lip, drawing blood as the tip of a key snagged her bra, peeling the cup from her breast.

"And your panties?" he demanded softly. "They're cut high, aren't they?" His other arm came down then, and he finally touched her. But it was just one finger—at the point of her hip. "About here?"

Exactly there.

"Yes." It came out on a hiss.

His head turned and lowered until his smoky breath was in her ear. "Relax, honey. I'm not going to kiss you. Not on this ship." The key grazed the areola of her breast, but still he didn't touch her. "I promised, *remember?*" The keys slipped lower. She knew where he was taking them— and she wanted it.

"Yes." The word was a shameless plea now. He had to have heard it. And she didn't care.

"No, not here." She gasped as the key circled the base of the nub, his voice thick and strained now. "But when I do kiss you, it's going to be right—" he scraped the tip *"—here."*

She closed her eyes then—and moaned. But the keys were gone. And so was he. By the time she opened her eyes, her door was closing.

She drew a deep, ragged breath as she heard the door to his stateroom open and shut. And when she heard the faucet running, she could almost see him shoving his head beneath the icy flood. But it didn't help.

Not one damn bit.

Chapter 13

"Will you look at that, less than an hour in port and he's already abandoned ship. This has to be a record, DCA—even for you."

Jade pulled her hand back from mid-knock on Reese's door and glared at Dillon. "What are *you* doing here? I thought Medical already sprayed this section for roaches."

Dillon smirked as he shoved a stack of papers under his arm. "Very funny. But that just proves your rapier wit isn't why Mack jumped ship the first chance he got, doesn't it? Must be because of your other—" he coughed "—*skills.*"

Jade rubbed the skin above her stitches as she fought the familiar urge to throttle him. "Okay, Mike. You obviously think you've swallowed a canary. You'd better spit out the bones before you choke on them."

He shrugged. "What's to swallow? I just find it damned amusing to see you panting outside Mack's door when he's not even on the ship."

Reese wasn't aboard? For a split second she stiffened,

almost believing him. But then she relaxed. "Since when does Reese clear his schedule with you?"

"He doesn't. But it looks like he doesn't clear it with you, either. Too bad. If he had, you'd know he split ten seconds after the brow hit the pier. And from what I saw, he looked anxious to leave. Maybe it had something to do with that hot date he had planned for tonight?"

Oh, God, he wasn't kidding. Even Dillon couldn't fake that pompous sneer. Reese really *had* left the ship. And he hadn't even bothered to tell her. She sucked up the shock as she cruised by Dillon and stabbed a key into her own lock. She twisted the knob, shoving the door open as she held on to her hope. Maybe—just maybe—he'd left a note in her room.

Dillon stepped up behind her. "Guess you weren't worth waiting around for again, eh, honey?"

"Drop dead, Mike." She slammed the door in his face, collapsing back against it as she glanced down at her desk.

Nope.

She straightened quickly, casing her rack, the mirror and, finally, the back of the door. Damn. No Reese, no note, no clue. No nothing. Just peachy. She pulled her dress-white cover off her head before tossing it upside down on her desk and hooking her keys into it.

Those keys.

She tore her gaze away before she succumbed to the memory and stalked over to the porthole, staring out at the frigate parked on the opposite side of the pier. Where the hell was Reese? Had he found something during his search of the staterooms? Something that forced him to leave the ship before she was able to break away from the bridge? Something so important he didn't have time to leave her an explanation—or even a *phone number?*

Sighing, she turned away from the porthole, pulled her overnight bag out of a drawer and began filling it with laundry. There was no sense sitting around. Liberty call would be going down any minute and she might as well be on it.

Rap, rap, rap.

Reese?

She dropped the bag on her rack and practically sprinted for the door. "Oh. It's you."

Karin arched her brows. "Nice to see you, too."

She flushed, swinging the door wide. "Sorry. Come on in. Just packing up to head home." She turned back to her laundry drawer and yanked out her dirty khakis, glancing over her shoulder as Karin shut the door and tsked.

"Such a long face. Could it be you were expecting Reese?" She whipped a hand from behind her back, dumping a box on the desk before brandishing an envelope. "Or maybe you were expecting *this?*"

Jade stared at the envelope, crossing her arms and reigning in her hope as Karin grinned and waved it tauntingly. "And that would be…?"

"From Reese."

Karin's dimples cratered as Jade snatched it from her hand. The only mark on the outside was her name. Her heart kicked into double time as she stared at the bold script.

"Well, are you going to open it and tell me what the key is for?" Karin's dimples rivaled the grand canyon as Jade glanced up in shock. "Yeah, there's a key. I held it up to the light. And I have a pretty good guess what it opens."

Right. In her dreams. She stared back down at the envelope, wishing Karin was right. But the odds were against it. It was probably the key Reese had been searching for. And on that chance alone, she couldn't afford to open it in front of Karin. She laid it carefully beside the box. "Is that for me, too?"

Karin rolled her eyes as she groaned. "I can't *believe* it. You're not going to put me out of my misery? That thing has been burning a hole in my pocket for the last four hours and you won't even give me the satisfaction of letting me know I'm right?'' She shot her a filthy glare as she huffed, ''Fine, see if I ever play messenger for you two lovebirds again.''

For once Jade welcomed the heat torching her face—because it got her off the hook.

''Stop that, it makes me feel guilty and you know it.'' Karin groaned again, snatching up the present as another wave scorched Jade's face. She thrust the box into her hands and turned back to the door. ''Sometimes, I think you blush on purpose just to get me to leave you alone.''

Jade managed to smile through the next blast. ''It works, doesn't it?''

Karin laughed. ''Yeah, it does.'' She jutted her chin toward the box. ''I held that back on your birthday because I wasn't sure you were ready for it, but now I think you are. See you at the hail-and-farewell party tomorrow.'' She paused at the door. ''You *are* going, aren't you?''

She wrinkled her nose. ''If I don't, I'm going to get a lecture by the Captain come Monday about how I snubbed the Supply Officer at his own party.''

Karin arched a brow as she opened the door to leave. ''Since when has that stopped you before?''

She grinned. ''Never.''

Her smile evaporated as the door closed. She slapped the box down and pounced on the envelope, tearing it open. The key dropped to the deck as she yanked out a slip of paper.

15 Camarillo Court. Had a meeting.
If you get home before me, turn down the covers.

R.

He'd sketched a map underneath.

She scooped up the brass key and stared at it. A house key. *His* house key.

His *trust*.

She swallowed quickly, wondering why she was getting choked up in the first place. Hell, who was she kidding? She closed her eyes and sighed. There was no use pretending—not anymore. For days her mind had been denying what her heart already knew. But she couldn't deny it any longer. She slumped back against the wall unit, the truth piercing her gut, twisting around for good measure, causing her to gasp with the double-edged joy and pain of it.

She was in love with Reese.

She pressed her head back as her heart and mind raced against each other for the second time in her life. Only this time her heart was ahead. By a mile. The only question left was, what was she going to do about it? Or specifically, how she was going to keep Reese from finding out?

She glanced back down at the box Karin had left behind, her curiosity managing to shove the turmoil aside for a moment while she pulled off the lid.

What the—

Hooking her fingers into the spaghetti straps, she slid the scarlet silk out of the box, dangling the teddy in shock. This was no innocent little nightie. Her fingers shook as she held it up to her uniform, the white fabric underscoring how little it would cover, should she *ever* dare to don it.

Heat suffused her as she turned to stuff it back in the box—but something else caught her eye before she had a chance. Her eternal furnace blasted out yet another round, her face no doubt darker than the silk by the time she finished reading the label on the box within the box: Prophylactics—100 Each.

Condoms?

Karin had given her a box of *one hundred* condoms?

She stiffened, clenching the wisp of silk in her hands. She was going to *kill* the woman. She was going to hunt her down with a heat-seeking missile and blast her off the face of the earth. She was going to—

She faltered, the fire within her dousing suddenly as the

real message behind Karin's gift cut through her haze. Karin was trying to tell her to follow her heart. To put aside the pain, fear and regret and just go for it. She was telling her to take another chance. To reach for what she really wanted.

Reese.

Jade picked up the key, glancing between it and the teddy. She didn't even have to make up her mind—because her heart had already made it up. She shifted the teddy and key to one hand and snagged a handful of condoms with the other before turning to drop them beside her bag.

And then she dumped out her uniforms and started to repack.

Jade pulled her jeep into the drive, her mouth gaping as she killed the engine. This was no crude bachelor pad.

It was a bloody *house.*

Still bemused, her gaze traced the adobe arch leading into a courtyard and the sprawling red-tiled ranch beyond. Maybe it was the wrong house? Her fifth glance at the number welded to the yawning iron gate finally convinced her she was in the right spot. Fifteen Camarillo Court.

Reese's house.

She left her bag on the passenger seat, slamming the door to her jeep before fishing his key from her olive shorts. She probably didn't need it. Even though her car was the only one in the drive, surely the open gate meant he was already home?

He was.

She was barely inside the courtyard when the double doors opened. Then Reese was standing in the doorway, that heart-stopping smile on his lips, looking too damn sexy for his own good in bare feet, faded jeans, a white T-shirt, with a cordless phone crooked at his neck. The only thing out of place was the holster under his left arm—and the Glock inside it.

He met her halfway, tucking her under his free arm as he hugged her fiercely.

God, he smelled good.

"Yeah, TJ, I'm still here. Did you get anything back yet on the ships I asked about?" He brushed his lips across her bangs, then lifted his head and sighed. *"Damn."*

He shook his head as she tried to move away and pulled her back to his chest. "All right, stick with it. I know it'll be rough getting it over the weekend, but I think he's going to move soon and we need to be ready."

Her breath caught as his fingers burrowed into her braid, pulling out the pins and rubber band, dropping them at their feet as he listened to the guy on the other end. She sighed as he dug his fingers in again, massaging two weeks' worth of drills, watches and sleepless nights from her scalp.

"Sounds good. One more thing, make sure you do a cross-check with the names I gave you. I want to know the second you come up with anything." He wrapped a swathe of hair around his hand and brought it to his lips. "You got it, buddy. Oh, try my pager first this weekend. Dan's watching the ship. If this guy does suspect me, maybe he'll make a move when I'm gone. I'll be back Monday morning. Fine. Talk to you then." The handset beeped as he severed the connection.

He didn't bother with preliminaries. He just tossed the phone to one of the teak chairs and plowed his hand deeper into her hair, sealing her body to his with the other one as he lowered his head. A groan escaped as he swept his tongue deep in her mouth, exploring every inch, laying waste to the fears that had plagued her the past few days.

She was breathless by the time he lifted his head. He stared into her eyes, desire burning clearly in his. "Hi, gorgeous. Welcome home."

Her lungs nearly stopped altogether as she realized he meant it. Oddly enough, it felt as if she *had* come home. But it had nothing to do with the house.

It was him.

It was also the way he couldn't seem to keep his hands off her. He kept running them over her, into her hair, down her neck, pausing to flirt with the collar of her cream T-shirt, then down her waist—as if he couldn't get enough.

She drew a shaky breath. "Hi, yourself."

She shuddered as he cupped her rear again, pulling her tight against his rigid form. And then he kissed her again, hard and deep, his breath shallow by the time they tore apart. "God, I missed you."

She managed a chuckle. "I missed you, too. And if you let me inside the door, I might even show you how much."

Reese groaned and damn near blushed at Jade's husky admonishment. She was right. He was so glad to see her he'd dropped the phone on TJ. In fact, there was no doubt he'd be taking grief the next time he saw the guy for turning incoherent when he opened the door. But he couldn't help it.

If Jade was beautiful in uniform, she was downright stunning out of it. He still wasn't sure how her legs could be that long—the top of her head barely reached his chin. But they were. And shapely, too. All the way down her dusky thighs and calves to those slender feet encased in sandals. And that T-shirt? What little it bothered to leave to the imagination, his memory was more than eager to supply.

But it was her expression that got to him most of all; for a second he'd seen the uncertainty before she'd masked it. From that moment on, all he could think about was gathering her close and reassuring her.

He hadn't meant to take her hair down—at least not so soon. He hadn't even realized what he'd done until it was down. By then, it was too late. He couldn't stop touching her. Hell, he'd practically ravished her on the front steps. So much for his ability to keep himself in check.

He framed her face. "You'll have to forgive me. I spent a very long, *frustrating* night alone. In fact, it's a good thing you had watch when you did because I was on the verge of picking your lock and slipping into your bed when you left.''

An impish smile curved her lips. ''It wasn't locked.''

''*Now* you tell me?'' He groaned as he pulled her close and dropped his chin to the top of her head. She would never know what it cost him to leave her standing in that room, alone. Hell, he'd shoved his head under that faucet so long, it was a miracle he hadn't sprouted gills.

The fire in his gut burned hotter and brighter as she looped her arms around his neck and stretched up to him. ''Does this mean you're willing to finish what you started last night?''

Oh, yeah.

And then some. He smiled as he slid an arm down her back, trying not to hustle her through the door. ''Why don't you come in and find out?''

They made it into the entryway before she stopped short. He glanced down at her quickly, praying she wasn't having second thoughts. ''Is something wrong?''

She shook her head, seemingly at a loss for words. Pink washed her cheeks as she took a deep breath and plunged in. ''My…ah…that is—'' she cleared her throat gently ''—I have a bag in the car.''

Yes! He glanced back at the door, casually. ''We'll get it later.''

She shook her head, her gaze sliding to the oak floor. ''It has something in it we'll need.'' Her gaze snuck back up, somehow bold and demure at the same time. ''Condoms.''

His heart started pounding so hard, his chest was in danger of splitting open. God, he loved her. He loved her brains, her beauty and her blushes. The way she was cool and confident one minute, and then shy and self-conscious the next. But most of all, he just plain *loved* her. Unfortunately, he couldn't tell her.

It was too soon.

What if he scared her off? How could he expect her to believe he loved her after just two short weeks when he'd only realized it himself last night? In fact, it was the realization that had given him the strength to leave her. For the first time in his life, he was terrified of screwing up.

Yeah, it was a damn good thing he hadn't known her door was unlocked. Because they'd needed to wait until the time was right for them to make love, until they were off the ship—and not because of the Navy.

Because of her.

Because no matter what, he wanted her to be able to look herself in the mirror in the morning. And smile. But she wasn't smiling now. In fact, she looked downright unsure. He had to reassure her.

Needed to.

He tipped her chin up and lost himself in her smoky gaze as he confessed, "Honey, I want you so bad, I think I sprinted down that pier. I even stopped at a gas station *before* I went to the office."

He was rewarded with a smile. A steamy, sultry, come-hither smile that slipped into his heart and simmered his blood all the way down to his toes. And right then, he knew without a doubt, if he didn't back away from her now, he was going to rip the clothes from her body and take her right here in front of the door.

He took a deep breath and stepped back, linking her hand in his. "Would you like to see the house?"

Just your bedroom.

Jade bit the words back in the nick of time. The last of her doubts had fled the moment Reese mentioned leaving the ship. But she couldn't very well jump him in the foyer, could she? Nope, she'd wait until they reached his bedroom. And *then* she'd jump him. Even if she blushed her way through it. But first, she had a house to see.

She took a deep breath and glanced around, for the first time noticing his home—and the fact that she was actually *in* it. Then she swung her gaze back and stared again. The entire house was almost one huge rectangle—and the cathedral ceiling made it seem even more so. Gleaming hardwood floors stretched out in every direction, broken only by a few scattered area rugs and grouped furniture. A sofa area off to the left, a dining area off to the right, what looked like the kitchen beyond—but in the center, beyond the open French doors—

"You have a *pool?*" The question was rhetorical. Of course he had a pool, it was right there. And it wasn't going anywhere, because not only was it in-ground, there was a stone patio surrounding it as well. She turned to stare up at him. "How on earth can you afford a pool?"

For a moment she was afraid she'd offended him. Fortunately, he knew what she was asking. Uncle Sam paid his salary just as he paid hers. And Uncle Sam wasn't known for his generosity—at least not on this scale.

He shrugged. "I started saving early and built up a pretty good portfolio. And when this place came up for foreclosure, I grabbed it. It needed a lot of work, but I didn't have much else to do in my off time." He took her hand and led her across the floor to the patio, pointing out various items as they passed. "My mother found the dining set and the buffet at an estate sale, the coffee table at an auction, I think. You'll have to ask her."

"Your mother's here?" She blanched and promptly thanked God she hadn't jumped him in the foyer.

He chuckled. "No. She stayed with me for a while after her divorce and did this—" he pointed to the ivory sheers on the French doors as they walked between them "—to thank me. Or so she says." His smile turned devilish. "Personally, I think she was tired of sitting on boxes."

Despite the sun beating down, Jade shivered as they stepped off the patio to stroll around the pool. No, she wasn't cold—it was Reese. He wouldn't stop touching her.

Her arms, her back, her neck, every inch of flesh he could reach.

He was driving her insane.

Here she was, strolling around a miniature Garden of Eden, and all she could think about was a bed.

His bed.

As in, how big was it? And where the hell was it? It was obvious from the way he was touching her he was thinking about it, too. So what were they doing out here?

He stopped near a bush at the edge of the pool and leaned down to pluck a pink bud. He stood, and her breath caught as he mimicked the path of the keys from the night before, sweeping the petals down her cheek and across her lips.

Damn him, he was smiling. He knew *exactly* what he was doing. And if he didn't stop, she was going to rip that stupid flower from his hands and attack him right here.

She glanced over his shoulder, at the privacy fence beyond. Hell, why not? If she couldn't see out, no one could see in, right? But wait, first they'd need a condom. And hers were in the car.

She took a deep breath and snatched the flower from his hand to preserve her sanity. "Did your mother plant these, too?"

He chuckled, the glint in his eyes telling her he knew she was changing the subject—and why. "No, I'm afraid I've turned into quite the gardener on my own."

He reclaimed the flower and her lids drifted shut as it slid down her neck. She could almost see him, bared to his waist, slick with sweat as he worked the ground with a shovel.

No.

She forced her eyes open. She had to get her mind off that, *now*. "You mentioned your mom lived close. How close?"

Smiling, he used the flower to tilt her face. "Why are we talking about my mother? Trust me, you'll meet her soon enough.'' He lowered his head. ''Next weekend, if you want. But not now, not this weekend.'' His breath turned hot as his lips brushed her ear. ''This weekend is *mine*. Just you and me. Someone else is watching the ship this weekend. So unless I get called in, they'll be no more talk of heroin, or the Navy, or ships. Or my mother.'' The flower fell away, forgotten as he claimed her lips in a slow, languid kiss.

And then it wasn't slow anymore.

Her breath caught as he molded her body to his, splaying his fingers over her thighs. She shivered as he found the edge of her shorts and then her panties. And then he was underneath.

He shuddered as she ground herself into his hand, fitting herself into his palm. She tasted his approval as he claimed her mouth in another ruthless kiss, plunging his tongue deep inside as his fingers bit into her rear. He dug his other hand into her hair and pulled her closer, wrenching a groan from them both as the kiss turned harder, deeper, almost savage as he tried to crawl beneath her skin.

She gloried in it.

In *him.*

And then, suddenly, he tore his mouth from hers, growling as he buried his face into her neck, nipping and sucking with less and less force, until she was afraid he was going to stop altogether. And then he *did.*

She moaned aloud in frustration. Condom and privacy be damned. She didn't care if Reese was having second thoughts about taking her in the backyard. She wanted him.

Now.

She wanted his body, his muscles, his skin. She wanted him wrapped around her. She wanted him smothering her. She wanted to smell him, touch him, taste him just as she had that night in her stateroom.

But this time she wanted more. She wanted *all* of him. His mind, his heart, his soul.

She wanted his *love*.

And, God help her, she wanted him forever.

But right now, she'd settle for his body. She'd settle for really seeing it. Because she hadn't.

Yet.

And they weren't stopping until she had.

She ripped his T-shirt from his jeans, shoving her hands beneath so she could touch him. But it wasn't enough. She raked her fingers down his chest, tugging at his shirt, trying desperately to pull it over his head. But it wouldn't budge. And then she realized why.

That damn Glock.

She tore at his shirt for a few more frustrating seconds until, mercifully, he helped her. His hands brushed hers away. A second later, the offending holster and his shirt were gone.

Shock and awe swirled together to drive the breath from her lungs. Good God, if he got this body from gardening, she was buying him a lifetime membership in the horticultural society. She took a jerky step back to admire the golden muscle beneath her palms—and yelped as she lost her balance.

Reese lunged forward, reaching for her as she teetered for a few horrific seconds at the edge of the pool. She sighed as he caught her just before she tipped out of his reach.

But it was too late.

Their combined momentum propelled them both back over with all the grace of a teenager doing a cannonball dive, and they went down together.

Chapter 14

Reese groaned as he and Jade sunk to the bottom of the pool like a pair of bowling balls.

Damn, he'd wanted this first time to be perfect.

For both of them.

He wanted to howl and gnash his teeth at the injustice. He would have, too. If he didn't think he'd end up swallowing half the pool. As it was, he came up sputtering just behind Jade as he used his strength to help her surface. For a moment, he thought she was going to scream as well.

But then she smiled.

And then she was laughing.

Really laughing.

So hard, her mirth was probably spilling over into tears— he might have even been able to tell if there weren't so many water droplets streaming down her face.

And then he was laughing with her. And it no longer mattered where they were. It didn't matter that they weren't in the bed he'd carefully turned down. That the candles he'd dug up from his mother's emergency stash weren't lit. That

the wine was growing warm. That her favorite jazz CD—
and his, too—wasn't playing in the background.

He smoothed the hair from her face and cupped her smiling cheek. No, none of that mattered anymore. All that mattered was that they were here.

Together.

And that it was finally time.

He could tell she agreed by the way her gaze darkened,
by the way she turned her face into his palm and brushed
her lips across his skin. An unexpected bolt of lust rocketed
straight through him as her tongue lapped the water from
his palm.

And then she pulled away.

He nearly gasped with the agony of her withdrawal. Until
he realized her intention. And then he did gasp. This time
in anticipation.

She smiled at him softly as she tugged the ends of her
sopping T-shirt from her shorts and peeled it up her waist.
His breath caught as the bottom of her bra winked at him.
And then white lace filled his view as the shirt plopped into
the chest-high water around them.

He barely remembered to breathe as his gaze traced the
scalloped edge where it hugged her breasts, the water turning her bra translucent. And then his gaze sank farther, until
it was riveted to the dusky nipples clearly visible. He nearly
groaned as her hands came forward, obscuring his view as
they opened the clasp. But then they were gone. And so was
her bra.

His breath came out on a shudder.

Magnificent.

He'd suspected her breasts would be when he'd seen the
curves peeking from her robe. By the time he'd explored
them with his hands and mouth, he'd *known* it. But nothing
could have prepared him for this. They were the perfect
combination of firm and plump, white and proud amid the
twin triangles of her tan.

And her *nipples*.

He did groan then. Because he couldn't breathe. He couldn't even tear his gaze away as her hands slipped beneath the surface to unzip her shorts and peel them down her hips. Not only did the water reach her nipples, it bisected them. Drawing a precise watery line from one to the other, right across the puckering tips, lapping at them with the most erotic, mesmerizing rhythm.

He grew hotter and hotter as he stared, certain the pool water would boil off any second. Somehow, he found the strength to rip his gaze from those perfect breasts and raise his eyes.

She smiled at him. And then she sank into the pool, tossing her shorts over her shoulder as she resurfaced.

Reese swallowed, letting his gaze rove over her body with greedy abandon—and then swallowed again. Because she was totally, incredibly, wonderfully nude. And he had to hand it to her, she was still smiling—right through the fiery blush that covered every square inch of her.

And that aroused him even more.

He reached out to touch the crimson tide darkening her breasts, wondering—not for the first time—if it was as warm as it looked.

It was.

She sucked in her breath as he grazed her nipples, puckering them even tighter. And then she stayed his questing fingers. "One of us seems to be overdressed—" she smiled softly "—and I don't think it's me."

He nodded solemnly. "What do you suggest we do?"

Her smile grew. "I think you should stay absolutely still, Mr. Garrick, and let a professional take over." A wicked gleam entered her eyes as she glanced below the water to his jeans. "After all, I *am* a sailor and this *is* an underwater operation. I'd hate for you to drown."

He nodded again, trying desperately to keep a straight face as she dipped below the surface.

And then it didn't matter.

Because as her fingers found the studs of his fly and popped them one by one, all he had to worry about was trying to breathe. She came up for air briefly as she finished the last stud, and his eyes followed the inky cloud swirling around her as she went back down to peel his pants—underwear and all—down his legs.

He kicked them away and was about to part her hair to see what was taking so long when suddenly he *knew*. The water surrounding his erection turned white-hot, merging with the firm erotic suction, ripping his breath from his lungs in one long hiss as he gave himself up to her intimate kiss.

He fought the temptation to close his eyes, regaining his sanity long enough to wrap his hands around her arms and pull her up. As much as he was loath to stop her, he was afraid for *her* air supply.

He needn't have worried.

He was gasping harder than she was when she surfaced. But their smiles were surely equal. She laughed softly as he stepped backward, into the deeper end of the pool.

"Reese, you're out of my depth. I can't stand there."

That was the point.

He wanted her so far out of her depth she'd have to hold on to him for the rest of her life.

He grinned as he tugged her into his arms and kissed her. "I guess you'll just have to hang on tight." He reached down and plucked the condom he'd felt her palm from his pocket before she stripped him, and tossed it onto the edge of the pool. There was no way he was losing track of that little gem. Not after the trouble he'd had getting it.

He'd told Jade the truth about stopping at a gas station. What he hadn't told her was he'd had to stop *three* times to find one in stock. Heck, he would have stopped at a hundred if that's what it took.

He still couldn't believe she wanted *him*. He'd dreamed

of this moment, fantasized about it. Hell, he'd spent most of last week *praying* for it.

But he also knew now that once would never be enough. Nor would forever. Not even eternity.

Not with Jade.

Because he loved her.

He also knew that for once, he *wanted* it to work. And it would. And they were going to start right now.

By the time he wrapped his arms around her, hers were already around his neck, her fingers twining in his hair as she treaded water. But she wasn't close enough to suit him.

Not by a mile.

He smoothed his hands down her curves, pulling her in tight. He groaned as she tangled her legs with his and slid them slowly up his thighs, the water giving her the buoyancy to wrap them around his hips. What he wouldn't give to delve his fingers into her dark thatch and explore the hot cavern rubbing sensuously against his stomach.

But he couldn't.

Because if he did, he'd be lost.

He also wanted to give her a taste of the pleasure she'd given him, to hear *her* breath hiss from her. Unfortunately, that would prove awkward given their present surroundings. It would have to wait for another time. He grabbed her rump instead, lifting her higher until he could reach her nipples. They were begging to be kissed.

And so he did.

Jade shivered as Reese darted his tongue from one nipple to the other with maddening repetition. Over and over until she was flooded with a steamy moisture that had nothing to do with the pool. Still he kept it up, flicking his tongue— and only his tongue—at the tips, keeping his mouth, and even his lips, from her.

He chuckled as she finally growled in frustration and grabbed his head, yanking him in hard and holding him there. And then mercifully, he settled on one, slowly closing his mouth over it. He sucked and licked every inch he could find—gently at first, then with more and more pressure until he finally clamped down on the whole thing, sucking the nub up to the roof of his mouth as he pulled on it relentlessly. She closed her eyes and dropped her face to his head, burying herself in his wet hair as she finally faced reality.

Reese really was driving her insane.

And he was enjoying every minute of it.

Determined to pay him back, she tried to unhook her legs—but before she could get an inch of water between them, one of his arms came lashing around his back, clamping her legs right back where they were. She tried scooting down so she could rub her bottom over his throbbing erection, and that he allowed.

But no more.

Hell, he was virtually holding her prisoner, turning her into a shuddering slave to his hot mouth and his hard hands as he fed the wave of need churning within her. She smiled through the sensual haze. He wanted to tease, did he?

Fine.

Two could play that game.

And she didn't need her lips or her hands. She dipped her mouth to his ear and gave voice to the passion he was weaving, gasping when he bit into her nipple, moaning softly as he soothed it with his tongue. Her every shudder and groan telling him without words she loved what he was doing to her.

Telling him that she loved *him*.

Soon his arms began to tremble and his fingers slipped back to her bottom. He caressed his way closer and closer to her opening. She hissed as he finally reached it. This time, as he slipped a finger inside, her moans were not for show. She ground her teeth in frustration as he slid his finger back to the entrance, rimming her again and again, teasing and tormenting her to the very brink of fulfillment.

She wasn't exactly sure when she started pleading with

him. Nor was she precisely aware of when he began to move toward the side of the pool. But by the time he reached it and pressed her back into it, she was eternally grateful he had.

Because then he was inside her.

For the life of her, she couldn't have said whether he was wearing the condom or not. Nor did she care.

All she knew was this was how she wanted to die, wrapped in Reese's arms, with his hard, slick body pounding into her, again and again. The water splashing up between them every time he pulled back, cooling her for a breathless moment before he came slamming back.

His harsh breath filled her ears, telling her almost as much as the way he groaned her name, over and over. And then suddenly, she caught the edge of the wave as it reared up again, swelling and growing to tidal proportions. She rode it higher and higher, praying Reese was still with her, calling to him, begging him to follow as she reached for the crest.

And then she was *there,* suspended for a few glorious moments, her entire world swirling and crashing in around her as he locked his arms tight and drove himself in one last time.

And then she was drained.

Drained down to nothingness.

So drained that if he wasn't still holding her as they panted out their last remaining breaths, she would have slipped down into the water and drowned—happily.

She smiled.

A lazy smile, filled with contentment, filled with Reese. It grew as she realized the most horrendously acrid scent in the world had just become her most powerful aphrodisiac.

Chlorine.

And then she laughed.

He lifted his head, smoothing the hair, sweat and water from her brow. "What is it?"

"I just realized I have no idea whether we played roulette.

What's more, I don't care." She grimaced. "And for the DCA of a ship, that's a pretty scary admission."

He grinned. "Does this mean I get a kiss if I tell you I took care of it?" He sighed and dropped his head to hers. "Though how I managed to get that bloody condom on, I'll *never* know. Personally, I think I deserve one of your medals for it."

She smiled in relief and slid her fingers underneath the water, caressing his rear. "You're right, you do deserve a medal. And when you're *up* to it—" her fingers inched around to the front "—I'll show you right where you can hang it."

He drew back slightly. "Why, Ms. Parker, I'm shocked." But he was smiling as he cupped her cheek. "If I'd have known what it took to cool your blushes, I'd have dumped you in my pool weeks ago."

She pinched his waist. "Hey, that's *Lieutenant* Parker to you, Macbeth." Her groan nearly matched his as he shifted her in his arms—but hers wasn't playful.

He froze. "Honey, what is it? Your stitches?"

She shook her head, wanting to tell him it was nothing, but it wasn't. "My back. I think I must have scratched it against the pool when we—uh, well—a few minutes ago." Only she'd been so involved it was just now starting to smart.

He released her instantly—so fast, she slipped straight down into the water. He grabbed her arms and hauled her back up.

She spluttered and coughed for a few seconds, wincing as he slapped her back—right over the sore spot. She hiccuped, adding dryly, "Thanks. Is this how you get rid of all your girlfriends after you've had your fill? By drowning them?"

He shrugged lightly. "I wouldn't know, you're the first one I've had over."

Her breath caught, and the words slipped out before she

could stop them. "But I thought you said you've lived here for three years?"

He smiled, answering both questions, spoken and unspoken, at the same time. "True. So I guess I'd better keep this one alive, huh? Since she's obviously too important to lose."

Reese held his breath, waiting for the meaning behind his words to sink in. He was terrified he'd pushed Jade too hard. But after the most incredible experience of his life, he was afraid of not pushing hard enough. Whoever said there was a world of difference between having sex and making love was absolutely right. Because, while he'd had his fair share of sex in his life, today—right now—was the first time he'd *ever* made love. And he liked it.

A lot.

So much so, he was ready to get out of this pool and carry her into his bed just so he could make sure it hadn't been a fluke. And then he'd make sure again.

And again.

For the rest of their lives.

But first, he wanted to get a look at her back. Lord knew Karin was going to kill him if she ever found out he'd dunked her stitches in water. In his own defense, though, he thought he'd done a damn good job of keeping Jade's head above water once they'd gotten going.

He grinned as he hiked his arms onto the cement and pulled himself up out of the water and then reached back to help Jade out. And then he frowned as he turned her around. Damn. He smoothed his finger alongside the scrapes on her back and cursed beneath his breath again. He thought he'd exerted a hell of a lot more control than this.

"Well? How bad does it look?"

He scooped her into his arms and headed for the house. "Bad enough."

She looped her arms around his neck and snuggled deeper. "You know, I could get used to this. First my head, then my back. What should I bump the next time I want to get you to hold me in your arms?''

He dropped a kiss on her lips as he padded down the hall to his room, then kissed her again as he lowered her to his bed. ''I'll give you a laundry list after I soothe some cream into your back.''

She tightened her arms around his neck and pulled him down on top of her, her wicked smile sending a fresh bolt of lust through him.

Or was that her busy hand?

She cocked her head toward the other two condoms he'd left next to the bottle of wine on his nightstand. ''It's a good thing you have refills handy, because the only soothing I'm interested in right now is the internal kind.''

He tried to protest. Really, he did. But her busy hand suddenly got busier.

And by then, he wholeheartedly agreed.

Reese hitched the towel around his hips as he stopped short in the doorway of his room, his breath catching as he watched Jade pick up the white panties she'd laid out on the bed prior to her shower. She lifted first one dusky leg, then the other, sliding the silk slowly up her thighs, totally unaware that she was turning him on for the hundredth time in two days. Oh, God, she *was* beautiful.

And hot.

He thought about saying something as she picked up the bra. He really couldn't bear to see her cover those perfect breasts. It shouldn't be so hard to watch her conceal them after spending all afternoon stroking and tasting them. But it was. He sighed softly, cursing the evening ahead for the thousandth time since he'd left the shower.

She turned back to his dresser, picking up the brush she'd dug from her bag when he'd finally bothered to go out and retrieve it last night. Of course, he'd only gone to stock up on the refills Karin had so thoughtfully provided. And if he hadn't, who knows how long Jade would have made him wait to see that tantalizing wisp of silk that had come along with them.

He grinned at the memory, growing hard yet again. Yeah, he much preferred keeping the scarlet off her head and on her body. For one thing, it was a hell of a lot more fun peeling it off.

She glanced up at the mirror, her brush in mid-stoke as she finally noticed him watching her, turning as red as the nightie in question as she read his thoughts. He was pretty sure it was his mind she was reading—since the towel concealed the most obvious clue. For a bit longer, anyhow.

"Hi, handsome."

He came up behind her, wrapping his arms around her waist and burying his face into the mass of damp silk trailing down her back. He inhaled her heavenly scent for a few moments, then raised his head and took the brush from her hands.

She sighed as he smoothed the bristles into her scalp and down her back.

"Don't," he choked.

Another sigh, deeper this time. "Hmm?"

"Don't make that sound or we'll never make it out of this room, let alone all the way back to the base and into the Officer's Club." He glided the brush down the glistening strands, clenching the handle as she did it again.

"Why?"

He curled his fingers into her hair and swept it away from her ear as he leaned close. "Because that's the exact sound you make the moment I enter you."

"Is it?" Damn her, she sighed *again*. His hands trembled as she met his gaze in the mirror. "Then don't run your fingers over my hair with that look in your eyes."

"What look?" But he knew.

"The one that says you'd rather be running your hands down my body."

He tossed the brush to the dresser and turned her around in his arms. "You're right," he confessed, just before he kissed her, letting his fingers do what she'd accused him of.

It was a full five minutes before they came up for air.

"Reese?"

"Hmm?"

"If you don't leave me alone, we're going to be late."

This time he sighed—deeply. "I know."

She tiptoed up and kissed his chin. "Don't look so glum. The sooner we get there, the sooner we get back. Who knows? I might even be in the mood for another midnight swim."

That got him motivated. He checked his lust long enough to snag the brush from the dresser and turned her around so he could finish her hair. Half of him still couldn't believe he'd agreed to spend their Saturday night at this damn party in the first place. But the other half knew why. Jade had been persuasive.

He grinned.

Very persuasive.

He ran the brush through her hair again, freezing as she gasped softly. Damn. In his haste, he'd dug the bristles too deeply into her hair, scratching her sore back. He dropped the brush and swept the length of her hair over her shoulder, leaning down to kiss the reddened area above her bra strap. "Honey, I'm sorry. I guess I'm a brute tonight."

She chuckled softly as she turned. "No, you were a brute this *afternoon*. But I don't recall complaining."

Neither did he. He grinned in memory. In fact, if she'd done anything, it was to encourage him. Still, she'd taken quite a beating since she'd known him—*because* of him. He lightly traced the stitches that should be coming out tomorrow.

She caught his hand. "Oh, no, you don't. Don't you go blaming yourself for that again." She frowned and trailed a finger down his abdomen, tracing the faint lines left by her keys. "Besides, if I remember correctly, I got a few licks in myself."

"True, but I don't recall complaining when you took the sting away." He sucked in his breath and grabbed her wrist as her fingers followed the faint trail below the edge of the towel. He lifted her hand and kissed her fingers one by one, smiling as her lids lowered. "But you never did tell me who taught you that particular move."

Please, God, let it be her father and not *Jeff*. He'd hate to be beholden to his ghostly nemesis.

She smiled. "Greg."

"Greg? As in Lieutenant *Coffey?*"

"The one and the same. Hey, don't look so surprised. He and some of the other guys in my ROTC unit gathered up the women and taught us a few things after we had a rape on campus."

Reese felt his jaw set. Damn, right now being in debt to Coffey sat just about as well in his craw as being in debt to Jeff. Especially after that little impromptu search he'd conducted during sea-and-anchor detail early yesterday morning. He glanced back at Jade—only to panic. She was looking at him funny. Which meant he needed to divert whatever thoughts his face had revealed.

Now.

Before she got suspicious. He did not need to put her in the position of lying to one of her best friends tonight. Not if he could avoid it.

He took a deep breath, grasping the only other topic he could find in his head. "So was Jeff one of the other guys who helped the women out?"

For a moment she just stood there.

And then she blinked.

He clenched his fingers together as he waited for her to say something—anything. Oh, God, what if she didn't say what he wanted? What if she didn't laugh the man off and tell her he'd never meant anything to her? Or worse, what if she said something that sounded like he still did mean something?

"What exactly do you know about Jeff?"

Crap. That note didn't bode well. He took a deep breath and formed his next words with extreme care. "Not much. Why?"

Her shoulders relaxed slightly. "Thank God, I was so sure Dillon had already gotten to you with Jeff's version of events."

He nearly choked at that. *Dillon?* The guy had known something about Jade all along, something that *might* have made pursuing her easier, and he'd kept it to himself? He was going to kill the bastard when the case was over, anyway.

Reese cupped her cheek. "Dillon and I never got beyond small talk where you were concerned."

Her eyes closed in relief.

Yeah, he was definitely going to murder the man. "You want to tell me about it?"

She opened her eyes. "No." But then she shrugged. "What the heck, you could hear the story from Coffey just as easily as from Dillon. Though I like to think Greg would be a little kinder in the telling." She picked up the green tank dress from the bed and slipped the soft cotton over her head. It skirted low on her calves as she sighed. "There's not really much to tell. Jeff was in ROTC, too. We met our freshman year, we dated, we fell in love, we planned to marry."

He stood there, rigid, as each razor-sharp sword sliced into his gut, trying to keep the agony from his voice. "And then?"

She pulled her hair back and started to braid it. The anguish in his gut eased slightly as he realized she was keeping her hands busy so she could get through this. He pulled her fingers from her hair and squeezed them. "You don't have to tell me this."

She smiled at him softly, almost regretfully. "Yeah, I think I do. For me."

He nodded. "Okay. But will you leave your hair down? For *me?*"

She stared at him for a few moments—the decision warring in her gaze—and then nodded. "Okay."

He caressed her cheek. "You really don't have to tell me."

She took a deep breath and ignored him. "Anyway, I didn't know Jeff was seeing another girl—one of the Anchorettes—on the side."

Now there was one he'd never heard. "Anchor*what's?*"

She smiled. "That's what I said during freshman orientation. It's sort of a little sister sorority for the midshipmen—emphasis on *men*—at the University of Texas at Austin. They're supposed to bake cookies and date the guys."

He didn't bother hiding his disgust. "Swell."

She laughed. "Isn't it?" Then her smile faded altogether.

He nudged her gently. "So you called off the marriage because Jeff was sleeping with another woman?"

She shook her head. "Actually, I didn't find he was doing that until a few weeks later. No, I broke off the engagement because he told me I had to make a choice—I could marry him or I could join the Navy."

"What?"

"He told me later he knew I didn't love him enough, that I'd never be able to put any man before the fleet." She sighed. "I guess he was right."

Reese stood there, rocked to his core as Jade pulled his world out from under him and slammed it into the garbage. His blood was thundering so loudly he could barely hear. And he certainly couldn't speak.

He was dimly aware of her telling him she had to touch up her face in the bathroom. He nodded numbly as she passed, still rooted to the spot, trying desperately to suck up the agony as reality smashed into his hopes and dreams grinding them into dust as he realized the woman he loved more than life itself would never marry him.

Chapter 15

"Well, it's about time you two showed. I was beginning to think you were trying to use the whole box by Monday."

Reese snagged a clean plate from the buffet table and turned to Karin, his smile real for the first time since he'd arrived. "We're working on it. And, by the way, thanks."

Karin laughed as she took the plate from him. "Good— and you're welcome." She loaded on the jumbo shrimp as he retrieved another. "I suppose I should warn you, the Captain trapped your date five minutes ago. If you want another crack at that box tonight, you'll wait five more and then spring her." She snared a champagne flute and took a sip. "So tell me, just how *did* you get Jade to come to this shindig?"

Huh? He shook his head, more than a little confused. "I don't understand—*she* invited *me*. Why does everyone keep thinking it's the other way around?"

Karin choked, slamming the flute back down to the buffet as he patted her back. "Sorry, I could have sworn you said *Jade* asked you to come tonight."

"I did." Wasn't that the way it worked? Didn't the social scene go with the job? Sucking up to the brass, pressing the flesh, anything and everything to get promoted?

"*Jade* asked *you?*" She shook her head slowly. "We can't be talking about the same woman."

She seemed so certain, he glanced across the room to where Jade was standing with the Captain and now the *Baddager*'s executive officer. He stared in shock and then stared some more.

Damned, if Karin wasn't right.

Even from here, he could see her eyes glaze over. She kept blinking them, as if she knew and was trying her damnedest not to let the boredom show. Her relief when the Supply Officer interrupted was practically palpable—at least to him. Reese grinned, because he had to agree. Snoozing through your Captain's sea stories probably wasn't the recommended path to promotion.

But still, how could Jade *not* get off on this crap? Hell, his old man had *lived* for it. Still did. His breath caught as her gaze found his. There was no mistaking the relief in her eyes, nor the look she sent him.

Save me!

Was it possible? Could she really have nothing more in common with his father than the uniform? He'd thought so—until she'd told him about Jeff. Afterward, he wasn't so sure. Now he didn't know *what* to think. All he knew was he couldn't marry her if the Navy came first. He just couldn't. Because he wouldn't survive.

Not this time.

He glanced back at Jade. She was smiling at him now, the look in her eyes definitely giving him hope.

I want you. Now. He heard the words as clearly as if she'd shouted them.

Karin tapped his arm. "Reese?"

He couldn't seem to break his gaze away as Jade made

her excuses to the Captain and wove a path to him. "Sorry, what did you say?"

He heard Karin sigh. "I asked if you were okay."

He nodded, still watching Jade, smiling when she tossed him a look of total exasperation as someone else stopped her. "Yup." He was just fine—and getting better by the second.

"Damn."

He finally glanced down as Karin's beeper went off.

She dug through her purse and groaned. "Rats, it's the ship. Tell Jade I had to go, will you? I've got a patient in sick bay I need to admit to the base hospital."

"Sure thing." He turned back to the buffet as she left, intent on loading a plate for Jade. Maybe he could use it as an excuse to get her away from the Chief Engineer. They needed to talk. About Jeff—and whether or not she really believed what she'd said.

"I think you're going to need the entire Fifth Fleet to help you eat that." Evidently she'd managed to escape without his help.

He smiled as he piled on another shrimp and turned. "Nope, you do. It's yours."

She shook her head, laughing as she stared at the plate. "Reese, there is no way I can finish all that."

He grinned. "Sure you can. And you'd better eat every bite. I don't want you fainting on me again." His grin spread as indignation competed with the pink he loved so well.

"Hey, I did *not* faint. I was *tired.* Good grief, you ought to know. You're the one who wore me out."

His grin turned downright wicked as he heaped another spoonful and passed her the plate before snagging a flute of champagne for her as well. "Then buck up and eat, because I plan on wearing you out again—and *again.*"

He bit back a groan as her gaze darkened. Hell, this was

not the place to be having the fantasy he was having. Because he couldn't do a damn thing about it.

Evidently Jade agreed, because her breath came out on a whoosh before she changed the subject. "So what did Karin have to say?"

He tucked the fantasy away for later and smiled. "She offered to refill the box for us tomorrow if we need it."

God, he loved that blush.

"Relax, I told her we'd need a week at least."

He chuckled around the shrimp she shoved into his mouth, then choked as she sucked a drop of cocktail sauce off her finger. Several lines of division later, he opted for changing the subject himself. "Actually, Karin seemed surprised to see us here. You especially."

Jade laughed. "Surprised? That's it, huh? And to think I was half-afraid to show in case she had a heart attack."

By God, it was true. But just to be sure, he pushed it. "You really *don't* want to be here?"

Her smile was tiny, yet full of promise as she leaned close to whisper, "Where would you rather be? Here or home in bed?"

She had to ask? He stared at her for several seconds, thoroughly baffled. "If you don't want to be here and I don't want to be here, *why* are we here?"

"Because of the case."

"The what?"

She chuckled. "Your case. You remember? Greg Coffey? Mike Dillon? The whole reason you came aboard. I haven't seen them yet, but they're bound to show—they both eat this garbage up. Anyway, I thought you might discover some clue tonight." She shrugged, almost in embarrassment now. "Well, you never know."

He was floored. She'd brought him here—somewhere she didn't want to be—simply because she thought it *might* help him solve his case? If he wasn't already in love with her, he'd be falling right now. As it was, he just wanted to get out of here. He wanted to take her home and celebrate all night long.

Because she *wasn't* his father.

He only regretted it had taken this damn party to force him to see it. Jeff was wrong, Jade could put a man before the Fleet. She'd been doing it all weekend. More important, even with all this Navy brass floating around, she'd been doing it all night. Whether she realized it or not, she *had* been putting him first.

And he intended to stay there.

"Reese?"

He stared down at her, putting his heart into his smile. "Hmm?"

She took a deep breath and smiled back. "Well, I was going to ask what you were thinking about so hard, but I think I have the answer."

"Oh, honey, you don't know the half of it." He took her plate and slapped it on the table, then reached for her flute. "Let's go and I'll explain it to you on the way home."

"*Chester?* Is that you?"

Damn!

Reese nearly snapped the crystal in two. For a split second he considered just grabbing Jade by the elbow and hustling her out of the club. But it was too late; she was already turning toward a voice from his nightmares.

He had to do something. Now. But what?

Maybe he could bluster his way through? Cut the man off at the crucial spot. *Anything,* just to keep the truth quiet a few more hours. Until he could tell her himself. And he would, orders or no orders. Because it was getting too damn dicey as it was.

"Chester?"

Slowly, he turned and forced a smile. "Hey, there, Admiral."

Admiral Moore's craggy face split into a grin. "Son of a

gun, it *is* you, Chester! And I've told you before, the name is Dan.''

He told himself Jade's stiffening was just surprise. Surprise to finally learn what the *C* stood for—maybe even surprise to learn he was on a first-name basis with an admiral.

She had *not* guessed the rest.

Relax, buddy.

If she hadn't made the connection by now, she wasn't bound to. Unless someone shoved her face into it. He clenched his fingers around the stem of the flute, praying Dan Moore wouldn't be the one to shove her face into it. He took a deep breath, combing his brain for some innocuous comment that would keep him out of the minefield.

''So, how is the old goat?''

He almost laughed in relief. How the hell should he know? Except for that clipped call the morning he checked aboard the *Baddager,* he hadn't heard from his father in three years. And then he'd only called to warn him to keep his identity a secret.

As if he wasn't smart enough to figure that one out on his own. ''Far as I know, he's just fine. How about yourself?'' *Smooth, buddy, keep it smooth.* He glanced around. ''I don't see Alice.''

The admiral laughed. ''Nah, she never could stand these things. I'm just here to congratulate Captain Kennings on his promotion.'' The man's gaze took in a clearly befuddled Jade—who so far had remained silent.

Thank God.

''So how about you, Chester? I don't see your father, so you must be on your own—unless this young lady is the reason?''

Jade offered her hand. ''Lieutenant Jade Parker, DCA, *USS Baddager.*''

Grinning, the admiral returned her shake. ''Well, I'll be damned. The DCAs are getting prettier every year.''

She smiled back—but her eyes were cool. "Thank you, sir."

Reese was more than happy to take the hint. He shifted the champagne flute to his left hand before cupping her elbow. "Well, sir, we have to mingle. It's been nice seeing you again."

"Great to see you, too, son. Almost like old times. Well, you take care—and tell that old sea dog of a father to get off his lofty perch and give me a call sometime. I'm over at SURFPAC."

"*Sea* dog?"

Ah, damn. He'd been so *close.* He nearly snapped the stem again. Hell, it was only a matter of time now. It was the "sea dog" that did it. And now that she knew his dad was a sailor, she was bound to make the next connection. His father was so high up in her chain of command, she'd have to be an idiot not to.

And Jade was not an idiot.

The admiral grinned. "Chester didn't tell you?"

Her smile was frozen in place as she turned to glare up at him. It thawed only slightly as she turned back to the admiral. "No, it seems *Chester* left a few things out."

"Well, hell, Lieutenant, it's no wonder. Seems Chester's a bigger chip off the old block than his father suspected. He used to do the same thing, you know." He leaned over to confide, "Liked to know the ladies were after him and not his old man's reputation."

Reese stiffened. "*Thank you,* Admiral. I think I can take it from here." There was no mistake regarding his tone. He didn't mean for there to be.

The admiral took the hint and left.

Reese heaved a sigh as he turned to face the music, trying to figure out how to put the truth into words. How to keep Jade from feeling as though all the lessons and insight she'd given so freely were *not* for naught. To keep her from feeling like a fool.

He needn't have bothered.

She *knew*.

"If you'll excuse me, I have a hail and farewell I need to return to."

Like hell, she did. He clamped down on her elbow. "Oh, no, you don't. You're going to stay right here while I explain."

Oh, man, was she furious. If she wasn't careful, that expression was going to freeze right on her face.

"Please *do*. Please explain why you've been lying to me for weeks. Please explain why you continued to play the naval idiot savant even after you told me your real name. Please explain why you didn't bother telling me I was sleeping with *my boss's son*."

Nope, no one could inject venom into a whisper like Jade. However, she was off on that last one. And it irked him. Enough for him to push it. "My father is *not* your boss."

"I beg your pardon, *Mr. Garrick,* but he most certainly is. *Admiral Arthur H. Garrick* is Commander Fifth Fleet and *that*—though several times removed—makes him my boss. Or did you fail to notice his striking portrait on the quarterdeck of my ship—*each and every time you passed it?*"

He brandished the champagne flute. "Okay, okay. I'll give you that. But come on, there are four fleet admirals. Not only that, it's no secret my father has a son who's DEA. If I'd told you my dad was Navy, exactly how long do you think it would have taken you—or anyone else on the ship— to figure out who he was? And then where would my cover have been?"

"That's not the point and you know it. You trusted me with the rest, why not this?"

She had him there. But this wasn't the place to get into his life history—nor the insecurities that stemmed from it. So he offered the only other argument he could, praying she'd understand. "Because that information was on a need-to-know basis. You're an officer, Jade. Surely, you can understand. Telling you was a risk I wasn't allowed to take.''

''A risk? Now you're telling me I'm a *risk?*'' She tried jerking her arm from his hand, but he refused to let her go.

He sighed. ''That's not what I said and you know it.''

''You're right, I do know it. I also know exactly how you feel about your father's family *business.*'' She bit the last word out as she tried jerking away again. ''Now, if you'll excuse me, I need to be somewhere else.''

''I'll take you.''

''Let me go.'' It came through clenched teeth.

''Jade—''

''I believe the lady asked you to release her arm.''

Reese ground his teeth as he glanced up. ''Stay out of this, Coffey.''

Lieutenant Coffey shook his head. ''I don't think so. Now, release her before I have to help you.''

Reese smiled grimly. Hell, he'd like to see him try. Unfortunately, the only thing he'd accomplish by smashing the man's face in would be to blow his case. And risk ticking Jade off even further than she already was. No, he'd have to bide his time. He'd give her a while to cool off and then they'd talk on the way home. She'd have to—her car was still at his place.

He stared down at Jade. ''We'll talk later.''

She jerked free and linked her hand into Coffey's crooked arm. ''Don't count on it.'' And then she left.

A second later he stared down at the stem of the champagne flute as it finally snapped.

''So are you going to tell me what that was all about?''

Jade stared up at the man who'd now helped her through two of the biggest heartaches of her life and shook her head. Boy, had she been wrong. Wrong about Jeff and wrong about Reese.

How could one woman be so *ignorant* when it came to

men? Heck, she was so good at picking the wrong men, she ought to be teaching the class. She could see the syllabus now: Incompatibility 101. Nope, better make that 401—this was definitely a senior-level course.

"You want to leave?"

Again, she shook her head. Perversely this time. She didn't know why she was still here. Heck, she'd done her duty, she could be long gone by now. She didn't even need Greg's help to do it. All she had to do was pick up the phone in the lobby and call a cab. Or walk, for that matter. She was already on base—the ship was fifteen minutes away at worst on foot.

But no, she'd rather stay here. Where else could she stand in a corner and watch Reese seethe? And he was seething. The amusing part was, he was glaring at Greg, not her. Well, let him glare. She might be a lousy judge of lovers, but she had a damn good head on her shoulders when it came to friends. Best friends.

God, why hadn't she accepted Greg's offer for a date all those years ago? Before they'd fallen in as friends and decided they'd be better off as buddies—because they thought it would last longer. Well, see? It *had*. Nine years longer. Long enough for her to know whom to trust.

And it wasn't Reese Garrick, that was for damn sure.

Coffey shook his head. "Okay, you don't want to talk about it and you don't want to go. What *do* you want?"

She pushed her hair over her shoulder and sighed. "I wish I knew."

"Will you be okay for a minute? I'm going to head over to the buffet and grab some champagne—I think the toasts and roasts are about to start."

She nodded absently, her gaze already slipping back to Reese. "Sure. Grab one for me, too."

"Will do."

She yanked her gaze away from Reese and turned to stare out the window beside her. It was one thing to glance his way when Greg was standing next to her, quite another when she was by herself. For one thing, she didn't need him thinking she was a lovesick puppy. Because she wasn't.

Who you trying to convince, Missy?

She sighed, her gaze skimming the surf breaking over the beach ten yards away. Dad was right, she was a liar. Only she was worse than lovesick. She felt like a dog who'd been kicked by its master and then asked to lick his hand.

Did Reese honestly think his feelings about the Navy wouldn't matter? And she *did* remember the things he'd said about his dad—and his *business.* She was sorry he'd had such a lousy father, but didn't he realize it wasn't the Navy's fault? The Navy didn't make bad fathers, people did. Surely he wasn't naive enough to think the man would have put Ward Cleaver to shame if he'd just been in another line of work, did he?

She rubbed her arms as a chill swept through her. Then again, maybe that was the real problem. Maybe his pain ran so deep he *did* believe it. Or at least wanted to. And where would that leave her? Out in the cold, most likely.

She felt her sigh all the way down in her toes.

"Do you want to talk about it?"

Reese.

"No."

He sighed when she refused to turn around. "Not here, not now, or not with me?"

"All of the above."

"Honey, please—"

"Well, I'll be damned, Mack. You did it."

She didn't need to turn around to know Reese stiffened—she could feel it.

"Get lost, Dillon."

"Take it easy, buddy. You provided the proof, I'm just man enough to admit when I lost and pay up."

Dillon a man? Now there was an oxymoron. She snorted and turned around, despite herself. "Okay, Mike, I give.

What are you trying to say? And make it quick, the Captain's about to start.''

"Ah, the ice princess speaks."

"*Spill it,* or do what he says—'' she jerked her head toward Reese ''—and get lost.''

Dillon's brow furrowed as he tsked to Reese. "Such a sweet disposition. You know, if she was a horse, you'd have to shoot her.'' He shrugged. "But it's your love life, buddy. And you *did* get her hair down. I'll drop the hundred bucks off Monday.''

"Do it, and I'll shove it up your a—''

"*Excuse me?*'' She gaped at them for several moments, before she recovered enough to narrow her glare on Reese. "You *bet* on me? And with *him?*''

She caught Dillon's sanctimonious smirk out of the corner of her eye. "Guess that's my cue. Bye.''

She kept her stare pinned to Reese. *"Well?"* She gave him all of two seconds to answer before she spun around and marched off.

Reese reached for Jade's arm as she stalked away—and missed. *Damn.* He nearly growled as he shoved his hands through his hair, torn between wanting to follow her and wanting to hunt Dillon down with an ax—a well-honed ax.

He didn't have a chance to do either. Because Jade's Captain, true to his impeccable timing, chose that particular moment to hail him into the wardroom. He froze as some hundred and fifty-odd pairs of eyes turned to stare at him.

Unfortunately, he hadn't heard the Captain's words, so he had no idea how to respond. Several seconds of awkward silence stretched to several more. And then, mercifully, someone else stepped up to the microphone.

Coffey.

"I'm afraid you've embarrassed Mack with your compliments, Captain. I'm sure he'll return the favor when he fills his father, *Admiral Garrick,* in on the best repair ship in the fleet.''

Had Coffey overheard—or was he the one?

For a split second, Reese thought he'd actually cursed out loud. But he couldn't have. Because if he had, everyone would be staring at him and not Coffey. And then they were. One by one, the entire room turned to him, stunned. In fact, he was the only one who didn't seem surprised.

And that was probably because he was *livid.*

He crushed his hands into fists as he tried to divert the rage coursing through him, knowing full well that no matter what the film critics said, tonight he deserved an Oscar. Because *somehow* he managed a smile. It even felt real. But it wasn't. And then his beeper went off.

He ripped it off his waistband as someone called out, "Must be your agent."

He forced his smile into a grin as he glanced down. And then it became real. TJ. And from the code his partner had attached, he was on to something.

Something big.

"It is. Sorry, guys, gotta take this. There's a role I've been waiting to hear about." He was across the room and at the lobby pay phone in twenty seconds flat. Another ten, and his call had gone through and TJ was picking up.

"Reese here. What do you have?"

"Hola, amigo. Your lady came in on the money."

Reese gripped the receiver. "How so? And be quick, I could have an audience any minute."

"I hear you. Okay, here's the lowdown. One of the cruisers on the list *did* run her reactor out of specs, just as Jade suspected."

He whistled.

"It gets better. I finally got hold of the cruiser's personnel records and did a cross-check against your boys."

"And?" He clamped down on the cord. *Please, God, let it be him.*

"Seems Dillon sowed his childhood oats in the same field as two guys off the cruiser—and one of *them* works in the reactor. Also, we got a match off the partial print you took off the key. Again, Dillon's.''

Yes! ''How soon—''

TJ chuckled. ''Way ahead of you, *compadre.* As soon as the judge signs the warrant, I'll beep you.''

''Great. Anything else?''

Another chuckle, this one knowing. ''When do I get to meet her?''

''Soon.'' And that was a promise. He hung up.

''Guess you'll be leaving now—right, Mack? Or should I say, *Mr. Garrick?*''

Reese held his fist in check as he spun around to face Coffey. Now was *not* the time. ''Where's Jade?''

There was a wealth of insolence in Coffey's shrug. ''Sorry. I'm just her friend, not her keeper. I leave the man-handling and lying to bastards like you.''

Okay, it was time.

He took two steps forward and slammed Coffey up against the wall before the guy had a chance to breathe. Then he was two centimeters away, glaring into pure shock as he ground his request out again. *''Where is she?''*

Chapter 16

Jade stopped at the end of the driveway to the Officer's Club and waited for the car behind to pull onto the road. It pulled up alongside her instead. Tucking her purse under her arm, she rounded on it, more than ready for battle if it was Reese. But it wasn't.

Unfortunately, it was worse.

The red Mustang's passenger window hummed as it lowered. "Well, well. Looks like Little Bo Peep has lost her sheep—and her ride back to the pasture as well."

"Get lost, Dillon." She kept walking, nearly groaning as a fat raindrop fell from the sky onto her face and rolled down her cheek. Just peachy. Then again, it was rather poetic, wasn't it? Or was that pathetic?

Dillon kept pace with her as he leaned across the front seat to pop the door. "Get in. I'll give you a lift back to the ship."

She stopped, glaring at the door, then over to him. "Why? Since when have you gone out of your way to help me?"

Apparently Dillon thought that was amusing as hell. His

laughter barked out. "Never. And don't get any ideas, either. It's on the way. Now, are you getting in or not?" He glanced at the windshield as a handful of droplets splattered onto it. "You've got two seconds to make up your mind."

Jade glowered at him for the first second, and then shrugged as she grabbed the handle and slipped inside. What the hell. As far as she could tell she had three choices. She could ride with Dillon, walk and get soaked, or go back and call a cab—and risk running into Reese again. For once Dillon was the lesser evil.

"I said, *where* is Jade?" Reese tightened his grip on Coffey's shirt, holding him against the wall as he cut the man's oxygen supply in half. "I'm not going to repeat myself."

He had to give the guy credit. Coffey managed to glare back even as his face lost color. "She *left.* I tried to give her a ride, but she said no. I don't know where she is."

Damn. She was probably already in a cab on her way to the house to grab her stuff. At least she was safe. He'd just have to wait until after he served the warrant to track her down.

That left Dillon.

He hadn't seen him since Coffey took it upon himself to blow his cover from here to Japan. He tightened his grip on Coffey's shirt. "Where's Dillon?"

"He left, too. I think he's got plans tonight. Why?"

"Damn!" Reese snapped his head back up. "Is he headed back to the ship?"

"What's it to you?" The moment he loosened his grip, Coffey twisted his collar free. "What the hell is your problem, Mack?"

Reese dug his wallet out of his boot, opened it and slammed it up against the wall next to Coffey's head. "The name is Reese Garrick and you damn well know it. And my problem is *you.* That and the fact that you just blew my cover clear out of the water."

In his own defense, Coffey turned white, then red as he stared at the DEA credentials. "Cripes, man. I had no idea."

Reese grimaced as he jammed his wallet into his back pocket. "I believe that was the point. Now, *where* was Dillon headed?"

"The ship, I think. Why?" He stiffened. "*Good God,* you don't think Dillon's involved in drugs, do you?"

"I don't think, I *know.* Listen, I need you to get me into the NSF. I've got a search warrant showing up any minute, but I can't afford to wait. After your little announcement, he'll probably move the heroin tonight."

Reese had the satisfaction of watching the remaining color drain from Coffey's face. Along with the last of his suspicions about the guy. "*Heroin?* You're telling me Dillon's got *heroin* in my shop?"

Nope, there was no way the guy could fake that. Still, he had one more question before he was certain. "When did you give Dillon the combination to the safe in your stateroom?"

"During the last deployment. Why? Wait a minute, how did *you* know Mike had the combination to my safe?"

Reese twisted out a smile. "Because he left me a present in it. The key to my stateroom. It also explains why that key was the only thing in it."

Coffey's eyes narrowed to slits. "Son of a bitch, the bastard tried to set me up, didn't he?"

"Looks that way."

"I'm gonna kill—"

"Stand in line. But first, the codes."

He stiffened as Coffey shook his head. "Sorry, I can't. Relax. I said I couldn't give them to you, but I *can* go with you."

Good enough. "Let's go." He yanked his car keys from his pocket and was halfway out of the club before Coffey could respond.

* * *

Jade breathed a sigh of relief as they finally pulled into the parking lot beside the pier. If she had to sit and listen to Dillon wax poetic about his latest conquest for one more minute, she was going to scream. At least the rain had let up. She grabbed the door handle and practically scrambled out of the car as he pulled into a slot. "Thanks, I owe you."

He grinned, knowing full well it irked her. "Don't sound too grateful, I'm liable to go into a diabetic coma."

She slammed the door as he got out. "Drop dead, Mike."

He laughed as he fell into step beside her. "Now, there's the viper I've come to detest. But don't loose all your venom on me. I'm sure you'll want to save a little for Mr. Garrick."

She stopped just shy of the guard shack at the end of the pier and gaped at him. "What…how…?"

A shiver ran down her spine as Dillon's eyes narrowed. "So you did know who he was all along. And here I figured you were just sleeping your way to the top."

Jade was still too shocked to take the bait. She flashed her military ID at the guard out of habit, pulling herself together as the Petty Officer saluted them through. "How did *you* find out?"

"By that, I take it you missed Coffey's little announcement."

"*What?*" *Greg* blew Reese's cover? Why? Why would he *do* that? Unless… Oh, God, did that mean *he* was the one?

Dillon stuffed his hands into his jacket pockets. "Hell, Jade, looks like you're not in the loop anymore, doesn't it?"

She managed to shake her head as they reached the base of the brow, still stunned by the implications of Coffey's betrayal. "Anymore? What *are* you talking about?"

Dillon grabbed her arm and nudged her up the metal steps. "I'm talking about your boyfriend and his *real* job."

She stopped a third of the way up, panic setting in as she

tried—and failed—to twist her arm from his grip. "What do you think you're doing?"

"Taking care of loose ends." His lips thinned as he jerked his chin up at the ship.

"*Oh, my, God.* It's not Greg. It's you."

He actually smiled. "Congratulations, there is a brain in that head. I was beginning to wonder."

Panic turned to dread as she glanced up the steep brow. The quarterdeck was clearly lit—but it was empty. The Officer of the Deck and his Petty Officer must be inside the shack. She sucked in her breath as Dillon's fingers dug into her elbow.

"Awww, does that hurt?" His smile widened. "Good. Now, listen up. You're going to smile at the Officer of the Deck and check aboard like nothing's wrong. Understand?" He jabbed something hard into her side. "Because if you don't, I'm going to have to give the Petty Officer of the Watch another chance to qualify with his .45—and I don't plan on informing him first. You got me?"

"You know, Mike, I always knew you were an ass." She spit the words into his face—and then grunted as he crammed the barrel of the gun into her waist. At least, she assumed it was a gun. And with two innocent sailors at the top, she wasn't taking any chances. "Yeah, I got you."

"See? The perfect little sailor. I knew you could follow orders." As soon as they were alone, she was going to rip that smirk off his face—with her bare hands.

But what was she supposed to do until then? Hope Reese came after her? Not after the way she'd skipped out. And even if he wanted to, he'd probably assume she went back to his house for her car. But, dammit, she had to do something!

But what?

Coffey pointed to a red Mustang parked near the entrance to the pier. "*There.* That's Dillon's car."

Reese nodded as he pulled his Bronco up alongside and killed the engine. He reached down into his boot and pulled out his Glock, double-checking the magazine more out of habit then necessity.

"Damn, you mean business."

He nodded grimly as he glanced across the cab. "I always do."

Coffey cocked his head at the pistol. "Jade know about that?"

"Yes." He returned the gun to his boot.

Coffey whistled. "And you still didn't tell her about your dad? You *do* like to live dangerously."

Reese slammed the door and dug his ship's pass out of Mack's wallet. "Not a word unless I give it." No sense jump-starting the grapevine until it was time to harvest.

"Understood." Coffey held up his ID as Reese flashed the pass. "But when this is done, you might want to consider giving the rest of that explanation to Jade. Including the three words she's waiting to hear."

His stride faltered as he stared at Coffey in shock. How the hell did he—

"It doesn't take a genius to figure it out. Besides, I know her, remember? She wouldn't feel nearly so betrayed if she didn't love you." Coffey waved him on ahead as they reached the brow. "Hell, she wasn't that mad when she found out Jeff was doing the horizontal tango on someone else's dance card."

Oh, man, that last should *not* make him feel so damn good. But it did. Because if Coffey was right, and Jade was that upset—it could only mean she loved him. And *that* meant they could survive his stupidity. Hell, it meant they could survive anything.

He reached the top of the brow, remembering just in time not to face the rear of the ship. Since the colors came down at sunset, there was no flag to honor.

"Sir, request permission to come aboard."

"Permission granted." Lieutenant Shale saluted Coffey aboard. "How was the Hail and Farewell?"

Coffey grinned. "Great. Hey, is Mike still aboard?"

Shale nodded. "Unless he left by the Midships brow. Want me to call down and see?"

Coffey shook his head. "That's okay. I'll do it."

Reese followed both officers to the guard shack but hung back as they entered, staring at the Chain of Command board hanging next to the oval door. Yup, there was Dad, all right. But other than the eyes, you wouldn't know it. And then, only if you were looking. He turned away as Coffey left the shack.

"He's still aboard, but not in his stateroom. I called down. I didn't think you'd want me phoning the NSF."

Reese nodded. "Good move." He wanted to keep the element of surprise as long as possible. Something caught his eye as Coffey went to stuff his hand in his pocket. He clapped his fingers around his wrist and tugged it up.

"Do you mind?"

His heart nearly pounded out of his chest as he stared at the necklace in shock. Jade's necklace. He'd know that heart anywhere. Especially since he'd spent a good deal of last night and this morning running his fingers over it as they lay in bed, talking. His gut nearly imploded with the implications.

Relax, buddy. It didn't mean she was with Dillon. Just that she was on board. He took a deep breath. "Where did you get that?"

Coffey was staring at him as if he'd pulled out his Glock and begun firing. "It was caught on the platform. Shale asked me to drop it by Medical. Apparently Karin dropped it when she came aboard tonight."

"That's not Karin's—it's Jade's."

"No, it isn't." Both he and Coffey turned to Shale, who was pointing at the chain. "I asked her just before she and

Dillon headed inside. She said it wasn't hers, but she'd seen it on Karin.''

"Crap!'' He and Coffey cursed simultaneously.

Reese ripped his badge out of his pocket and shoved it at Shale. "Special Agent Reese Garrick, DEA. Secure the ship. Do *not* let Lieutenant Dillon leave.'' He dug a card out of the wallet and slapped it into Shale's palm. "Call TJ Vasquez at this number. Tell him I need backup. *Now*.''

Coffey shoved the necklace into his pocket. "Damn, we can't even call a security alert. Dillon knows the routine. Shale, I'll contact the Command Duty Officer personally and get him to open the weapon's locker.''

"The codes.''

This time, Coffey didn't hesitate. He repeated them twice before Reese nodded and raced down to the NSF, praying all the way.

Jade shoved another package of heroin into the black carryall. "You'll never get away with it.'' *Come on, Dad, help me out here. I need you.*

Stay calm, honey, just stay calm. I'm on my way.

Jade stiffened. That was *not* her father's voice. It was Reese's! What the hell was *he* doing in her head? And where was her father?

Never mind. Just keep your wits about you and look for an opening. I know you can do it, baby. I've seen you stare down an entire ship on fire.

Stunned, she almost turned around to look for him, certain he was in the room. His voice was that clear, that *real*. But, of course, that was ridiculous. Her mind was playing tricks on her. It had to be.

Dillon laughed. "Sure, I'll get away with it. I'll be so far south by morning, lover boy will have to take the Berlitz crash course in Spanish to track me down. And that's too bad, because he won't have the time. He'll be too busy looking for you.'' He jammed the tip of his pistol into her back. "Now, hurry up. I've got a border to cross and a tequila to order."

Jade yanked another package of heroin out of the ship-to-ship transfer box as Reese's chuckle echoed in her brain.

Shows how much he knows. I already speak Spanish. Now, slow down. I want you to get him mad. If he's mad, he'll make a mistake, create an opening. And then you take it, okay?

What the hell was going on? She slowly reached for another mottled brown package and gave up wondering why her subconscious was projecting Reese's voice into her head. It didn't matter. All that mattered was that by doing so, she was remaining calm. And she was thinking.

Get Dillon mad?

Yeah, she could handle that. And Reese—rather her unconscious—was right, moving at sub-snail speed would be the perfect place to start. She just wished having his voice in her head when she needed it didn't emphasize that *she* hadn't been there for him when he needed her.

When Greg blew his cover.

Stop it, honey. Don't go there, not now. It doesn't matter. All that matters is you get through this.

But it did matter. It mattered because she'd let her memories of Jeff's betrayal get in the way of giving Reese the chance to explain.

She sucked in her breath as Dillon smacked his hand across the back of her head—hard. "I said, hurry up."

She ground her teeth and picked up another kilo, or unit—or whatever the heck Reese called it—and slowly placed it in the bag.

Unit. Now, start getting his goat. Gradually at first, so he doesn't suspect. And then I want you to blister him. Come on, baby, I know you can do it. I've had a taste of your acid a time or two myself.

Man, she had a healthy imagination. Jade laid the unit on top of the others and slid it to the side. "So why'd you do it, Mike? Still ticked off at Uncle Sam for not recognizing your superior intellect?'' Her tone left no doubt she found him lacking there as well. ''Still sucking your thumb and mewling because you got stuck on a repair ship instead of getting an aircraft carrier?''

She bit back a groan as he smacked her head again—harder this time.

She heard Reese growl. *I'll kill the bastard for that.*

''I'll take that as a yes.''

''Shut up, bitch.''

She pulled the last package out of the box. ''Bitch?'' She managed a laugh. ''You've got a gun to my head and that's the best you can come up with?'' She sighed. ''I guess it's no surprise. I mean, you never did think well under pressure, did you?'' A grunt finally escaped as he whaled on her head—with the butt of the gun this time. Her head began to throb in concert with her screaming nerves.

Another growl, followed by a string of curses that would have made her chief blush. *I'm going to strangle him with my bare hands.*

Dillon smacked her again and snarled, ''What the hell are you trying to do, get me to kill you here?''

She closed her eyes until the nausea and dizziness ebbed. No, she had no intention of dying. Here or anywhere else. But it was working. Dillon was mad.

But not mad enough.

She needed him so pissed he wasn't thinking clearly. ''You're not going to kill me, Mike. You can't. You don't have the guts. You didn't have the guts to pull Erickson off that transformer and you didn't have the guts to try CPR. And you *certainly* don't have the guts to admit you froze. You're chicken. You always have been and you always will be.'' She forced another laugh. ''Hell, Mike, you're so shriveled, if the ship had a choir, you'd be singing lead soprano.''

That did the trick. She watched the shadow of his hand

rear up on the bulkhead on the far side of his desk. Still, she waited. Timing was crucial.

Now!

And then she made her move.

She spun around, using her motion to swing the heavy bag up into his face, smashing it into the side of his head. She was rewarded by a loud grunt, and then metal banging into metal as the pistol went sailing out of his hand and into the bulkhead on the far side of the office. She took advantage of his shock, jerking her knee up and ramming it into his groin. He went down with a thud, writhing and moaning as he clutched himself.

Run!

She headed for the door, clawing at the watertight lever, heaving it up, listening and praying for the welcoming buzz as the electronic seal severed.

It never came.

She grunted as Dillon crashed into her, grabbing a fistful of her hair, yanking her head back so hard, she thought her neck was going to snap. And then her head exploded into blinding pain as he smashed her forehead into the watertight door. And then he did it again and again, slamming her head into the steel harder each time.

And then, mercifully, he stopped. But the pain was still pounding into her skull, beating her mind down to mush. She was so foggy, she was barely aware of being dragged off the door by her hair before he slammed her down to the deck. She moaned, fearing her sanity crossed over into the abyss when she finally heard the electronic lock buzz. And then she knew she was losing it because now, not only could she hear Reese, she could *see* him as well. She whispered to him, anyway, "I'm sorry, Reese. I tried."

But it was too late.

Reese knew he'd lost the element of surprise the second the lock buzzed. But by the time he entered the space and saw Dillon about to slam Jade's head into the deck, he didn't care. Because pure, undiluted rage carried him through.

He was across the space before Dillon could finish turning his head. He snarled his fury as he crushed his fingers into the bastard's throat, ripping him off of her and slamming him down on the closest desk. Then he pounded him some more.

Reese paused to pick Dillon up by his shirt and pitch him over the desk. The man smashed onto the other side with a satisfying thud. Reese vaulted over the desk for another round. He was barely aware of the lock as it buzzed again, and by the time Coffey reached him, it took him and two other guys to pull him off Dillon's limp body.

He growled out one last curse as he stood. But as he turned to go, Dillon groaned and slid his hand underneath the desk. Reese shot out a foot, stomping the bastard's wrist into the deck as he leaned down to cram his Glock into Dillon's face. "Go ahead. Give me a reason. *Please.*"

He didn't.

Dillon dropped whatever was in his hand, and Coffey snaked his underneath the desk and pulled up a gun.

Reese turned his back on Dillon's moans and vaulted back over the desk to Jade. Her eyes were closed, and the only color left in her face came from the bruises already darkening her forehead. He lifted her gently, not even caring if anyone saw the tears scorching his cheeks as he cradled her close. His voice was hoarse as he glanced back at Coffey. "Find Karin. Tell her I'm coming. And then keep this bastard here until TJ arrives. Don't let anyone touch anything."

Coffey nodded grimly as he reached for the phone. "You got it, buddy."

"I'll be right there." Karin slammed the phone back into its cradle and tore out of the wardroom, the only thought in her head that never before had she heard that note in Coffey's voice. But she'd recognized it instantly.

It was fear.

And it was about Jade.

She rounded the corner in the passageway and ran smack into something solid and alive. She tore at it blindly, not even bothering to use manners—let alone apologize—as she yelled *"Move!"*

When it didn't, her adrenaline kicked into hyper-drive and she flattened the muscle against the bulkhead and careered past, ignoring the sharp *oomph* and Spanish curse that followed.

Too bad.

And if anyone else got between her and Jade, they'd suffer the same fate—if they were lucky.

She nearly ripped the door to Medical off its hinges as she smashed it open. The duty corpsman was waiting, pointing to the first exam room as she barreled past. Seconds later, the exam door suffered a similar fate.

"Oh, my God!" The words tumbled out before she had a chance to reign them in. Fighting back tears of fear and fury, she leveled a glare on Reese as she approached. "What the hell did you do to her?"

Jade fought the dizziness swirling inside her brain long enough to turn her head on the exam table and focus on Karin. Surely she didn't think *Reese* did this? She squinted her eyes at the rage blazing across Karin's face.

Oh, Lord, she did.

And Reese wasn't even denying it.

She swallowed the sawdust in her throat and croaked, "Not him."

The denial didn't seem to faze Karin. She just pointed to the door. *"Out."*

Reese stiffened, but he didn't move.

Jade squeezed his hand. "It's okay. I'll explain."

"Are you sure?" His gaze softened as he stared at her.

She nodded.

Only then did he leave, though obviously still not enthralled with the idea.

Karin was running her hands down Jade's body before the door even closed, probably checking for broken bones. She was fairly sure she didn't have any, though quite a few bruises felt like it. Jade gasped as Karin found one.

"Oh, honey, I'm sorry." She wiped back a tear and picked up her stethoscope.

Jade managed a smile and found her hand. "It's okay. Now, listen—Reese didn't do this."

Her fingers fumbled over her pulse. "I don't understand, Greg said—"

"I don't care what he said. Reese didn't do it. Dillon did."

"Dillon?"

She swallowed another lump of dust. "He decided to play one last game of basketball before he jumped ship. Unfortunately, he used my head as the ball. Besides, I know you. You didn't wait for the whole story, did you?" She almost managed a chuckle as Karin flushed—but it came out as a cough, followed by a groan instead.

The blush faded as Karin began the exam in earnest. "Hush, not another word until I finish."

Reese paced the narrow passageway outside the exam room for the hundredth time. What the hell was taking so long? He glanced at his watch and growled. At this rate, Dillon would be serving his prison term by the time Karin finished. He reached the end of the corridor, spinning around as a door opened.

TJ.

Damn.

"Nice to see you, too, *amigo.*"

Reese cut him off with a glare. "Don't start."

TJ was smart enough not to push. "Sorry, man." His

partner ran a hand through his shoulder-length black hair as he met up with him at the door to the exam room. "Your lady, she's okay?"

"I don't know." And it was driving him insane. He took a deep breath, desperate for anything that would keep his mind off the wait. "What have you got?"

TJ flashed his crooked grin. "Plenty. Seems Dillon's homeboys aren't as loyal as he thought. As soon as Ricky showed up with the warrant, one of the guys started composing a song—and didn't quit till the end. Upshot is, the heroin was weighed down and dropped off the side of the pier before the ship pulled into Korea. The diver dude would snag it during routine maintenance, stash it in his gear and pass it off to his buddy in engineering—"

"So it *was* packed in the coolant valves."

TJ nodded. "Looks that way."

Son of a gun. In spite of his mood, Reese smiled. They really should consider recruiting Jade. She was *good*.

TJ joined him in pacing the passageway. "We're still waiting on the statement from the guy in Engineering—but from the look on his face when he found out the outside was radioactive, I'd say yes. Especially after he begged to see a doctor when he discovered he'd handled it himself, however briefly." His smile turned grim. "It would serve the bastard right if he was contaminated."

Reese stopped short, doing an about-face as another door opened. Relief flooded him as Karin poked her head out and waved him in. *Thank you, God.*

But he hadn't taken more than a step before TJ sucked in his breath and grabbed his arm, nearly wrenching it from the socket.

Reese glanced back, managing a grin—because Karin *smiled* before she slipped back inside. His grin deepened as he stared at his partner. "I'll give you an intro later, Romeo—now, get lost." He didn't wait for TJ to argue as he headed back into the exam room.

Karin stepped back from the table as he entered. "She's going to be okay. I'd like her to stay aboard tonight so I can keep an eye on her, though. But we can discuss that when I return, *Mr. Garrick.*" That last let him know she'd had a few other things she wanted to discuss as well. He didn't care. Later, he'd tell her his whole damn life story if that's what she wanted—as long as she gave him a few minutes alone with Jade now.

She did.

He slipped his hand into Jade's as the door closed, smoothing his other down her bruised cheek, wishing he'd gotten a few extra whacks into Dillon before Coffey had pulled him off. She was so damn pale—where she wasn't purple—he was afraid to speak.

And then she smiled.

He was nearly overcome with the urge to pick her up off the table, carry her out of Medical and off the ship. He wanted her home. In *their* home—and it *was* her home, too. Hell, she already had his heart, she might as well take everything else he owned.

As long as she took him, too.

Oh, God, he did not deserve her. Not after the way he'd lied to her. But God forgive him, he wasn't letting her go. He couldn't. Not now and not ever.

He took both her hands in his. "Jade, I'm so sorry. I—"

She shook her head and pressed her fingers to his lips. "Shh. It doesn't matter."

He kissed her fingers and brought the hand down, squeezing it gently. "Yes, it does. I just don't know where to start. I could tell you what I'm supposed to tell you—what I was *ordered* to tell you. That no one was supposed to know about my father because of the case. But I can't. Because that's not the truth—at least not the *whole* truth."

He took a deep breath, drawing strength from her as she squeezed his fingers back. "Honey, the truth is, I was scared. Scratch that—I was *terrified.* By the time I realized

I'd gotten in over my head with you, I knew you well enough to know you wouldn't put up with my prejudices about the Navy. I also knew I couldn't ask you to get out. But I couldn't let you go, either.''

''Why not?''

It was now or never. He knew that. But what if she wasn't ready? What if she was *never* ready? He stared into those gorgeous gray eyes for a few more moments, then cleared his throat. It was time to find out. ''Because...I love you.''

She took a slow, deep breath and then exhaled just as slowly—but by the time she finished, her eyes were glistening just as brightly as the hair slipping through his fingers. ''I suppose that's a good thing—since I happen to love you, too.''

He closed his eyes, savoring the words. It didn't matter that Coffey had already told him. He'd needed to hear it from her. And frankly, they sounded a hell of a lot sweeter coming from her lips. So sweet, he leaned over and kissed her. He grazed his thumb across her bottom lip as he pulled away. ''So what do we do now?''

''Get married?''

He froze. ''Did you just say what I think you did?''

Jade's heart stopped as Reese stared at her, obviously in shock. Oh, God. Why did she say that? It was her head, that was it. She must have taken one whack too many because now she'd gone and blown it for good. Why did she have to assume just because Reese said he loved her, he wanted to marry her? She was such an idiot! He couldn't have made it more plain than he already had. He wasn't taking on the Navy.

Ever.

She swallowed another lump—this one of tears and not sawdust. ''I'm sorry. I—I shouldn't have said that. You just told me you couldn't live with the Navy.''

He cupped her face as he leaned close. ''*Yes*, I'll marry you.'' Then he stunned her again as he grinned. ''You'll have to forgive me—and my surprise. I was all set to convince *you* we had to get married, but you beat me to it.'' He took a deep breath and squeezed her hand, firmly this time. ''And I *can* live with the Navy. I know that now. What I can't live without is *you*. Just, please, don't ever ask me to join the Navy Wives Club.''

She chuckled through a fresh wave of tears. ''I don't think they've called it that for years. But, okay, I promise you—I'll never ask you to join.'' She sighed as he leaned over and kissed her again—though he ended it much too soon as far as she was concerned.

''Good. Then it's a done deal.'' He smiled that gorgeous smile of his, the one that warmed her from the inside out. It actually caused the pain in her head to ebb. ''Besides, how can I turn down a lifetime with the most incredibly sexy woman on this planet, who drives a ship better than any man I know, can blush one minute and turn into a tigress the next—*and* thinks my kisses rate a twenty?''

''What?''

Karin. There was no other explanation.

She struggled to sit up. ''I'm going to *kill*—''

''I eavesdropped.''

She blinked—and then laughed.

He folded both her hands into his and leaned close, staring deep into her eyes. ''And, for the record, I did *not* make a bet with Dillon. He did that all on his own.''

She flushed. ''I know. I figured that out about ten seconds after I left the club, but I was too stubborn to go back in and tell you.''

He hugged her gently then, lifting her up off the exam table and into his arms as he buried his face in her hair. She wrapped her arms around him as he shuddered. ''God, I will *never* forgive myself for not being there for you.''

''But you were there.''

He drew back and stared at her, as confused as she had

been when it happened. But she wasn't confused anymore.
Jeff was wrong. She knew that now.

She didn't *have* to put a man first.

But if she ever did, she now knew she could. It just had
to be the right one.

This man.

She nodded, smiling. "You were there, Reese. In my
mind. I guess I was so scared I'd never see you again—that
I'd never be able to tell you I loved you—that I just conjured you up."

She forgot to breathe as he lowered his head and stared
deep into her eyes, his own burning steady and blue as his
grin lit up her entire world. "I love you, *Lieutenant Jade
Parker.* I love *you.*"

And then she cupped his face and kissed him. Because
that was all she needed to hear.

* * * * *

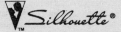

If you enjoyed what you just read,
then we've got an offer you can't resist!

Take 2 bestselling
love stories FREE!
Plus get a FREE surprise gift!

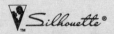

Coming in June 1999 from

Silhouette® Books...

Those matchmaking folks at Gulliver's Travels are at
it again—and look who they're working their magic
on this time, in

HOLIDAY
Honeymoons

Two Tickets to Paradise

For the first time anywhere, enjoy these two new
complete stories in one sizzling volume!

HIS FIRST FATHER'S DAY   **Merline Lovelace**
A little girl's search for her father leads her to
Tony Peretti's front door...and leads *Tony* into the
arms of his long-lost love—the child's mother!

MARRIED ON THE FOURTH   **Carole Buck**
Can summer love turn into the real thing? When
it comes to Maddy Malone and Evan Blake's
Independence Day romance, the answer is a
definite "yes!"

Don't miss this brand-new release—
HOLIDAY HONEYMOONS: Two Tickets to Paradise—
coming June 1999, only from Silhouette Books.

Available at your favorite retail outlet.

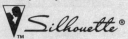

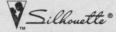